CW01067239

Bristol Library Service

AN 2999261 3

SEARCH THE ENDLESS SEA

SEARCH THE ENDLESS SEA

Frederick Harsant

BRISTOL CITY COUNCIL	
Askews	22-Feb-2007
	£16.99

Book Guild Publishing
Sussex, England

First published in Great Britain in 2007 by
The Book Guild Ltd
Pavilion View
19 New Road
Brighton
BN1 1UF

Copyright © Frederick Harsant 2007

The right of Frederick Harsant to be identified as the author of
this work has been asserted by him in accordance with the
Copyright, Designs and Patents Act 1988.

All rights reserved. No part of this publication may be reproduced,
transmitted, or stored in a retrieval system, in any form or by any
means, without permission in writing from the publisher, nor be
otherwise circulated in any form of binding or cover other than
that in which it is published and without a similar condition being
imposed on the subsequent purchaser.

All characters in this publication are fictitious and any
resemblance to real people, alive or dead, is purely coincidental.

Typesetting in Baskerville by
IML Typographers, Birkenhead, Merseyside

Printed in Great Britain by
Antony Rowe Ltd, Chippenham, Wiltshire

A catalogue record for this book is available from
The British Library.

ISBN 978 1 84624 101 7

To my daughter, Jill, who patiently deciphered the untidy writing of the earlier versions of this manuscript and saw me through the mysteries of transferring it onto the computer.

Contents

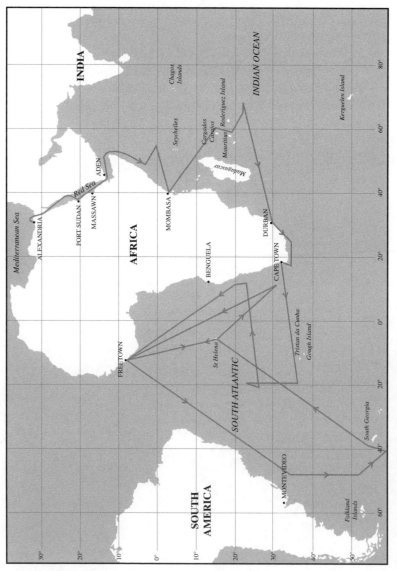

Map showing routes taken by Peregrine and Consorts

Author's Note

In 1941 HMS *Eagle* searched the Indian Ocean and South Atlantic for the German raider *Atlantis*. I have used this search as the basis of my novel. Many of the events described are based on the experiences of my friends and myself aboard *Eagle*. The characters, the romantic story and the end of *Hohenlinden* are all fictitious.

Chapter 1

Janet and Ann

Janet Hall and Ann Turner talked in a desultory fashion as they waited in the lobby of the Naval Hospital in Alexandria. Janet was a fair-haired, tallish, slim girl, not quite twenty years old; her friend, Ann, of a similar age, was dark-haired, shorter in height and rather cuddly. Both girls were VAD nurses working in the Naval Hospital. The year was 1941 and, as it was the end of March, the air was warm and dry.

The girls were waiting for their friends, Bill Hewitt and Killer Compton, naval aviators from HMS *Peregrine* with whom they expected to spend the evening dining and dancing at the Carlton Hotel. The boys were already fifteen minutes adrift.

'I don't like the look of it,' said Janet. 'It's unlike either of them to be late. I wonder if they've gone off to sea again.'

'The carrier was in harbour this morning,' said Ann.

'Perhaps they've returned to the Western Desert.'

The two officers the girls were discussing were Midshipman (A) Bill Hewitt, RNVR, an observer in 999 Squadron, and Sub Lieutenant (A) Compton, known generally by his nickname, Killer, a pilot in the same squadron. Both officers had seen much action at sea in the Eastern Mediterranean and in the Western Desert. At different times both had been wounded and had been nursed by the girls at the Naval Hospital. Bill had been shot down and captured and, with his pilot, 'Holy'

Temple, had escaped from a prisoner convoy by hiding under the sand and walking eastwards until picked up by a long-range army patrol.

The girls had been out with the boys only the day before. Bill and Killer had been in a despondent mood. Friends of theirs had been caught in a sirocco in their Swordfish aircraft and lost at sea. The girls had met them at the Naval Club, where they had done their best to encourage them out of their despondency, with some success. They had arranged to meet that evening for dancing at the Carlton.

Janet was attracted to Bill. Janet's father was a stockbroker and well-off. Bill, she knew, came from a relatively poor home. He had obtained a scholarship to a grammar school, passed his higher certificate, and obtained a commission in the Fleet Air Arm. When she had first met him, at a party of naval officers and VADs arranged by Ann, he had been hesitant and unsure of himself, coming alive only when he was dancing. She remembered, now, the slow, languorous dance steps, Bill's complete mastery of the slow foxtrot, and the dreamy, trance-like way in which she had followed his lead.

In hospital Bill had been confined strictly to bed with his leg wound, and Janet had spent some of her free time with him, learning more about him. He had been interested in ancient history at school, and Janet had found a book for him on the history of ancient Egypt. He was interested in everything around him, in the extremes of wealth and poverty in Egypt, in the sights and sounds of Alexandria, the men in jellabas, the women in yashmaks, the water-carriers, the hookah-smokers; he had described them to, and discussed them with, Janet.

She knew that on New Year's Eve, whilst confined strictly to bed, he had broken out of hospital by climbing through a window and had gone to a night-club where he had met and made friends with a Greek, called Socrates, and his wife.

Through them he had spent part of his sick leave in Cairo. Something had happened in Cairo because on his return he had been a different person, more sure of himself, more mature. Janet suspected the influence of another girl. She was not sure about this, but was surprised to find herself jealous.

Half an hour later the girls decided that the boys were not coming.

'It's most unlike Killer,' Ann said sadly. 'I feel sure he'd have phoned if he could.'

Ann remembered the sturdy, shortish figure, the puckish face, the twinkle in the eye, the strong, lively character. She had first met Killer when he was delivered into her ward as a patient with a leg wound. His Swordfish had been shot down somewhere in the desert and he had been rescued by a senior officer in his squadron, someone called Bolo Hawkins.

From their first meeting Killer had tried to make a date with her, flirting outrageously. At first she had resisted, but Killer had a way with him. She liked his banter and his sense of fun. She remembered her first dance with him at the Carlton, a waltz. Killer had approached it in his usual determined way, plodding firmly forward with hopelessly untrained steps. Ann was light on her feet, but it had taken all her skill to avoid his feet. She had left him feeling well-pleased with his efforts.

She remembered the change when she danced with Bill – so easy to follow, such a good dancer. Yet she preferred the easy, outgoing personality of Killer to the introspective, hesitant manner of Bill. She knew that Janet favoured Bill and she thought what a happy quartet they made.

'I wonder what the boys are doing now,' she said, as they made their way to the nurses' lounge. 'I expect they're at their desert landing-strip. It seems horrible to think of them flying into anti-aircraft fire in their Swordfish.'

3

'I was horrified when Bill showed me his aircraft in the hangar. It seemed so ancient, a biplane made of canvas.'

Janet was referring to the wardroom dinner party two or three weeks before, when, after the meal, the boys had taken the girls on a tour of the hangar and the flight-deck. They had shown them their aircraft and introduced them to their maintenance crews.

'Killer told me something then that partly explains his character,' said Ann. 'His father is a doctor in the country somewhere, and that's what Killer wants to be after the war. The first thing he wants though, is to defeat Hitler and bring this war to an end. Only then, he said, will he be ready to give up being "Killer" Compton and take up his role as Dr Compton.'

'And I thought he wasn't serious about anything!' said Janet.

'If that were so I don't think I'd be as interested as I am,' said Ann. 'Underneath all that banter is a very serious man. That is what attracts me to him.'

'People aren't always what they seem, are they?' said Janet. 'Take Bill. At first he seemed so young for his age, awkward, even gawky. Then I danced with him. It was heaven! When he's doing something he's good at he's mature and confident.'

'I think we're lucky,' said Ann. 'I always thought that the Fleet Air Arm would be a hard-hitting, hard-drinking crowd, but they aren't a bit like that. Think how well all the officers aboard the *Peregrine* treated us at the party. I hope we see a lot more of them.'

The next morning the girls were asked to see Matron in her office. Ten nurses were assembled there, with Pat Harding, a nursing sister. The girls looked at each other questioningly, wondering what was up. Matron certainly didn't look angry, so they knew they weren't in trouble.

4

'As you know, girls,' Matron began, 'we've had a large number of wounded naval personnel over the past month. Since the Italians invaded Greece the war at sea has stepped up. Many ships have been sunk or damaged, with large numbers of casualties. It has been decided to ease the situation here by sending some of the walking wounded off to South Africa. The hospital ship *Carpathian* will arrive shortly in Alexandria and a hundred naval casualties are to go aboard for transit to Cape Town. You girls have been chosen to look after the naval party. Sister Harding will be in charge, and you will come under the overall control of the ship's matron. There are, of course, resident doctors and nurses, but these will be required mainly for army casualties. Are there any questions?'

'Yes, Matron,' said Janet. 'When do we leave?'

Janet was concerned that she could lose touch with Bill.

'Shortly after the *Carpathian* arrives and as soon as we can complete the arrangements for the transfer; almost certainly within the next fortnight.'

'Shall we be returning here, Matron?'

'I'm not sure. Most of the patients will stay in South Africa until they are well; some of them, I believe, are due to go all the way to England. You might well be asked to accompany them onwards.'

For the next three days the girls were kept busy, preparing for the move. During this time they tried telephoning the *Peregrine* and HMS *Grebe*, the Naval Air Station at Dekheila near Alexandria. Their questions were met with silence. No information was available.

Could they pass messages to the two officers?

That wasn't possible.

On the fourth day they decided to beard the lion in his den. With some trepidation they boarded a felucca and asked to be taken to *Peregrine*. The Arab handled his craft, with its single lateen sail, with great dexterity and soon

5

brought them alongside the landing platform of the *Peregrine*. Paying the boatman and dismissing him, the two girls ran quickly up the boarding steps of the carrier.

'Here, miss, you can't come up here,' said the sailor who greeted them.

'Well, we are here, and we've come to see the Commander.' Janet turned to her friend for support.

'Have you an appointment?'

'No, but I am sure he'll see us. Tell him that we met him at dinner aboard the ship three weeks ago.'

'Here's the Officer of the Watch. You'd better have a word with him.'

The two girls turned to a bearded lieutenant RN who greeted them. They had purposely retained their uniforms, thinking quite correctly, that these might help them get through the first barrier. The officer regarded them quizzically. He saw two young, attractive ladies, wearing determined faces as well as uniforms. He decided to give in gracefully.

'I'll send a message down to him.'

'Please tell him that we met him at the party here and that it's very important that we see him.'

The messenger was sent and, while they waited, the lieutenant enjoyed the company of the two girls.

When he returned, the messenger spoke in an undertone to the lieutenant, who turned to the girls and said, 'The Commander will see you now. I'll take you to his cabin.'

Followed by admiring glances from the deck-party and every other sailor they passed, the girls accompanied the lieutenant through a maze of corridors and hatches until they came to the officers' flat and finally the Commander's cabin.

Bidden to enter, the lieutenant introduced the girls to the Commander: 'Miss Hall and Miss Turner, VADs from the Naval Hospital.'

With a smile, the Commander greeted the girls courteously.

'I remember you,' he said. 'We met at the dinner party three weeks ago. You were with ...' He paused.

'Sub Lieutenant Compton.'

'Midshipman Hewitt.'

The girls answered simultaneously, and then laughed. The tension was broken and between them they told the Commander of their dilemma. They had tried to contact the officers to tell them they would be leaving on the hospital-ship and to arrange forwarding addresses, but had met impassable barriers when they telephoned the ship and Dekheila, so they had decided to approach the Commander.

The Commander was not unaware of the determination shown by the girls in getting into his cabin and he had a good deal of sympathy for them – his own daughter was not much younger – but there was little he could do for them.

'I'm afraid I can't tell you where they are at present,' he said. 'The squadrons are away on a secret mission and it's more than my job is worth to tell you where.'

'Will they be back before we leave in the hospital-ship?' said Janet.

'I can't answer that, but let me say that it's highly unlikely.'

'We've written letters to them,' said Ann. 'Could they be delivered?'

'I'll personally see that they receive your letters if you would like to leave them with me.'

The girls knew that this was as far as they could go. At least they would establish communication with their friends. The Commander, however, had not yet finished.

Taking the letters from the girls, he said, 'Perhaps you would like to join me for a cup of tea.'

When a steward brought the tea, the Commander soon had the girls relaxed and talking about their work. He was interested to hear that they were the nurses who had tended the wounds of the two officers. He sent them away feeling much happier and confident that their letters would be passed on.

A week later the *Carpathian,* a peacetime passenger ship converted into a hospital-ship, arrived in Alexandria. Shortly after her arrival, the VADs were invited aboard to meet the matron and her nursing staff and familiarise themselves with the ship. Most of the cabins had been converted to take two or four patients. The dining room and one of the lounges retained some of the ancient splendour and were used as originally intended. Other lounges had been converted into wards. An air of clinical efficiency pervaded the ship, symbolised by the white-painted upper works and the large red crosses displayed on either side of the hull and on what used to be the sports deck, the uppermost deck of the vessel.

The VADs were shown to their cabins and Janet found she was sharing one with Ann. This suited the girls who had become firm friends, a friendship that had really developed after meeting the Fleet Air Arm officers. They had enjoyed the evenings spent in the Carlton with the boys and swimming with them at the Sporting Club. These shared experiences had drawn the girls together.

Ann was happy usually to leave Janet to make any arrangements required. Ann herself was placid by temperament, but she was no pushover. Above everything else she liked helping the sick and the wounded and she had a natural talent for this. Many of her patients had had a rough time when their ships were sunk or damaged. Some had minor wounds, but others suffered distressing injuries. All were very far from home, and most felt the need of a woman's touch, a woman's sympathy. She was gentle with her patients and responded to their needs without ever allowing them to take liberties with her.

Killer Compton was the only man she had been out with since arriving in Alexandria and she had been careful to have other girls present. At first she had playfully rejected Killer's advances. She did not know enough about him or his background. The Fleet Air Arm was an unknown quantity. She felt happy tending the men in the wards, but was not ready to go out with one of them. Gradually, when Killer was a patient, as he teased her and joked with her, she responded to his efforts. He was not exactly handsome, nor was he a romantic figure, but he was persevering and sure of himself and he had a way with him.

Janet, on the other hand, had very quickly become interested in Bill Hewitt. She had first met him when, at Ann's request, she had agreed to make up a foursome with Ann, Killer and Bill. At first, Bill had been diffident, perhaps even nervous. Janet had noticed that he seemed to leave the organising and ordering to Killer. Bill seemed to be shy and watchful, observing and taking in points. Killer had led the conversation, was the life and soul of the party and soon had the girls laughing and responding. It was on the dance-floor that there was a reversal of roles. Killer was awkward and clumsy; Bill was accomplished, sure of himself and a dominant partner, leading easily and gracefully and taking his partner with him.

That first dance had opened Janet's eyes. She became aware of a hidden fire in Bill, of forces as yet untapped and unknown. She was nineteen years old; he was perhaps twenty, young and naive, but with a maturity and force of personality waiting to be released.

When Bill, in his turn, became a casualty in Ann's ward, occupying the same bed that Killer had occupied, Janet became a frequent visitor in her spare time. She became aware of the breadth of Bill's interests, his love of ancient history and architecture, of music and poetry. Bill told her something of his background, the large family, hard-working father who was a bookkeeping clerk, the terraced house in a mean London street that was all they could afford. Bill told her of his early childhood: playing in the street; going on to grammar school and growing away from his early companions; the Roman Catholic Church where he served at mass every morning; the church club, when he was seventeen years old, where he had learned to dance; his search for a simpler religion.

All of this was so different from her own life. She was an only child, had gone away to boarding school, and met other girls and boys at parties carefully organised by her parents or the parents of her friends. Life for her had always been ordered, organised. It still was to some extent, for Matron and the sisters kept an eye on their young colleagues. Bill, on the other hand, she thought, had been a free spirit, learning to fend for himself in the streets, fighting a lonely spiritual battle, escaping from his background into a new and demanding culture and doing it with the same spirit of enterprise he had shown when escaping from the Italians.

A few days later she was aboard *Carpathian,* awaiting the arrival of the naval contingent of wounded. The coaches arrived and the men were registered in the ship as they entered. The VADs helped to settle the arrivals in their new quarters. The officers, petty officers and more severely wounded were given the cabins, whilst the less seriously wounded men were billeted in the newly created wards. The cabin allocated to Janet and Ann, like all the other staff accommodation, was situated on the boat-deck.

An atmosphere of excitement pervaded the ship as patients and staff settled down for the voyage. The patients were clearly delighted to be aboard the ship and the air of festivity was not marred by the convalescent state of the passengers.

The next day, the *Carpathian,* escorted by *Peregrine,* the cruiser HMS *Lancashire,* and three destroyers, left Alexandria. Janet and Ann stood by the swimming pool at the stern of the hospital-ship and watched the receding harbour. Janet's feelings were mixed. She had enjoyed her year in Alexandria and had found the work interesting and rewarding. However, as she glanced at *Peregrine,* astern of the *Carpathian,* she thought of Bill and the squadron. Surely, if *Peregrine* were escorting them, she would meet up with Bill. So where was Bill? Where were the two Swordfish squadrons?

Chapter 2

The *Orsini*

At that moment, one of the two squadrons, 999 Torpedo Bomber Reconnaissance (TBR) Squadron, led by its commanding officer, Lieutenant-Commander Simpson DSC, RN, was flying south from Port Sudan in the Red Sea towards Massawa. Massawa was under siege by the victorious British Fourteenth Army, which had driven the Italian East African Army eastwards through Eritrea to the one-time capital and principal port. A British brigade, on the coast north of Massawa, was being bombarded by an Italian destroyer. A wireless call to Port Sudan had resulted in 999 Squadron being dispatched to take care of the destroyer.

The squadron was flying in loose formation on the long flight south, keeping to seaward of the coastline. Bolo Hawkins, the Senior Pilot of the squadron and leader of the third sub-flight, relaxed in his cockpit and let his mind go over the events of the past fortnight.

The two TBR squadrons from the aircraft carrier HMS *Peregrine* had done what they had been sent to do – defend Port Sudan against an assault by an Italian flotilla of six destroyers, based at Massawa. The squadron had undertaken a hazardous flight from Alexandria, a thousand miles down the Nile and five hundred miles across the desert, landing every three hundred miles on hastily prepared airstrips to refuel. This had been followed by several days of searching and patrolling amongst the islands to the north of Massawa. Then had come the day when five of the Italian flotilla had broken out from their base to make their assault on Port Sudan. Their intention had been to bombard the port and scuttle themselves in the harbour, thus blocking Britain's only deep-water refuelling base and coaling port in the Red Sea.

A search across the Red Sea had discovered the enemy ships only sixty miles from Port Sudan, heading for the port at full speed. A day-long battle between aircraft and ships had ensued. Sunk or damaged, the Italians had been thwarted and turned away only twenty-five miles from Port Sudan, and the two surviving destroyers had headed for the Arabian Coast, where they had finally been abandoned in a sinking condition.

That should have been the end of the story, Bolo reflected ruefully, but now this destroyer had appeared on the scene. It must be the sixth destroyer of the Italian flotilla they had defeated, the *Orsini*. The Swordfish should be able to sink the *Orsini* once it was spotted. The squadron was now very experienced after several months of continuous action in the Eastern Mediterranean and the Western Desert, making torpedo attacks on ships at sea and in harbour, and dive-bombing ships, troops and storage depots.

The Western Desert! Bolo recalled the long nights in the desert, under the stars, when he had come to terms with his growing love for Joyce. In 1938 Bolo had been an up-and-coming Sussex fast bowler. Corny Wilde, his old friend and mentor at the cricket club, had introduced him to his daughter, Joyce, then eighteen, just finishing school and five years younger than himself. Bolo was the son of elderly parents. His mother had died when he was young and he had never known a real family life. Corny had been like a father to him. When he met Joyce he treated her as his young sister. They had spent many happy hours together at Hove where they lived, walking on the Downs, or motoring in the New Forest. Joyce had opened Bolo's eyes to the world of nature, flowers, animals and birds seen on their country walks, and to music and poetry at her home.

It was in the desert that Bolo had come to realise how much Joyce meant to him. The many incidents he recalled having shared with her took on a new significance and he now knew that he had fallen deeply in love with her. After a particularly demanding spell of action in the desert, Bolo had written to Joyce a simple, direct letter, expressing his feelings. By nature Bolo was direct, with the straightforward approach of the fast bowler rather than the guile of the spinner or googly bowler. His nickname had come from his former profession.

Joyce's reply had arrived just before they had left the *Peregrine* for Port Sudan. She had loved him from the moment she had met him. She knew that he had treated her as his young sister and she had been hard put to contain her feelings for him. The letter was in the breast pocket of Bolo's shirt.

Bolo had learned to fly in 1938 and, at the outbreak of war, had volunteered his services to the Fleet Air Arm. He was accepted immediately and found himself, as a sub lieutenant, piloting observers on their training course at Lee-on-Solent. At Lee he had learned to be a good naval officer as well as a good naval pilot, and six months after joining he was promoted to lieutenant. When Italy had entered the war in 1940 he had been posted to 999 Squadron in *Peregrine* as a replacement and, shortly afterwards, because of his seniority and experience, had been made a sub-flight leader.

Bolo was pilot of K-King. To his right he could see 'Snowball' Kennedy, the observer of L-Love. Snowball had been one of the oldest members of his course and Bolo had known him as a trainee at Lee-on-Solent. Snowball's nickname came from his hair, blond almost to the point of whiteness. A steady officer, he had a steadying effect on his young pilot, Killer Compton.

Killer was one of a group of young RNVR HO (Hostilities Only) midshipmen and sub lieutenants that had joined the squadron six months before, when it had lost four experienced RN crews at a disastrous strike on Rhodes. For six months their replacements, these young RNVR officers, had been heavily involved at sea and in the desert and were now very experienced. Killer, who had been a midshipman when he first arrived and had been promoted to sub lieutenant on his twentieth birthday, had derived his name from his recklessness. He had, so to speak, 'killed off' the enthusiasm of several observers because of his dangerous piloting. Snowball Kennedy had survived and stuck with him, and he had had a steadying effect on him. Killer was no longer foolhardy, but in action he had been courageous and enterprising. Bolo thought what a good team they had become.

Beyond L-Love, Bolo could see Midshipman Bill Hewitt, the observer of B-Baker in the CO's flight. Bill also had been one of Bolo's trainees, on the same course as Snowball Kennedy. Bill, Bolo knew, had done well in his course, passing out in the first five, but because of his age was ranked midshipman instead of sub lieutenant. Bolo had noted Bill's developing maturity, particularly after he had been wounded and shot down in the Western Desert and escaped with his pilot, 'Holy' Temple. Bill was now a first-rate observer, intelligent and showing confidence and initiative.

'Message from the Army, Bolo.' This was the voice of Lieutenant 'Dicky' Burd RN, Bolo's observer, coming through his Gosport tube. 'The destroyer has broken off the engagement and is making away to the south-east.'

'The CO said this might happen,' replied Bolo. 'I expect the Italians have spies along the coast and they have reported us. We are to remain in formation until the CO gives a signal; then we split up and search the islands for the destroyer.'

'Yes. We follow diverging courses until we are five miles apart, then parallel courses to the south-east. Whoever sights must jettison his bombs and stay to report and shadow the enemy.'

'Message from the CO, sir.' The voice of PO Mercer, the telegraphist-air-gunner, broke into their conversation. 'The CO says we are to break off for the search when he waggles his wings.'

Bolo acknowledged the message. He reflected on how primitive communication was in the Fleet Air Arm. They relied entirely on W/T and hand signals or the waggling of wings. R/T was as yet untried in TBR aircraft.

'There's the signal!' exclaimed Dicky. 'The first course is one-one-eight degrees.' Bolo had seen the signal and was already turning.

Bill Hewitt in B-Baker had also seen the signal and he gave his pilot, Holy Temple, his new course.

'Steer one-six-five degrees, Holy,' he said. 'We'll keep that course for twenty-three minutes, then turn on to the search course of two-two-five degrees.'

'Right, Bill. Turning now.'

Bill watched as the CO, in A-Abel, slanted away from him to the right and 'Hatters' Dunn, in C-Charlie, bore away to the left. The remaining aircraft of the squadron were on diverging courses until they were five miles apart. Ahead, a pall of smoke lay low over the sea for many miles to the east of Massawa. This would be the smoke of battle blown out to sea by the prevailing wind. It would be difficult to see the enemy ship in the murk. Just as well they were only five miles apart, Bill thought.

Like all the other crews, the crew of B-Baker was well practised. Bill knew that he could rely on Holy to steer the course he had given him so he could concentrate on the search, using his binoculars to try to pierce the gloom that enveloped the islands ahead. Off Massawa was an archipelago of numerous islands, many of which could provide refuge for the destroyer. The most likely, however, was Nocra, a harbour on the large island of Dahlac Chebir. At the briefing, Sandy Sandiford, the Senior Observer, had told them that if they had to search for the destroyer Nocra would be the reference point for navigational positions.

The smoke was thicker to the north of Massawa and Bill thought he could hear the rumble of gunfire. He tried to imagine the battle, with the Italians digging in round the outskirts of Massawa and the British Army, with tanks and light artillery, trying to penetrate the defences. He remembered some of the scenes in the Western Desert where General Wavell's Eighth Army had driven the Italians back across Libya, in particular the night when B-Baker was engaged in harassing the enemy front line by dropping one bomb every ten minutes on enemy forward positions. One of their bombs had fallen on a fuel dump, setting it ablaze. At the same time B-Baker had been hit by an enemy shell and its engine put out of action. Bill had been wounded, but Holy had made a superb landing on the roadway alongside the burning fuel dump. The crew had been captured but had managed to escape with the help of a long-range British patrol unit.

Bill no longer had a fear of going into action. At first that had been the fear of the unknown. He had come to realise that at the moment of action there was so much to do and see that there was little time for fear. Now he was busy with his binoculars. He noted the many craft that seemed to be leaving the port. Once he directed Holy to investigate a larger ship appearing round one of the islands, but on closer inspection it proved to be a passenger ferry.

A few minutes later he caught sight of a wisp of foam a few miles ahead, barely seen through the gloom.

'Something ahead, slightly to port, Holy,' he exclaimed. 'Let's have a look at it. Keep it to port and go round its stern.'

'I've got it!' said Holy.

By now they were only two or three miles away and puffs of shell bursts appeared ahead of them.

'It must be the destroyer,' said Holy.

'Yes. I'm sure it is. I'll get off a sighting report.'

Bill was writing quickly on a pad in simple code.

Enemy destroyer in position 280 degrees Nocra 15 miles. Course 100 degrees. Speed 30 knots.

'Here, get that off, Black,' Bill said, passing the message to his telegraphist-airgunner.

'I'm jettisoning the bombs,' said Holy.

Bill felt the plane judder as the bombs left. This was in accordance with the operational orders. B-Baker must stay and shadow. They must not risk being shot down.

'Message passed, sir,' said PO Black.

'I'm turning now,' said Holy.

The manoeuvre, which Holy carried out smartly, put the Italian gunners off their mark, for the shell bursts that had been following them closely ahead were now left well behind. Suddenly PO Black's voice cut in like a whiplash.

'Enemy fighter abeam – port.'

PO Black was already manning his Lewis gun.

'I've got it! It's a Macchi fighter. Now on port quarter, distance one mile,' exclaimed Bill. 'Stand by to evade.'

He had gone smoothly into the defensive tactics evolved by the squadron at the Fleet Air Arm base at Dekheila, in the aftermath of the disastrous raid on Rhodes. 'Fighter one thousand yards, port quarter. Stand by to corkscrew port.

'Five hundred yards.

'Four hundred.

'Three hundred. Corkscrew. Go. Go.'

Just as the fighter came into firing range, Holy made a violent turn downwards and to port, at the same time closing his throttle and using the drag of his wings to slow the aircraft.

The effect on the Macchi was startling. Unable to turn inside the tight circle achieved by the Swordfish, he hurtled past harmlessly, and as he did so PO Black gave him a burst of Lewis gunfire.

Holy pulled out at five hundred feet and steadied on a northerly course, once more crossing the track astern of the destroyer. The destroyer had stopped firing, no doubt leaving it to the fighter, Bill thought.

The Macchi was now turning for a second attack.

'Enemy fighter astern, one thousand yards,' chanted Bill. 'Stand by to corkscrew starboard.'

Again Holy tensed, waiting for the signal to turn. Again PO Black prepared to fire his Lewis gun.

'Five hundred yards.

'Four hundred. Stand by to corkscrew.

'Three hundred. Go. Go.'

The order was marginally earlier this time, and the enemy pilot was just beaten by the turn. His tracers were outside the turning circle of the Swordfish.

Holy threw his aircraft into a twisting corkscrew turn downwards and to starboard, pulling out almost at sea level. He was using his own skill and the marvellous manoeuvrability of the Swordfish to defeat a superior enemy aircraft.

The enemy pilot made a fatal mistake. He tried to bring his aircraft round so that his guns could bear. As he came level PO Black gave him a long burst. Too late the pilot realised his error. He was too close to the sea. Bill watched the wing of the Macchi touch the sea. He watched as the pilot fought his machine, trying to haul it clear. He saw the wing dip in further, and then the Macchi cartwheeled and disappeared in an enormous splash of water.

Only now did Bill feel his legs weaken and a need to subside onto his stool.

'Well done, chaps,' came the voice of Holy. 'Now let's get back to the target.'

'That must have been one of the last Italian planes left at Massawa,' said Bill.

'Look, sir,' cried PO Black. 'The Swordfish are attacking.'

B-Baker was now four miles away, hurrying back towards the Italian destroyer. The presence of the other Swordfish was marked by the shell bursts that followed them in.

The CO was attacking in A-Abel, with C-Charlie astern of him. Bill watched as the two Swordfish, at four thousand feet, began their run in. The CO was almost over the destroyer when he began his dive. Bill watched the destroyer making the tightest of turns to port. The CO dropped his bombs at a thousand feet – and missed the ship to starboard. Hatters Dunn, following behind in C-Charlie, over-compensated. The enemy ship turned back to starboard and Charlie's bombs missed to port.

By now Biddy Bidwell's sub-flight was closing up. Biddy ignored the shell-bursts and circled, waiting for his sub-flight to come up with him. They formed line astern and attacked one by one, dive-bombing and dropping their bombs at a thousand feet. The destroyer captain was very good. He turned his ship in towards the aircraft to try to make them overshoot and at the critical moment, as their dives became steeper and their bombs were released, he jinked his ship one way or another, causing the bombs to miss.

Bill realised what a difficult target a fast-moving, fast-turning destroyer was.

'Here come the other Swordfish,' said PO Black.

In L-Love Snowball, Kennedy had heard the sighting report and had given Killer a course to intercept the enemy. At four miles he saw the shell-bursts following the second sub-flight in and the dramatic escape of the Italian destroyer. Then, in the gloom, he saw a light blinking ahead of him, spelling out the letter K.

'There's Bolo ahead in K-King, Killer,' he said. 'He's waiting for us to close up on him.'

Bolo was indeed waiting for his sub-flight, coolly circling at four thousand feet about three miles away from the destroyer.

'M-Mike coming up astern,' called his TAG, L/A Gibbons.

Snowball looked and saw the Swordfish about three miles astern of them. Killer formed up loosely in his accustomed position on Bolo's starboard quarter. A minute or two later, Sub Lieutenant Bing Crosby had formed up on Bolo's other side.

The destroyer had settled again on its course for Nocra, its fire now directed at Bolo's sub-flight.

Snowball thought that Bolo seemed to be completely untroubled by the enemy gunfire, although he himself was feeling tremors in his stomach. He saw Bolo wave the sub-flight into line astern and he took up his position in the open cockpit hard against the forward bulkhead, looking over Killer's shoulder. In his hands was his camera. Snowball had been a newspaperman before joining up and now he was determined to get pictures of the actual attack.

He watched as Bolo went into a steep dive. He saw the bombs release. He took a picture as they burst alongside. He saw the sky and the sea revolve about him, and felt his stomach move up towards his head from the negative G as Killer began his dive. He saw, over Killer's head now, the ship beneath him. A sailor was running from a gun-post to take shelter behind a bulkhead. The close-range weapons were opening up at them. Tracers approached slowly and then flashed past on either side at great speed. He took a photograph. Time stood still.

The destroyer was turning fast; Killer with it. Their altitude was one thousand feet and no bombs gone. The destroyer was turning back. That was what Killer was waiting for. An aileron turn and the ship was again in his sights, huge and menacing.

Five hundred feet. He felt a judder through the plane as the bombs were released. Then he was sinking to his knees with the weight of gravity as Killer pulled out at sea level. Now he was back to his camera to catch the bombs bursting across the destroyer's foc's'le. Two hits. The destroyer was slowing down, going down by the head. The men were taking to boats. The madness was over.

'Well done, Killer,' said Snowball quietly.

Any other comment would have been out of place.

'We're short of fuel,' said Killer. 'Can you give me a course to Mersa Teclai?'

Mersa Teclai was an RAF airstrip only a hundred miles away. Returning to Port Sudan was beyond their range. They had used the airstrip before in the battle against the destroyers.

'Get this off, Black,' said Bill Hewitt in B-Baker.

He passed the message reporting the destroyer bombed and sinking, the crew having taken to their boats.

'Fuel is getting short,' said Holy Temple. 'Time to go.'

'Here's the course,' said Bill.

Following the rest of the squadron, Holy turned his Swordfish on a course to Teclai and Port Sudan.

Chapter 3

HMS *Peregrine*

The next day, 998 Squadron, the other squadron from HMS *Peregrine*, was on duty. Their call-out came early. This time, British positions were being shelled by an Italian armed merchant-cruiser. 998 Squadron took off and flew the long flight to Massawa and searched the islands until their fuel was so low they had to return to Teclai. They saw nothing of the armed merchant-cruiser, and it was thought that the enemy vessel had either hidden amongst the islands or was making the hazardous journey south through the Gulf of Aden and out into the wilderness of the Indian Ocean.

Rumours and flaps abounded, and later in the day B-Baker was sent to look for a hospital-ship that was expected in Port Sudan and had failed to arrive. Bill Hewitt plotted a square search, which Holy Temple followed conscientiously. Bill scrutinised the sea through his binoculars, looking for debris or lifeboats, or hopefully the ship itself. The following morning they learned that the hospital-ship had been held up at Suez.

Two days later another call for help came from the British Army. Progress north-west of Massawa was blocked by a concentration of guns and tanks. Could the Navy help? Bolo Hawkins was dispatched with his sub-flight and two aircraft of the second sub-flight. Each of the five aircraft was equipped with eight 100-pound fragmentation bombs. Bolo's plan was to fly at low level seawards of the coast to avoid detection, turn into the land at the last minute and make a low-level run over the enemy positions.

'We know where the target is,' he told the assembled crews. 'Ten miles out along the coast road that runs north-west from Massawa. We shall make one run only, in line astern. We'll climb to one thousand feet just before we turn in, make a shallow dive towards the target to build up speed, and release our bombs at about five hundred feet. Remember, we are not dive-bombing and the bombs will be spread out, so don't leave it too late before you press the tit. And don't get too low or you might get blown up by your own bombs. We'll be tight for fuel so as soon as we've dropped we'll make for Teclai to refuel.'

Two and a half hours after take-off Bolo could see the battle smoke ahead of him. It might have been an industrial city that was concealed by the smoke, which hung low over the ground, filling the horizon; but this was the Sudan, not Europe, and the smoke came from guns and dust raised by bursting shells.

In the murk, he climbed to a thousand feet and turned in towards the target, waving the two sub-flights into line astern. His speed increased to a hundred and thirty knots as he put his nose down slightly. The sea beneath him was littered with craft of all sorts, fleeing the harbour, like a miniature Dunkirk. The surprise was complete; hardly a shot was fired at them as they crossed the coast.

'Can you see the target, Dicky?' Bolo asked his observer.

Dicky Burd, standing up in the cockpit, was looking over Bolo's shoulder, searching through his binoculars. In the rear cockpit PO Mercer was manning his Lewis gun, ready to use it whenever he saw a chance.

'I can see the road from Massawa, about three miles ahead,' said Dicky, 'and, yes, there's the target, five degrees to port.'

24

'I've got it!'

Bolo could see the tanks strung across the road in a slight curve, their guns pointing and firing to the north-west. Behind them was a line of field guns, also firing. Bolo was approaching at right angles. He could take either the tanks or the guns.

'I'm going for the tanks,' he called.

Dicky could see men aiming their rifles and machine guns at the aircraft, but he was not aware of the bullets passing. It was not like an attack on a ship or on port installations, where shell bursts and tracers would have greeted them.

They were almost over the tanks. Dicky could see faces staring at him, men trying to line up guns, men turning to run for shelter. The bombs were falling, a long line of them, starting at one end and running along the line of the tanks. Then Bolo was pulling away and Dicky saw that two of the tanks were hit. He could see Killer in L-Love, coming in lower than he should, also aiming for the tanks. Again the bombs followed the line and more tanks were hit.

Bolo had climbed to a thousand feet and was circling to one side of the target area. Dicky saw Bing Crosby, in M-Mike, attacking the line of guns, up-ending three of them with direct hits.

Now it was Biddy Bidwell's turn and he was going for the guns. More were hit. Into the dust and smoke flew Hank Phipps, the American pilot of G-George. His bombs burst in the centre of the concentration.

Forty bombs had fallen within the target area, delivered with the precision that the Fleet Air Arm specialised in. The defence concentration was in chaos and already Dicky could see the British, in light tanks and armoured cars, surging forwards.

With the squadron forming up on him, Bolo made one low-level pass over the British troops, waggling his wings in acknowledgement of their waving arms. Then it was time to go. They had enough petrol, but only just enough, to get to Mersa Teclai.

A week later, the British occupied Massawa. Italian resistance had crumbled. The East African war was over.

Lieutenant Commander Simpson led his squadron in a fly-past over Port Sudan. 'Wings', Commander Flying from *Peregrine* who had organised the defence of Port Sudan, was piloting H-Howe, replacing Sub Lieutenant Andy Andrews who had been lost at sea. All the aircraft were tucked in tightly, in three vics of three, in immaculate formation. Over the airfield they flew, then over the Red Sea Hotel that had been their home for a month, where all the staff were on the roof waving to them, over the harbour and out to sea, heading north-east.

All nine aircraft were present. Amazingly, no aircraft had been lost in the battle with the Italian flotilla. Two had been hit by gunfire; B-Baker had nearly been lost when, on a search near the Arabian coast, four scraper rings had gone. Holy Temple had nursed his aircraft all the way back across the Red Sea to Port Sudan, crossing the coast at twenty feet and landing on the beach. Sand from the desert landing-field had penetrated the engine, causing the damage. Squadron mechanics had repaired the engine and air riggers had repaired bullet holes in other Swordfish. In the primitive conditions maintenance had been limited but effective. 'Chiefy', Chief Air Artificer Tom Stillson, in charge of aircraft maintenance in the squadron, wanted the Swordfish back on board where he could see that all aircraft had a thorough overhaul.

B-Baker was tucked in on the starboard side of the CO. Its observer, Midshipman Bill Hewitt, had plotted the course given by the Squadron Senior Observer, Lieutenant Sandy Sandiford. The carrier HMS *Peregrine* was sixty miles away from Port Sudan, escorting a hospital-ship, with the cruiser HMS *Lancashire* in attendance and three destroyers providing anti-submarine cover. Peering intently through his binoculars, he saw the faintest streaks of white, twenty miles away. As they drew near, the streaks became the wakes of ships, the ships became toy models, like those in the ship-recognition room, and then his heart lifted as he recognised *Peregrine*. There was the old lady, majestic and beautiful. They were coming home.

Ahead of the carrier was the hospital-ship, with *Lancashire* leading the column. The CO led his squadron, still in tight formation, down the starboard side of the column and up the port side. After the fly-past, all ships turned until they were heading into the wind. One of the destroyers took up a position on the port quarter of the carrier, to retrieve the crew if an aircraft went into the sea. The affirmative was hoisted on a yardarm and the CO waved his squadron into line astern. They circled the carrier, four hundred yards behind each other. The Deck-Landing Control Officer, 'Bats' as he was affectionately known, in position on the port-side after-end of the flight-deck, was holding a bat in each hand, controlling the approach of each aircraft landing on. Wings was the first to land. The arrester wire brought him to a halt and his aircraft was wheeled forward by the deck-handling party to the forward lift.

Bolo Hawkins watched the familiar scene. He saw Wings touch down. The CO, backing up two hundred yards astern, was making his approach. Had Wings been waved round, the CO would have been brought in to land. As Wings had landed safely, the CO was waved round again. So was Holy Temple in B-Baker. As Hatters Dunn approached in C-Charlie, Bolo saw the lift come up and Bats bring the aircraft on to another good landing. Biddy Bidwell, in F-Fox, and Hank Phipps, in G-George, were waved round. Now it was Bolo's turn. Setting his pitch for landing, Bolo put his aircraft into a nose-up position, hanging on to its propeller, so that his hook, towards the tail end of the plane, could catch on

27

one of the arrester wires. He saw the DLCO standing motionless, his bats horizontal. Then the bats pointed downwards. He was too low. A touch of throttle to gain height. The bats had gone above the horizontal. He had over-corrected and was now too high. Ease the throttle slightly and let the aircraft sink towards the flight-deck. The DLCO brought his bats diagonally across each other, pointing downwards. Cut the engine and let the aircraft sink, in a three-point landing, onto the flight-deck. He felt the hook catch on the arrester wire and he was down.

Men in the deck-party released the arrester wire and wheeled the machine forwards to the waiting lift. The wings of Bolo's aircraft were folded and the lift carried him down to the hangar where squadron crews were waiting to push him into his place where the Swordfish was carefully picketed to ring bolts in the hangar floor. In the meantime, as the lift ascended, the next aircraft was approaching to land on.

Soon all the aircraft had landed, and a noisy throng gathered in the wardroom anteroom for pre-lunch drinks. The ship's commander duly passed the girls' letters to Killer and Bill.

'Janet's in the hospital-ship!' exclaimed Bill.

'So's Ann,' echoed Killer.

'We'll have to try and contact them,' Bill said.

Later that day they learned that the ships would remain in Port Sudan for three or four days for the hospital-ship to take on casualties from the East African campaign. Killer arranged for a message to go to Ann after the two ships berthed:

Bill and I are free tomorrow evening. Can you and Janet meet us for dinner and dancing? We shall be at the foot of your gangway at 1900 hours.

Love,
Killer

The afternoon was spent in the hangar, checking aircraft and discussing problems with the maintenance crews, visiting the squadron office to catch up on the bumph, settling into cabins and reading the mail. A month's mail had accumulated in the ship and this was eagerly claimed by the Port Sudan party.

Bolo took his three letters from Joyce to the privacy of his cabin. In the first, Joyce had included a recent photograph of herself. She was now twenty-one years old and in her third year at Cambridge. The following term she would be taking her finals in English.

Bolo studied the photograph. The girl he saw had a beautiful, serene face, with eyes set wide apart, and a look that was saved from being too serious by the suspicion of a twinkle in them. The tiny dimples in her cheeks enhanced the smiling mouth that promised so much more. Joyce's dark hair curled to her shoulders, adding grace to her poised and slender figure.

'To think,' Bolo reflected, 'I once thought of her as a sister.'

Now, mentally, he reached out to her and pulled her to him for the kiss he had not yet been able to give her. In her letter Joyce told him more about her life at Cambridge, about the books she was reading and the music she had been able to listen to.

'Do you remember,' she went on, 'when I came to visit you at Lee-on-Solent a year ago? What a wonderful Easter that was! We were listening to Brahms' Fourth Symphony and when it came to the slow movement the pizzicato was like a plucking at my heart, I was so full of love for you. You were so near to me and I wanted to reach out and hold you. The music was expressing what I couldn't say. I dared to hope you had similar feelings, but I wasn't sure. You were always so careful and correct with me. I was the daughter of your friend, Corny Wilde; I was like a sister to you. If only you had known; I didn't feel the least bit like a sister. ...'

And I don't feel like a big brother, Bolo thought ruefully. He was now twenty-six years old, the second senior member of his squadron, well used to leading men. He had faced enemy guns and enemy fighters; he had seen his friends die; he was hardened by battle and by hard living in the desert. Yet he had a melting, yielding feeling when he thought of Joyce, of her softness against his hardness. We two are one in spirit, he declared to himself. He longed for the time when the two could be one in the flesh.

Bolo thought again how Joyce had opened his mind to a wider horizon. Through her he had learned to feel the power of music; with her he had discovered art. He well remembered how they had travelled up to London to the Tate Gallery. First they had visited the Turner Room, where, with Joyce, he had been entranced by the hazy, magical, shimmering seascapes, truer to life than the reality. Of the post-Impressionists, Cézanne had particularly appealed to him. When Joyce pointed out the geometric shapes made by the landscapes and the colours that faded with distance, Bolo had cried, 'But that is just how I see a landscape from the air when I fly over it.'

Bolo realised that he had come a long way from the simple-minded cricketer of twenty-three that he had been when he first met Joyce. Now, once more, he picked up his pen to write to her to tell her of his love.

An air of suppressed excitement and anticipation had been developing in the carrier throughout the day. The ship was complete again. The squadrons were back. The operation had been a success. It was time for a party. The galley had prepared a special meal for dinner; the officers had dressed for the occasion in mess undress – a short white jacket over black trousers and cummerbund, and wing collar and bow tie.

Bill had something special to celebrate: he was now twenty years old and his promotion to sub lieutenant had come through. His wine bill was now increased to two pounds per month instead of the fifteen shillings allowed to midshipmen. With beer at sixpence a glass, whisky or brandy threepence and gin twopence, spirits were cheaper than beer, and in the hot evenings long drinks were popular. After dinner, wardroom stewards had been busy serving horses' necks and John Collins.

Now the squadron officers were grouped round the piano, which Dorrie Dorrington was playing. Dorrie was a great friend of Bill's. An observer from the same course as Snowball Kennedy and Bill Hewitt, like them he had been flown by Bolo Hawkins during his flying training at Lee-on-Solent. Unlike Bill, Dorrie came from a wealthy family and had attended a well-known public school.

Dorrie's bed had been next to Bill's when they had first joined the Fleet Air Arm as leading airmen at HMS *St Vincent*, a training establishment at Gosport. They had become firm friends and at Greenwich Naval College, where they had their induction as naval officers, and throughout Bill's first few months as an officer, Dorrie had quietly steered him through the difficulties of social adjustment.

Dorrie was popular in the squadron. He was a gifted pianist with a large repertoire, from popular songs to Mozart concertos. Now he had fitted his long, slim, elegant body beneath the piano and was thumping out a popular tune. Around him were grouped the officers singing lustily. Stewards moved amongst the officers, replenishing glasses. It had all the makings of a good party.

From popular songs Dorrie moved to favourite flying tunes. When Bill had first joined the *Peregrine* he had been shocked by the coarse nature of some of the songs. He had soon come to realise that the cruder the words, the more the young officers were able to let off steam, particularly after hazardous operations. Now he sang with the best of them.

There's a balls-up on the flight-deck
And the Wavy Navy's done it.
There's a balls-up on the flight-deck
And they don't know who to blame.

Without a pause, Dorrie ran through the songs: 'She was poor, but she was honest', 'A lady was barfin 'er baby one night', 'Lydia Pink', 'Eskimo Nell'; and 'I don't want to join the Navy'. One after the other the songs were sung with gusto, until Dorrie came back to the carrier's own song:

We are the carrier, *Peregrine,*
The best ship you have ever seen.
We search the seas for an enemy fleet
In winter cold or summer heat
And never return till the search is complete
And never have sight of an enemy fleet
And still you will find we are keen.

We fly our Swordfish aeroplanes
Whether it snows or whether it rains,
Except when the engine will not start,
Or wings break off and fall apart,
Or the looker cannot find his chart,
Or the sparker cannot raise a spark.
And we start all over again.

By now, glasses were empty and stewards were removing the debris. Suddenly across the hubbub came the cry:
'At 'em 999 Squadron.'
With practised skill the two squadrons found themselves locked in a gigantic rugby scrum. Laughing and shouting encouragement, they pushed against each other. It was a mighty, but even, battle. First one way the scrum moved, then the other. Ship's officers joined in if they saw one side giving

32

way, until eventually the whole company collapsed in a shouting, struggling, laughing heap of humanity.

Then a second order rang out:

'999 Squadron – Dogs o' War – Bill Hewitt.'

Bill was horrified. He knew what was going to happen. He had seen it before after other promotions. He tried to escape through the door, but he was unsuccessful. In very quick time his trousers were removed and he was hoisted bodily above the squadron in his shirt tails.

This marked the end of the party.

Chapter 4

Port Sudan

The following evening Killer and Bill were waiting at the foot of *Carpathian*'s gangway. They had received notes from Ann and Janet confirming that they were free for the evening. Both officers were in mess undress. The girls came down the gangway to greet them, dressed for the evening in attractive short evening gowns, Ann in pale blue and Janet in ivory.

'Fancy meeting you here!' exclaimed Killer, laughing.

'I don't know why we are meeting you,' Ann retorted. 'You stood us up last time we were going out to dinner. Remember?'

'So we did. So we did,' said Killer. 'And we couldn't even pass a message to let you know why. I'm sorry about that.'

'Why didn't you write?' Janet asked.

'We were earmarked for what was then a secret mission,' Bill replied. 'All leave was stopped and we weren't allowed to telephone or even send a letter. We thought we had lost contact, until the Commander gave us your letters.'

'He gave them to you personally?'

'Yes.'

'What a nice man he is!'

Janet then told the boys about their visit to the ship and tea with the Commander.

'So this is Port Sudan!' said Ann.

They had come to the town centre with its market square, surrounded by old, colonial buildings. Small native-style shops were still open, owned by Greeks and managed by Sudanese. The girls were intrigued with the 'fuzzy-wuzzies', from a tribe of fierce warriors, whose jet-black hair, plastered in dried mud, curled upwards and made them appear to be seven feet tall. They carried strangely carved knives, like kukris, in their belts.

'I had a funny experience with one of them,' said Killer. 'I'll tell you about it over dinner.'

At a corner, camels were drinking from a stone trough. The desert was never very far away and a dry, hot wind was blowing into the town. The carrier and hospital-ship seemed huge in the small harbour.

'This is very different from Alexandria,' said Ann.

'And a far cry from England!' echoed Killer. 'What would my mum say if she could see us now?'

The girls laughed.

'I expect she'd think we were on a film set,' said Bill.

'It is a bit unreal, isn't it?' said Janet, 'What with your flying in the desert and our being on a hospital-ship and meeting you like this!'

'Wait till you hear my story,' said Killer.

The group had now arrived at the Red Sea Hotel and Killer led the way into the comfortable lounge. They were in the middle of their drinks when Killer jumped up and said, 'Come on, Bill. Let's show the girls our bedroom.'

The girls looked at him in astonishment and some alarm. Janet was even more astonished when Bill took her arm and, stifling her protests, led her after Killer and the reluctant Ann. Bill had not been like this before, she thought. She had always felt safe with him.

Up the stairs the girls were hurried, through swing doors and out onto the flat roof of the hotel.

'This was our bedroom,' said Bill, laughing. 'The hotel was

so crowded that the junior officers slept in camp-beds on the roof.'

'It's beautiful up here,' exclaimed Janet.

The small town snuggled beneath them, its life hidden in the shadows of buildings. Out to the west they could see the desert and, to the east, the harbour, guarded by its cranes that stood like sentinels, and beyond the harbour the sea. The whole scene was bathed in moonlight that added to the magic and mystery. The girls were enchanted.

'I used to lie here at night-time,' said Killer, 'with the stars very bright overhead and the crescent moon looking down at me, and I used to dream of you, Ann.'

'Oh, go away with you!' exclaimed Ann, laughing.

Bill and Janet laughed, too. This was the Killer that the girls remembered, half serious and half joking. You never quite knew how to take him.

Over dinner, the girls pressed Killer to tell his story of the fuzzy-wuzzy.

'After the battle with the Italians,' began Killer, 'some of us thought we'd like to visit Suakin.'

'That's a town and harbour about forty miles down the coast,' interjected Bill. 'The harbour silted up,' continued Killer, 'and the town is now deserted. It's still intact, almost the same as when the people left. Now there's no one there at all. Its claim to fame, though, is Kitchener's Fort, which was built to defend the town against the Mad Mullah in the uprising against General Gordon. Did you see the film *The Four Feathers*? In that it was the fuzzy-wuzzies who were attacking the British troops.'

'I expect they used some of the fuzzy-wuzzies here as extras. They wouldn't have needed anything in the way of costume,' said Bill.

'The Governor of Port Sudan put three cars at our disposal, and a group of fifteen of us, including Bill, here, and Yank and Dorrie (I think you met them at the Carlton)

36

set off down the desert road to Suakin. We were warned that the natives were not too friendly and that we should take pistols with us.

'It was a strange experience. Even the ride was strange. At one point we saw a camel-train making for Port Sudan; at another, we passed a herd of wild gazelle; but the strangest sight of all was the mirage. The desert was shimmering in the heat when quite suddenly the mirage of a town appeared, complete with minarets and tree-lined streets. We all saw it.

'When we reached Suakin we were dropped at Kitchener's Fort and left to our own devices. We discovered that Suakin is divided into two parts: one the native quarter on the mainland, which still flourishes; the other the white quarter on the island, which is connected by a wide bridge to the mainland.

'As the island was deserted we decided to leave our pistols in the car. I set off with Bill, Dorrie and Yank, but we soon lost Dorrie and Yank. Then I stopped to take a photograph of the minaret of an imposing, but deserted, mosque, and when I looked round Bill had disappeared. Just then a strange wailing noise came from the minaret. It was the muezzin calling the hour of prayer at three o'clock. It was quite shattering because, remember, the place was supposed to be deserted, and the profound silence afterwards put me on edge. However, I set about exploring in real earnest and poked around in one or two houses, looking for souvenirs, but without success. The more promising ones were locked up.

'Eventually I came to a door which ought to have been locked but was not. I pushed it open and went inside. I was startled by what I saw. About twenty weapons, spears, swords and knives, were leaning or hanging against the walls, and some pairs of sandals were lying just inside the door. A mat and a stool were the only other furniture. I took two of the knives, rather like the ones carried by fuzzy-wuzzies, encased in leather sheaths, and stuck them down my shirt. I was just about to select a sword when I heard a creaking noise behind me. I froze.

'The door opened and I could feel the presence of a man behind me. I turned slowly. A grizzled, bewhiskered and altogether fierce-looking fuzzy-wuzzy, ten feet tall – well, seven at least – stood there, eyeing me with definite hostility. He was carrying a large, thick staff horizontally behind his neck and a knife in his belt. I decided to put on a bold face and hope for the best. "*Sayeeda,*" I said, as cheerfully as I could. That's the native greeting.

' "*Sayeeda,*" he growled, still looking hostile.

' "You – live here?" I asked slowly, in case he could speak English.

' "*Aywa,*" he replied. That means yes.

' "Nice – place – you – have!"

' "This mosque," he broke in, waving one hand around.

'Then I realised my offence. If this were indeed a mosque I should not have entered. In any case, one must be bare-headed and put on the sandals provided.

'I hastily took off my cap, begged his pardon and made a quick exit. He stood aside to let me pass. I believe I walked off calmly enough – British and all that – mustn't let the side down – but my heart beat faster when I heard footsteps dogging me. I stopped. The footsteps stopped. I turned left. The footsteps followed me. Not a soul was in sight and the only sound was the warbling of wild pigeons and those almost silent footsteps. Once a stray cat darted out from a doorway and made me pull up with a gasp. I began to wish I had my pistol with me. I turned another corner and darted into a doorway. Soon the man came into sight. It was my friend from the mosque. He saw that he was observed and now followed me openly a hundred yards behind.

'I realised that his intention was only to see that I did not return to his dwelling so I continued on my way more cheerfully, until I became aware of human voices whispering and laughing. I looked round, but I saw only my silent shadower. We came to a stone trough at the corner of a street, rather like the horse-troughs you used to find in England. Beside the trough were three native girls, regarding me intently. They beckoned me to go with them. I decided I'd had enough for one day so I took the right hand turning and increased my pace. Then I saw Bill coming towards me. He asked me about the fuzzy-wuzzy who appeared to be following me. I told him what had happened.'

'It's true,' said Bill. 'Killer and I tried to retrace his footsteps to find the mosque with the weapons. We did not find it nor did we see the three girls again, though we searched carefully. We tried all the doors, but they were all locked. The place was deserted, a city of the dead. The only inhabitants we saw were pigeons and stray cats. Even so, we both had the feeling that unseen eyes were watching us, and this feeling persisted until we sighted the others at Kitchener's Fort. Killer still has the knives he found.'

Killer had told his tale well and the girls had listened spellbound to the strange story.

'I reported it to the authorities,' said Killer. 'Their comment was that there were pockets of anti-British feeling and this was probably one of them. They would look into it.'

Ann shivered.

'Are we safe here in Port Sudan?' she asked.

Killer laughed.

'You are so long as you are with intrepid birdmen.'

They all laughed.

'What about your story?' said Bill. 'What's happened to you since we left you?'

Janet told them how they had been selected with eight other VADs to escort a group of naval casualties to Cape Town.

'We'd been told we were esorting a hospital-ship to Cape

Town,' said Bill. 'We'd no idea that you'd be on it until we had your notes yesterday.'

'Bill was sent out to look for a hospital-ship that was missing,' said Killer. 'We were told the next day that it had been delayed at the last port.'

'That must have been us,' Ann said. 'There was talk about engine trouble and we were held up at Suez for two days while the ship's engineers fixed it.'

'Well, we're all here now, thank God. The dance we're going to is at the Red Sea Sports Club,' said Killer. 'I hope you like it.'

The girls were captivated by the setting at the club. A dance-floor had been constructed on the lawn, lit up by coloured lights set in the trees and shrubs around it. Floodlights illuminated the small dance-band at one end.

'It never rains here,' said Killer, 'so they can have their dances in the open. Even the cinema is out of doors.'

Tables were set round the floor and there was a large table from which Sudanese waiters were serving drinks. Killer escorted the party to a vacant table and the girls were able to take stock of the scene. Only four couples were dancing. There seemed to be a large number of men, army and navy officers in uniform and some civilians.

'The civilians are mostly from the Greek population here,' said Killer. 'They keep very much to themselves and it's been difficult to find a girl to dance with.'

The two naval officers were looked at with some envy as they asked their partners for the first dance. Killer was first away, and Bill watched with amusement as Killer set off in a determined fashion, ploughing through the quickstep. Ann was a good dancer, very light on her feet and able to follow Killer's awkward steps. She made him look and feel like a good dancer.

From past experience at Alexandria, Janet knew that Bill

was an excellent dancer. Then, as now, he had led with confidence and skill. The floor was half empty and Bill was able to indulge in clever, little running-steps and delicate half-chassés, as he led her round the floor. Janet was not quite sure how it happened, but she felt that she knew what variation Bill was making almost before he made it. Bill was an intuitive dancer and she responded intuitively to him. But he had to have been taught.

'Where did you learn to dance like this, Bill?' she asked.

Bill laughed.

'It was at the church club,' he said. 'I was a practising Roman Catholic when I was younger and the church had a social club that met once a week to dance and play table tennis. One of the men taught me the basic steps, but there were several very good girl dancers who taught me the more intricate steps. I think it was through them that I polished up my dancing.'

Janet was intrigued with this glimpse of Bill's youth, which was so different from her own. She wanted to know more about him, but she knew he was diffident in talking about himself. She marvelled at the maturity he displayed on the dance-floor.

This was very much in evidence in the next dance she had with him. After a romping Viennese waltz with Ann, Bill turned to Janet for the slow foxtrot. His steps were long and languorous and Janet felt her body yielding to his. She danced as in a dream, effortlessly, unconsciously. She was aware of the soft, coloured lights, the shrubs and trees in half-shadow around them, the moon beyond, large and low, the shadowy figures of other dancers, but most of all the hardness of Bill's body against her softness. She laid her cheek against his and gave herself up completely to the dance. At the end of it Bill stood for a few moments, holding her, letting the experience slip away quietly before taking her hand and escorting her back to the table.

41

The evening was a great success. More nurses arrived from the hospital-ship to balance the numbers. Killer's light-hearted banter was in sharp contrast to Bill's quietness, and this contrast was repeated as they made their way back to the ships. Killer and Ann were walking ahead, arms around each other's waists, in animated conversation. Bill and Janet walked hand in hand, in silence. It was a companionable silence, as if their dancing had said it all, leaving them now relaxed. Janet had been strangely disturbed by the evening. The unusual setting, Killer's strange story at dinner, dancing with Bill, had drained her emotionally. She wondered if she were falling in love. She knew little about Bill other than that his background was very different from her own. We are both very young she thought, practically. And then she thought, what has that got to do with it?

Chapter 5

Enemy Submarine

The next day all leave on the *Carpathian* was cancelled. The wounded soldiers arrived in ambulances and lorries, to be carefully fitted into the accommodation aboard. In all there were two hundred army casualties in addition to the hundred naval patients. Some of them were stretcher cases, in need of hospital treatment. The *Carpathian* was their hospital. All the VADs, with Sister Harding, from the Naval Hospital in Alexandria, turned to help. The following day, the small convoy sailed. All the flying crews attended a special briefing in the wardroom after breakfast.

Wings spoke to them first. 'The war in East Africa is virtually over,' he said. 'However, we know that an armed merchant-cruiser escaped from Massawa and at least two submarines are unaccounted for. We shall send out a search party each morning, and throughout the day anti-submarine patrols will be maintained. The most dangerous area will be between Port Sudan and Aden. During that part of our journey we will have two anti-submarine patrols, an inner one and an outer one.

'Our first stop will be Aden, where we'll take on fuel. We expect to be in harbour for three days before continuing to Mombasa. Once we get into the Indian Ocean, south of Aden, we'll mount regular searches. We believe the Italian armed merchant-cruiser that escaped from Massawa may be

43

trying to contact the German armed merchant-cruiser *Hohenlinden*. Both of these are a threat to our shipping.'

The ASO, or Air Staff Officer, followed Wings:

'The inner anti-submarine patrol will be five miles ahead of the fleet, extending to five miles either side, and the outer patrol will be fifteen miles ahead, extending to fifteen miles each side of the fleet's course. A/S aircraft will each carry two depth charges. Wireless silence will be maintained unless you have a contact with a submarine when an immediate warning signal must be sent before you attack. Today's flying-programme has been posted on the wardroom notice board.'

Killer and Bill studied the list on the noticeboard. 999 Squadron was on A/S patrol duty and the list gave the order of flying. It also showed the changes made by the CO as a result of the death of the crew of H-Howe. The new crew had arrived in the *Peregrine,* pilot Midshipman (A) Cartwright RNVR, observer Midshipman (A) Saville RNVR, TAG Leading Airman Beale. Following his usual practice, the CO had put an experienced pilot with a new observer and vice versa. Snowball Kennedy had moved from L-Love to join Midshipman Cartwright in H-Howe and Midshipman Saville was to fly with Holy Temple in B-Baker. Although Bill Hewitt, observer of B-Baker, was sorry to be leaving Holy with whom he had seen much action, he was happy to be joining his friend, Killer Compton, in L-Love.

999 Squadron

Anti-Submarine Patrols Friday 18th April

Time	A/C	Pilot	Observer	TAG
1000	A	Lt.Com. Simpson	Lt. Sandiford	CPO Cutter
	B	Sub Lt.Temple	Mid. Saville	PO Black

44

1230	C	Mid. Dunn	Sub Lt. White	L/A Naylor
	F	Lt. Bidwell	Sub Lt. Weston	PO Jarman
1500	G	Sub Lt. Phipps	Sub Lt. Dorrington	L/A Kirk
	H	Mid. Cartwright	Sub Lt. Kennedy	L/A Beale
1730	K	Lt. Hawkins	Lt. Burd	PO Mercer
	L	Sub Lt. Compton	Sub Lt. Hewitt	L/A Gibbons
Reserve	M	Sub Lt. Crosby	S/Lt. Lloyd	L/A Davey

'I see we have the dusk patrol,' said Killer. That's a good time for sighting a submarine, particularly in the last half-hour before landing on.'

After tea, they were in the hangar checking their aircraft with their engine mechanic, Naval Airman Bailey, and their air-rigger, Naval Airman Riggs. Next to them, Bolo's aircraft, K-King, was being prepared by Leading Air Mechanic Hapwell and his friend, Air Rigger Tiny Rawlings.

They all stopped to listen to the Tannoy, blaring forth its message: '999 Squadron range two aircraft.'

'Here, that's us,' said Bailey. 'Come on, Tiny, we'll give you a hand with King if you help us with Love.'

Under the control of a petty officer, the four men released the picket lines anchoring King to the hangar-deck and wheeled the aircraft forwards onto the lift. Slowly, as befitted the age of *Peregrine*, the lift rose to the flight-deck, where the deck-handling party, under the sharp eye of the Deck Control Officer, wheeled it to the flying-off position at the after end. Here, its wings were unfolded and locked into the flight position. In the meantime, Love was manhandled onto the lift and taken up to the flight-deck to be positioned on King's starboard quarter. Hapwell and Rawlings and Bailey and Riggs now attended to their own machines. With the riggers winding up the engine-starters, the mechanics sat in the cockpits and, when 'contact' was made, started the engines. Each mechanic now nursed his engine until it was running smoothly. The air-gunners by this time had joined their aircraft and were busy tuning their wireless sets.

In the meantime, the pilots and observers had assembled in the operations room for final instructions. Killer and Bill learned that they were flying the inner patrol in L-Love whilst K-King would fly the outer patrol.

At 1715 they sauntered down to their aircraft, Bill with his canvas holdall containing his chartboard and navigation instruments and Killer carrying his pilot's parachute. Riggs passed up Bill's navigation equipment whilst Bailey exchanged places with Killer. Now, fitter and rigger took their places at the wheels of the aircraft, ready to pull the chocks away when signalled by the pilot.

The carrier was already turning, until the wisp of smoke at the forward end of the flight-deck was blowing fore and aft. Both air and ground crews fitted easily into the smooth routine, and soon the pilots were running up their engines on the brakes and chocks preparatory to take-off. Wings had come to the side of the bridge and was staring down at them, waiting for a signal from the Deck Control Officer. When all was ready he waved a green flag and Bolo was off. Then it was Love's turn. They were manoeuvred into the starting-position. Wings waved his green flag; Killer waved his chocks away at a signal from the DCO and revved his engine hard, holding the plane back on its brakes; then Killer released the brakes and the plane trundled forwards, at first slowly, but quickly building up speed until it was ready to take off. He let the Swordfish fly itself off and as Bill looked astern, over the air-gunner's head, past the tail fin, he could see the flight-deck falling away from them, and beyond it the destroyer stationed on the carrier's quarter in case of accident. He could also see the first of the returning aircraft already making its approach.

As Killer flew into his allotted position, five miles ahead of the fleet, Bill swept the sea with his binoculars. The surface was faintly ruffled in the slight breeze and Bill searched carefully for a telltale fleck of foam. At most he might expect to see a periscope. The light was too good for a submarine to risk surfacing. Ten miles further ahead, Bill knew that Bolo would be making a wider sweep.

Backwards and forwards Killer flew, monotonously, endlessly. The first hour passed, then the second. Still the three air-crew concentrated on their task, Killer and L/A Gibbons searching directly, Bill using his binoculars. He divided the sea into sections, searching each section diligently before passing onto the next. He had no need to bother about navigation. Killer was quite able to judge his position and turning point visually from the fleet only five miles away.

Slowly the sun descended in the west. Still the small fleet kept perfect formation to the north of them, zigzagging every fifteen minutes to make an attack by submarine more difficult.

By 1930 Bill was feeling tired. Killer was bored with the endless flying to and fro.

'I wonder what's on for dinner tonight, Bill,' he said, stifling a yawn. 'I'll be glad to finish this patrol. It doesn't look as though we'll sight anything now.'

'If there's a sub about, this is when he's likely to show up,' said Bill. 'I'll keep looking until we pack it in.'

Ten minutes before the end of the patrol, the sun had disappeared behind the rim of the sea, setting up a golden glow in the west. In that direction the sea was clear and bright. Nothing moved. To the east it was darker, the sea melting into a dark purple.

Suddenly a faint movement caught Bill's attention, a cat's-paw of wind – or what? He focussed his glasses onto it, carefully. And then he spotted the slim pillar, creating the slightest trail of foam. A periscope.

47

'Submarine red one-oh, about three miles away.' He spoke urgently into his Gosport tubes, keeping his eye on the target.

Killer responded immediately, turning on to the bearing, still unable to see the periscope with his naked eye.

A minute later: 'I've got it!' he called.

Bill scribbled a hasty message in simple code: *Submarine bears 210 degrees from you, distance five miles.*

'Get that off to the carrier quickly, Gibbons,' he said, passing the message to his TAG.

Killer had put his nose down and built up speed to a hundred and thirty knots. 'I'm going straight in,' he said. 'Stand by!'

Bill was sure the submarine had not seen them. He could now see the periscope clearly, less than a mile away. He clipped on his jockstrap, which secured him to the floor of the aeroplane, a necessary precaution in action to save him from being thrown out of the open cockpit.

'Message passed,' called Gibbons.

Killer was in a perfect position for his drop, approaching the submarine from its port beam. He was down to fifty feet, with the submarine only four hundred yards away. At two hundred yards, Bill saw a surge of water and the periscope disappeared.

'He's seen us,' he called.

In seconds Killer was over a spot slightly ahead of where the periscope was last seen.

'Depth-charges gone!' he called.

He continued on his course, to put distance between the plane and the exploding depth-charges. Anxiously Bill watched astern. He thought he heard the crump of the depth-charges over the sound of the engines, as two huge fountains of water cascaded over the probable position of the submarine. Then, nothing. The surge caused by the explosions died away. Killer brought his Swordfish round in a tight circle. Bill kept his eyes glued to the dying turbulence, disappointment welling up inside him.

Then all three crew shouted as one. The submarine was breaking surface, stern first. Bill watched as the hatches opened and men appeared in the conning-tower and by the gun-mountings The submarine was stationary, but men had already manned the three-inch high angle gun and the Bofors and were aiming them at Love. Shell-bursts appeared ahead of the Swordfish and tracers from the Bofors arched towards them, bright in the dim light. As always, the enemy failed to appreciate the slow speed of the Swordfish, now back to its cruising speed of ninety knots, and the tracers, too, passed ahead.

Killer steered the Swordfish just out of range of the Bofors and circled, easily avoiding the shell-bursts of the three-inch gun. The scene, Bill thought, was frozen in time, a tableau on a tapestry of sea, lit faintly by the dull glow of the dying sun.

Just one mile away to the south the submarine lay motionless. Four miles to the east the fleet had made a ninety degrees turn and was steaming away from the danger. One of the destroyers had picked up its skirts and was now three miles away, rushing in to attack. Gibbons completed the picture for Bill.

'Swordfish approaching, four miles west.'

Quickly Bill looked to the west and saw K-King racing in, in a shallow dive. The submarine had switched its gunfire to the approaching Swordfish, putting up a curtain of shells and tracers between itself and the aircraft.

'He'll never get through,' cried Killer. 'I'm going to divert their attention. Man your guns, Gibbons, and fire whenever you can.'

Already Killer had turned. Bolo, in K-King, was approaching from the submarine's port bow; Killer now dived towards it on its starboard bow, his single front gun spraying the submarine's deck. Gibbons, too, had joined in, firing as soon as his gun came to bear.

At the critical moment for Bolo, Bill saw the submarine's guns swivel round to meet the new menace, leaving Bolo a clear run in. Jinking from side to side, to avoid the shells, Killer completed his run just before Bolo arrived over the submarine. Bill watched Bolo's depth-charges fall in a perfect straddle of the submarine. They had been set to a shallow depth and the explosions came almost immediately. The submarine half rose out of the sea and then settled back in a sinking condition. Men came tumbling through the hatches, releasing rubber inflatables and wearing life jackets. Soon the sea was littered with the debris of battle. Some of the survivors had managed to get into the inflatables; some were clutching at the side of them; some were swimming or floating near by. The submarine was going down.

Before it disappeared, Bill saw Bolo drop a flame-float a short way away from the survivors. In the rapidly growing darkness, this was all there was to guide the approaching destroyer to the rescue. Only when the destroyer had begun to take the survivors aboard did Bolo leave the scene and, with Killer forming up on him, fly in the general direction of the fleet.

By now it was quite dark and Bill felt a surge of relief when out of the darkness ahead of them a searchlight was beamed straight upwards. Soon the two aircraft were circling the carrier. Bolo had once practised some night deck-landings, but Killer had never attempted one. Bill watched as Bolo made the first landing. He could see the two lines of lights, dimly illuminating the flight-deck of *Peregrine* and the navigation lights of King as Bolo made his approach. The carrier and the Swordfish themselves were the vaguest of blurred shadows. The lights of the Swordfish settled on the flight-deck and became stationary. K-King was down. Now it was their turn.

Bill stood up in his cockpit, leaning against the forward bulkhead. He could see over Killer's head and was able to watch their approach. As Killer came out of his turn, astern of the carrier, Bill could see the two lines of lights along the flight-deck, and on the port side, near the carrier's stern, the batsman's lights. At first the lights remained steady, one either side of the batsman. Then Bill saw the right-hand light drop down to the batsman's side, leaving the other outstretched: 'You are too fast. Reduce speed.' They were getting close now and then Bill saw the batsman's lights lowered below the horizontal. 'You are too low,' he was saying.

Events happened very quickly now. Suddenly the left light facing the Swordfish was whirled round and round in a circle. 'Go round again.'

Bill heard the roar of the Pegasus engine as Killer opened the throttle wide. He felt the surge of the plane as it gathered speed. He saw the shadowy shape of the round-down barely a yard beneath them as the plane roared past. It was touch and go at one point whether they would avoid the round-down. Then they were clear and Bill released his breath in a long sigh.

'We need to practise this a bit more,' Killer was saying. 'It's not so easy as in daytime.'

Killer's voice was calm, much calmer, Bill thought, than his own.

In a few minutes Killer was making his second approach. Again the lights were level: 'You are OK. Keep coming on.' Bats pointing upwards: 'You are too high.'

Killer eased his throttle and allowed the aircraft to sink, tail down. Bats level. A touch of throttle to stop the aircraft from sinking too quickly.

The batsman suddenly flung his arms across each other. 'Cut your engine and touch down.'

Killer closed his throttle and held his plane steady. Bill

51

heard the thump as the Swordfish hit the deck and then he braced himself against the drag as the arrester wire caught their hook. They were down. Killer had completed his first ever night-landing on a carrier.

Chapter 6

Aden

Janet and Ann were fascinated by the scene that greeted them when they came on deck. They had been on duty whilst *Carpathian* was anchoring, but as soon as they were free they had hurried out to see the sights. *Carpathian* had anchored in the Inner Harbour. Stretching away from them was the dusty, brown peninsula of Aden, with the town of Aden skirting the harbour. Close by they could see *Peregrine* at anchor and beyond her *Lancashire*, but it was the colourful scene around their ship that attracted them. Dozens of feluccas and other boats lay just off the side of the hospital-ship, with brown figures in white robes offering their wares to the many soldiers and sailors gathered on the promenade-deck: handbags and wallets in tooled leather, animals and figurines in wood or ivory, garish cotton cloths. All were offered with much gesticulation and shouting by the Arabs and good-natured approval from the soldiers and sailors.

To one side was a vessel like a punt from which small boys were diving. As the girls watched, they saw coins flung by the soldiers being caught by the boys as they glistened in the sun on their way to the bottom. Thirty feet below they could see some of the bigger boys scrabbling on the seabed for the coins that had been missed. A fat man in white with a red fez seemed to be in control. As the boys scrambled aboard the punt they handed their prizes to him before making their next dive.

The attention of the girls was caught by a boat leaving the *Peregrine*, and with pleasure they recognised the figures of Killer and Bill. They had sent a message to the carrier inviting the boys to lunch and to see over the hospital-ship. This was the reply. They hurried to the gangway to greet Killer and Bill as they came aboard.

'Do we or don't we?' said Killer as he came up the steps.

'Do what?' exclaimed Ann, laughing.

'Salute, of course,' said Killer, 'as we do on a naval ship.'

'I've never seen a doctor salute when he comes aboard,' said Ann.

'What a lot of brown jobs!' Killer said, as they made their way through the throng.

'We took on two hundred wounded soldiers at Port Sudan,' Janet explained. 'The ones you see are the less seriously wounded, like most of the Navy boys. The worst casualties are confined to bed in cabins or wards.'

'I like this,' exclaimed Bill, as Janet opened the door to their cabin.

The cabin was small, with a bed on either side, separated by a dressing table. Above the dressing table was an open port hole. Two wardrobes stood at the bottom end of the cabin and two armchairs completed the furniture.

'Well, it's a little bit spartan,' said Janet.

'Luxurious by our standards!' Killer exclaimed.

'Leave your hats here, and we'll take you down to the lounge,' said Ann.

As they made their way through doorways and corridors and finally down a rather grand staircase, the young officers commented on the ship.

'It's very different from the carrier,' said Bill, 'more elegant, even though it's all painted white. You know you are in a hospital-ship, though, with the nurses in uniform, the doctors in white coats and the smell of antiseptic.'

'We've just time for a drink before lunch,' said Janet, 'and after lunch we'll show you over the ship.'

Two other differences were noted by the boys when they entered the lounge. The drinks were soft and the majority of the inhabitants were female.

'Of course, we have many more nurses than doctors aboard, and our nurses are all female,' said Ann. 'On this ship the nurses and doctors use the same lounge and dining room. The patients have separate facilities.'

A number of VADs crowded round the naval officers as the girls ordered their drinks. Among them Bill recognised Maggie and Pam whom they had met in Alexandria. Bill seemed overwhelmed by the crowd of girls, but Killer was enjoying himself hugely.

'There I was,' he declared, 'at nought feet, with five huge fighters coming at me all at once.'

'What did you do?' cried Ann.

'Why, I put on my diving-suit and ducked under the sea.'

'Is he often like this?' Ann asked Bill.

'Very often,' Bill replied, 'particularly on soft drinks.'

Accompanied by all the VADs, Janet and Ann led the boys to the buffet lunch, set out on a table. They helped them to the choicest meats and the freshest salads, and it was a hilarious group that found its way to a vacant table.

'Hello, then! What's all this?'

The voice came from a good-looking doctor, probably in his early thirties. 'The opposition!' grunted Killer.

The chattering stopped.

'These officers are from *Peregrine,* Sub Lieutenants Compton and Hewitt,' said Janet to the doctor. 'And this is Doctor Lovemore, one of our surgeons.'

'You wouldn't by any chance have had anything to do with the submarine that was sunk?' said the doctor.

Killer and Bill looked at each other, saying nothing.

'You don't mean to say you were flying one of those Swordfish!'

Again Killer and Bill said nothing.

'You were!' cried the doctor.

'My hero!' exclaimed Janet, laughing and giving Bill a big kiss.

'Here, I had something to do with it,' said Killer.

All the girls now joined in the fun, taking turns to kiss the boys and express their approval. The information had quickly passed round the tables and there was a spontaneous clap from all those in the dining room.

Bill was embarrassed by the acclaim, but Killer enjoyed every moment of it.

'Wish my CO appreciated me like you lot,' he said, grimacing.

Lunch was a lively affair and, with eight ladies to contend with, the naval officers were hard put to keep their end up. That they did was largely due to Killer's unrestrained sense of fun and Bill's unfailing courtesy.

After lunch, Janet and Ann took the two naval officers on a tour of the ship. Along the promenade-deck were several large cabins, now converted into wards, each with four bunks.

'The VADs are nursing the naval casualties,' said Ann, 'and these are some of our more seriously wounded.'

She opened the door and Killer and Bill found themselves in a large, pleasant room, with an open porthole giving access to light and fresh air. The four bed patients, young naval officers, greeted the girls by name.

'Harry Tucker, Ben Brown, Tom Watkins and Ken Riley,' said Ann, introducing each of the naval officers in turn.

'Killer Compton and Bill Hewitt from *Peregrine.*'

Three of the officers were from destroyers that had been in action, north of Crete. Ken Riley was from *Warspite.*

'I got this ashore in the Western Desert,' he said, indicating the bandage round his chest. 'I was liaising with the Army when *Warspite* bombarded the Italian troops. I was spotting for *Warspite.*'

'That must have been the time when we were there, Bill,' said Killer.

Were you flying those Swordfish at Sidi-Barani, dropping one bomb every ten minutes?' Ken asked.

'Yes, that was our job. Each Swordfish flew over the Italian positions for one hour, dropping one bomb every ten minutes,' said Bill. 'It was supposed to keep the Italians awake and soften them up for the British attack.'

'I don't know about the Italians, but it certainly kept me awake. I was near the front line at the time. It was weird. We could hear the aircraft stooging around, then suddenly out of the darkness came a woomph and a burst of flame from the Italian position. It went on and on, all night long.'

'How did you get your wound?'

'Well, I thought while I was there I would have a look at the front line and see how the Army did it. I'm a gunnery officer in the *Warspite*.'

While the men were chatting, the VADs, professionals that they were, had quickly gone from bed to bed, tidying a sheet here and plumping a pillow there and checking bedside charts. The girls let the men talk. They marvelled how these young men that they had come to know so well could chat casually about the terrible actions they were involved in, often joking about them, as Killer had done at lunch.

From the ward, they took the boys to the operating theatre. It was not in use, but here they met Doctor Lovemore again. He greeted them in friendly fashion, showing them the operating table and the instruments he used. Bill thought that he would much rather face an enemy fighter than an operating table where he might have to carve up another man. Killer, however, showed a different side of his character. He was serious and knowledgeable and showed great interest in what Doctor Lovemore had to say.

The last port of call planned by the girls was the swimming pool. At the after end of the promenade-deck, it would have been a centre of social activity in the days when *Carpathian* was a passenger ship. Now it was used for therapeutic purposes and the group stood for a while watching the dozen or so men in the water. Some were swimming painfully, exercising muscles or nerves that were coming back into use after serious injury. Others were being helped by nurses who were in the water with them, encouraging tired or wasted limbs to re-establish themselves.

'Do you do this, Ann?' Killer asked.

'Not as a rule. These girls are trained in orthopaedics and know what they are doing. We go in sometimes to help, though, particularly when the weather's hot.'

'Just looking at you in a bathing-costume would be a big help,' said Killer.

Ann offered a blow at him, but Killer caught her hand and kissed it, grinning.

As they strolled along the promenade-deck, Bill was impressed by the number of patients that spoke to the girls. Janet and Ann greeted them all by name and spoke a few words to each. Bill became aware how popular the girls were and how good at their job they must be. The thought crossed his mind that a little more than two years before these girls, like himself and Killer, had been at school, finishing their education. He looked at Janet again, seeing her as the professional and experienced nurse, not the slim girl yielding to him in the dance or softly brushing her lips against his. Perhaps, he thought, one of the good things about the war is that it has cut through barriers and allowed us to be ourselves with each other.

'Time for tea now!'

Janet cut into his thoughts, taking his arm and leading him to the sports-deck where there were loungers for the private use of the staff. The girls hurried away, leaving the boys to reflect on their experiences in the hospital-ship. Soon they returned with trays of tea and cakes to complete a relaxing afternoon. Bill and Killer returned to their carrier much refreshed.

The stopover at Aden was a short one. No shore leave had been allowed, and the next day the fleet, having refuelled, left harbour to head for Mombasa. Very soon anti-submarine patrols were established and the squadron settled down to its wartime routine.

Janet stood at the stern of *Carpathian* looking at the aircraft carrier astern. She was off duty and had come to watch the aircraft taking off and landing on. Two aircraft were lined up on the deck of *Peregrine* with their engines running. Small figures emerged from the island, the superstructure on the starboard side of the carrier, and scurried, heads down, to the aircraft. Was one of them Bill? The figures were too far away to recognise.

Bill. He was very much in her thoughts these days. What were her true feelings towards him? She found him an interesting person, even, when with Killer, an exciting one. Killer, so often playing the buffoon, was more likely to get into scrapes because of his daring; Bill, so often serious, was more likely to get out of them. How would he fit in with her friends and family at home? When she had first met him, he had been unsure of himself, uneasy in his officer's uniform. Now, he fell easily into the role of naval officer. She guessed that he would be a very good observer; his intelligence combined with his ordered approach to life would guarantee that. He would probably be good at anything he attempted so long as he was interested in it.

Bill had told her a little about his stay in Cairo. He had been the guest of Charlot Agussis, the brother of Socrates. Charlot was a Greek diplomat, with a French wife, pretty high up in Cairo society, Janet guessed. This had undoubtedly influenced Bill's development. She had known him before his visit to Cairo and she thought he had returned from it

59

more sure of himself, more at ease with others. He was a quick learner and mixing in Cairo's high society had left him more relaxed and confident.

He had spent much of the holiday in the company of Louise, the daughter of Charlot and Helene. Louise had shown Bill Cairo's everyday life, the small craft establishments where silver or leather goods were produced, the diamond merchants in the Khan khalil, and the mosque Al Ashar; she had introduced him to her friends and taken him to parties; she had taken him to see the Pyramids. What had happened at the Pyramids? Bill had shied off the subject when she had pressed him about the visit. She guessed that Louise had been an exotic Latin beauty. Had Bill made love to her? Or, more likely, had Louise made love to him? She experienced a pang of jealousy, and yet she knew instinctively that Bill was happy with her. In some way, however, she felt that Bill had become more mature sexually since his visit to Cairo.

'Hello, Janet, what are you doing here?'

Doctor Lovemore had come out for air and was leaning on the taffrail beside her. The second aircraft was landing on, and Janet did not want to miss it. It might be Bill.

'Watching your boyfriend, I suppose.'

The aircraft had landed safely.

'As a matter of fact, Doctor Lovemore, I am,' she replied quietly.

'I do have another name, Janet,' Doctor Lovemore said. 'Most of my friends call me George.'

Janet turned to the man beside her. George was taller than Bill, and older, and handsome in an Adonis kind of way. He was smiling at her, inviting more intimacy than already existed between them. He had been making up to Janet for some time now and always seemed so sure of himself, so sophisticated. He irritated Janet.

She turned to him and smiled sweetly.

'I'm very interested in those boys on the carrier, George. They do a wonderful job, protecting us, don't you think?'

George glanced towards the *Peregrine* where the last aircraft was descending in the lift.

'Yes, I suppose they do,' he admitted. 'But they've gone now and it's lunch-time. Are you coming in, Janet?'

Quickly Janet looked around for one of her friends. The other girls had already gone in and there was no excuse she could make. The best thing was to go in gracefully.

In company with several officers from the squadron, Bill was enjoying the sunshine on the goofers' platform. This was a deck space on the island used exclusively by flying-crews when off duty. Most of them had an unquenchable desire to watch the effort of their colleagues, taking off or landing on. Bill was no exception. He watched now, as C-Charlie and F-Fox were lined up on deck ready for take-off on their anti-submarine patrol. A-Abel and B-Baker were circling the carrier preparatory to landing on. The fleet turned into wind and this brought the *Carpathian* into view, now steaming on a parallel course on the port bow.

Bill could just make out a group of nurses on the stern of the hospital-ship. He wondered if Janet were among them. For some time now, Janet had been constantly in Bill's mind. He admired her slender grace, her deep sense of service to her patients, and her sense of fun. He himself was rather serious by nature, but he always found himself responding to Janet's lighter mood. She seemed to bring him out of his introspective self, make him feel more sure of himself, less conscious of his humble origins. He remembered their first dance in the Carlton Hotel. He had been sexually aroused by her close contact with him, and self-conscious and embarrassed because of it. Janet had instinctively made him feel at ease with himself and her.

Bill wondered how Janet would react if she visited his

home. He was sure she would get on well with his mother and father, but what would she think of the small, terraced house, with no front garden, a small backyard, the children playing in the street? This was where he had grown up, playing marbles on the pavement, cricket against a lamppost and tip-cat in the road. Could he himself go back to it? The Navy had introduced him to a new and at first terrifying, world that he had now become accustomed to and accepted as normal. His experience in Cairo had added some finishing touches. He had experienced a home where the inhabitants dressed for dinner, where the man helped his partner into her seat before sitting down himself, where the men stood up when a lady entered the room. At first he had been worried by these practices, then come to view them ironically as superficial, and finally come to accept them as normal, everyday behaviour.

Louise, the daughter of the house, had been a new experience again. She was gay and vivacious and anxious only to entertain him, but she was young and hot-blooded and looking for more than friendship. He remembered the moonlight camel-ride from the Pyramids to the oasis, where Louise's flirtation had become more demanding. Fortunately, Louise was young and demanded no more than passionate kissing and cuddling. Bill felt at the time that he would go no further. He did not want to betray the trust of Louise's parents nor his feelings for Janet. His own upbringing, as a Roman Catholic, had instilled in him a deep sense of the relationships between sex, children and family. Louise, on the other hand, had left him with the feeling that sex could be fun. In a vague way he hoped that at some future date he might, with Janet, bring these two concepts together.

He was a little troubled by the thought of Doctor Lovemore. The doctor was clearly a mature and attractive man, and if he set his cap at Janet, Bill wondered what chance he himself would have. The doctor was already well established in his profession and could offer a secure home. What future had Bill? Would he even survive the war? Already, in less than a year, more than half the squadron had been lost. And after the war, what would he do? He had obtained a good pass at highers before joining the Navy, and a place at university awaited him. His main interest had always been ancient history and literature. He did not fancy teaching. Could he become an archaeologist or perhaps a writer? The post-war future was too far away and Bill was unable to develop his thoughts further. In the meantime he must live in the present. He was attracted to Janet. The second aircraft had landed on. It was time to go into lunch.

Chapter 7

Search for an Armed Raider

The next day started quietly. 998 Squadron was carrying out the A/S patrols and 999 Squadron had a rest day. This did not mean a rest from work, only a rest from flying. All the officers in the squadron had secondary duties and this was a day when they could catch up on them.

Bolo, as Senior Pilot, was responsible for the availability of the aircraft. Soon after breakfast he was in the hangar, making his rounds with Chiefy. The hangar, in *Peregrine,* was a huge metal box, at either end of which was a lift for taking aircraft up to the flight-deck. Between the lifts were long lines of Swordfish, with folded wings, in echelon formation, each tethered to ringbolts in the floor of the hangar. The walls and deckhead were festooned with spares of all sorts, rudders, tail-planes, upper and lower, port and starboard main planes, wheels and landing-hooks, propellers, engines and engine cowlings, and all the many bits and pieces that go to make up a Swordfish aircraft.

An aircraft-carrier might be detached from its shore base and must be capable of effecting any repairs required, if necessary rebuilding an aircraft from the fuselage upwards. *Peregrine* did not carry spare fuselages, but it had been known to use the fuselage of a badly crashed Swordfish and rebuild it into a complete aircraft. All these spares had their own place in the hangar and each was fastened securely in its place.

64

The whole scene was lit by arc lights, which revealed the many activities going on. B-Baker was having an engine service, and two engine-fitters had the engine-cowling off and were tinkering with the engine. Bolo and Chiefy stopped to talk to them. 'Any problems?' Bolo enquired.

'Mr Temple reported a drop in the oil pressure,' said Leading Air-Mechanic Robson, B-Baker's engine-fitter. 'We haven't found the trouble yet.'

'Have you tried the scraper-rings?' said Chiefy. 'We've had some trouble with them after the desert operations, with sand or grit getting into them.'

'We haven't tried that yet, Chiefy, but we'll get on to it,' Robson said.

F-Fox was having its controls checked. Its air-mechanic was in the cockpit, operating joystick and foot pedals, whilst the air-rigger checked the movement of ailerons and rudder. K-King, Bolo's own aircraft, was having the starboard lower main plane removed and replaced.

'We patched up the damage you had when you attacked the Italian sub,' said Chiefy, 'but I thought we'd take this opportunity to replace the whole wing. We can then give the old wing a thorough overhaul in the workshop.'

'Good idea,' said Bolo.

He watched as Leading Air-Mechanics Hapwell and Rawlings, the fitter and rigger of K-King, carefully fitted the new wing into position with the help of a team of squadron air-mechanics.

Killer Compton's machine, L-Love, was also having a thorough overhaul, and Bolo was not surprised to find Killer with his aircraft taking an interest in the work, discussing it with his fitter and rigger, naval airmen Bailey and Riggs.

On all of the aircraft, air-gunners were checking their guns and consulting the squadron armourer about any problems they had.

Some of the maintenance crews were still in the uniform

of the RAF, a hangover from before the war when the Fleet Air Arm was serviced by men of the Royal Air Force, but increasingly these were being sent home and replaced by young, new recruits to the Fleet Air Arm.

Above the hangar ran a gallery that housed workshops, stores depots and squadron offices. In 999 squadron office Dicky Burd, the squadron adjutant, was working with his assistant, Wes Weston. Wes was updating the squadron copy of *King's Regulations and Admiralty Instructions*, the bible for all naval units, with the latest additions and amendments that had arrived with *Peregrine*. Dicky was checking through the records of the maintenance crews. It was his duty to keep an eye on their qualifications and promotions, and he did this conscientiously. Dicky was a lieutenant and sooner or later would be promoted to senior observer in another squadron. Wes was getting experience and training so that he could take over when Dicky left. In this way the Navy trained their young officers for positions of greater responsibility.

Biddy Bidwell, a sub-flight leader, was also Squadron Stores Officer, and he was in the squadron stores depot checking over lists with PO Young, the Squadron Stores Petty Officer. This was an important job. Damage from action or accident meant that there was a constant demand for replacement parts. It was Biddy's responsibility to see that these were available when required, and PO Young's to see that they were ordered in good time. In practice, they worked together as a team, occasionally bringing in Leading Writer Ball, the squadron secretary, from the office, to help out with the paperwork.

In the recognition room, Sandy Sandiford, the Senior Observer, was holding a class on ship and aircraft recognition. He was responsible for the training and efficiency of all observers, but, on this occasion, pilots not otherwise engaged had joined the class, led by the CO. About a dozen officers were involved. Using models and photographs, Sandy was presenting to the group representations of ships from ahead, abeam, or any other angle, and asking them to identify and write down the name or class of the ship. The ship could be Italian, German or British, battleship, cruiser, destroyer or frigate, and whilst some of the more bizarre mistakes created laughter, there was an underlying seriousness in the endeavour, emphasised by the presence of the CO.

That afternoon, immediately after lunch, the CO was at another meeting, in the Captain's cabin. With him were the CO of 998 Squadron, Wings, the ASO and the ship's Commander. The Captain was discussing the future movements of *Peregrine*.

'A German armed merchant-cruiser is at large,' he was saying, 'at present in the Indian Ocean but believed to be heading for the Atlantic. It is believed to be an ex-German cargo-passenger ship, the *Hohenlinden*, now with six six-inch guns plus a number of smaller weapons. The Germans have been unable to maintain supply ships for it in the Indian Ocean, but have several ready in South America to replenish it in the South Atlantic. It will be our job to hunt it down.

'We have our present escort because of this danger. We are escorting the hospital-ship to Cape Town, where fresh orders will be given us.'

'Have we heard anything of the Italian armed merchant-cruiser that was seen at Massawa?' asked Lieutenant-Commander Simpson.

'No,' the Captain replied. 'It may now be in the Indian Ocean, possibly making for the Maldives or Chagos Islands, or any of the numerous islands dotted about the Indian Ocean. Many of them are uninhabited and it is possible that our German raider has been using one of them as a base. Possibly the Italian ship is making for the same base. The area must be a good hunting ground for raiders. There is still considerable unescorted traffic between Australia and New Zealand and South Africa.'

The Captain's suspicions were confirmed all too soon. At 1900, *Peregrine*'s wireless office reported an SOS signal from SS *Coomba*, that it was being attacked by an unknown merchant ship. It reported its position, three hundred miles south-east of the convoy. No more was heard from it.

Captain Bentley was the senior officer of the convoy and he came to an immediate decision. A signal was sent to *Carpathian*, telling her to continue with two of the destroyers to Mombasa. *Lancashire* and *Peregrine* with the destroyer *Heron* would increase speed to twenty knots and head for the last known position of the enemy. At first light 999 Squadron would carry out a nine-aircraft search, with 998 Squadron standing by for a dive-bombing attack.

Bill Hewitt stood on the quarterdeck of *Peregrine*, watching the departing ships. The *Carpathian* and her two destroyers bore away to starboard. *Peregrine*, with *Lancashire* and *Heron*, had turned to port, in search of the Italian armed merchant-cruiser. It was a quiet group that attended dinner that evening. Apart from the two newcomers, the squadron was now very experienced and knew what to expect on the following day.

The next morning Bill was awakened by a torch flashing in his eyes.

'Six o'clock, sir, time to get up.' This was the voice of the marine sentry. Killer was shaking himself out of sleep in the berth above Bill's. Little was said as the two young officers washed and shaved and made their way to the wardroom, where they joined their equally silent colleagues. Tea and coffee were on offer and the officers sipped their drinks and thought about the operation.

After dinner on the previous evening the CO and Senior Observer had gone over the operation in detail. Sandy Sandiford had addressed them first.

'The weather is set fair,' he said, 'so we can maintain a good distance between search lines, that is twenty miles. We'll drop a smoke-float as a starting-point. The tracks to be made good are due east or south depending on which side of the carrier you are searching, then southeast. You will proceed along this track at ninety knots until it is time to turn to be back at the carrier three hours after departure. The carrier will maintain a south-easterly course at twenty knots. Your position in the search is on the squadron notice board in the wardroom.'

As Bill took down the figures he thought of the four-vector problem involving a return to a moving base in an aircraft flying at a set speed. He could solve that problem easily enough. True accuracy, however, would depend on his establishing an accurate wind and Killer flying an accurate course. It was teamwork between pilot and observer that would make the search efficient.

Sandy concluded by giving the squadron their wireless frequencies and call signs, and repeating that wireless silence should be broken only by an enemy report. The CO followed his Senior Observer.

'The object of this exercise is to find the Italian raider,' he said, 'so we'll not be carrying bombs. If you sight the enemy you must report it and stay to shadow it until it's time for you to return to *Peregrine* four hours after departure. You've fuel for four and a half hours and that leaves only half an hour to spare, so no heroics. We don't want to lose any aircraft. Do not stay over time. Observers will need very accurate navigation and pilots very accurate flying. All observers will take cameras. Take pictures of any ship you sight, even though you think it is not the raider.

'There will be a short briefing in the operations room at 0630 tomorrow, when Schooley will give you the latest weather gen and the ASO will give you up-to-date information, if any.

'In the meantime,' he concluded, 'get an early night in. It could be a long day tomorrow.'

For most of the squadron this was a routine operation with which they were now familiar and few of them had the qualms and uncertainties they had experienced in their first operations in the Mediterranean. Shortly after they assembled in the wardroom for tea or coffee they heard the message on the Tannoy.

'999 Squadron range nine aircraft.'

For the past hour the hangar had been the scene of considerable activity as the maintenance crews performed their daily checks. Now it was time to move the aircraft. Each Swordfish was manhandled onto the lift, with its engine-fitter in the cockpit operating the brakes, the rigger on the tail-trolley, steering the machine, and a team of squadron mechanics pushing it. 999 Squadron occupied the forward end of the hangar so they used the forward lift. The manoeuvre was made to look simple because of the expertise of the men. In reality, each movement of aircraft was quite a complicated one. The Swordfish had to be steered round the tethered machines, along a narrow space little wider than the aircraft. It was further complicated by the roll of the ship and its tendency to take charge of the operation.

Once the Swordfish reached the flight-deck the deck-handling party took over from the squadron, to push each aircraft into its allotted position at the after end. There it would wait, with wings folded, until brought into position for take-off by the deck control officer.

By the time Bill and Killer made their way to the operations room all the squadron aircraft were on deck. Mechanics were already running up the engines to warm them; riggers were standing by the chocks; and TAGs were in their aircraft checking their wirelesses and guns.

The briefing was indeed brief. The wind was light, from the south-west; visibility was good, up to twenty miles. There were no further orders. Pilots and observers made their way down from the island to the flight-deck, past the whirling propellers, to the machines where maintenance crews were waiting to help them with parachute-harnesses and navigational gear.

It was already dawn when the ships turned into wind. One after the other the Swordfish were brought into the starting-position, their wings unfolded and clipped into flying position, their engines given a last-minute run-up, waiting for the green, and then the off.

Each machine trundled forwards, slowly at first, then building up speed until it ran out of flight-deck. There was the familiar dip as it left the deck and its re-emergence from below flight-deck level as it built up speed and climbed to its starting point, three thousand feet above the smoke-float dropped by the CO.

The time was 0715 when Bill gave his first course to Killer. That meant that he must return to the carrier by 1015. L-Love was the third aircraft out to the east from the carrier. His first track, therefore, was fifty miles to the east, then south-east until 0900, then 282 degrees back to the carrier.

Visibility was good, about fifteen to twenty miles, so the search would be fully covered by the parallel tracks of the searching aircraft. The wind was no more than force three from the south-west. Bill checked this a half an hour after take-off, using the Fleet Air Arm's system of wind finding. Using his stopwatch, he dropped an aluminium dust marker and instructed his pilot to make a rate-two, 180-degree turn to port and fly on a reciprocal course for exactly ninety seconds, when his pilot made another rate-two, 180-degree turn to port. By taking bearings of the dust marker he was able to measure the exact bearing and distance of the aircraft from the dust marker at three minutes, and from this compute the direction and speed of the wind at three thousand feet, the height at which they were flying. He

71

applied this wind to the course they were steering and so found the actual track he was making good over the sea. A slight correction to the course brought him back on the track he actually wished to make good.

This was all routine navigation to Bill. He worked quickly and accurately so that he could give as much time as possible to the search, first quartering the sea with the naked eye and then following that up with a search of the horizon through his glasses. He was assisted with the search by Leading Airman Gibbons, his telegraphist-air-gunner. Gibbons had already unwound his trailing aerial and satisfied himself that his wireless set was operating efficiently. Now he had nothing to do but listen out and at the same time search the sea.

As pilot, Killer Compton's main task was to steer an accurate course. Experience had taught him that watching his compass continuously was not the best way of keeping on course. This led to a lack of concentration. There were several alternative methods of keeping a good course: if there were a suitable cloud he could keep this on a constant bearing; or he could keep the sun on a constant bearing; or he could use the direction of the swell of the sea beneath him. In effect, he used all three of these and the occasional glance at his compass showed that he was rarely off course. All of this enabled him, too, to sweep the horizon, and this he did continually, adding his effort to those of the others.

By 0855 Bill was beginning to think of his return course to the carrier. He decided to make a last sweep with his binoculars. Starting from ahead, he carefully focussed his eyes on the horizon and moved slowly along it on the starboard side until he was looking dead astern. Then he moved his eyes forwards along the port side. At five degrees from dead ahead on the port side he thought he could see something. He removed the binoculars, wiped the lenses and applied them again to his eyes. Now he was sure. A tiny wisp of smoke could be seen, at least twenty miles, and possibly thirty miles, ahead of them and slightly to port. He spoke into his Gosport tubes.

'Killer, there is a ship about twenty miles, red oh-five. I can just see it through the glasses.'

Killer stared intently in the direction indicated. 'I can't see it,' he said.

'No, you won't see it with the naked eye; it's too far away. The point is – should we investigate? We're almost due to turn back to the carrier. If we investigate it could add another hour to our flight.'

'That means just over four hours flying altogether,' said Killer. 'That's near our limit, but I think we can manage. I think we should go and have a look.'

'So do I,' said Bill. 'Alter course five degrees to port.'

Fifteen minutes later they could all see the ship, a tiny break in the sea on the horizon. Through the glasses Bill could see it clearly, making smoke. It must have been the smoke that first caught his eye.

In another fifteen minutes they were circling it at one thousand feet. It was a cargo ship, possibly ten to fifteen thousand tons, with a large bridge structure that must have contained a number of cabins. Along its decks were large, wooden boxes that seemed to be a deck cargo. It flew a Dutch flag.

'I'll call it up,' said Bill.

Taking his Aldis lamp, he began flashing.

'What ship?'

'*Van Hollern*' came the reply, flashed slowly and laboriously.

'Where from and where to?' Bill flashed slowly, making allowance for a foreigner not good at morse.

'Jakarta to Cape Town' was the reply.

'Must be a Dutch East Indies ship,' said Bill, reporting the message to Killer. 'I think we'd better take some pictures, just in case. Fly down it, up-sun.'

Killer brought his aircraft round to the same course as the

Van Hollern, flying past it about four hundred yards away. Bill took a series of photographs.

It was time to go. With a waggle of his wings, Killer turned his aircraft onto the course of 285 degrees that Bill had given him for the return to the carrier. Bill noted the time of departure – 0940. They had been circling the *Van Hollern* for thirteen minutes. They had to fly a hundred and twenty miles to rejoin the carrier, an hour-and-a-half's flying. They would arrive back at the carrier at about 1110, near the end of their endurance.

During the first hour of the journey back Bill completely rechecked his navigation, a prudent precaution. With such a small margin of endurance he could not afford to be wrong. There would be no fuel left for a square search if he missed the carrier.

Killer hummed a tune to himself as he piloted his aircraft homewards. He was confident in his own piloting and in Bill's navigation. By nature not given to worrying about things that might not happen, he set his mind to thinking about the ship they had investigated, in particular the wooden boxes stacked on deck. He wondered what kind of cargo they could contain.

An hour later Bill was having the nagging worries that all navigators have when they are nearing their destination. For the fourth time he searched ahead of the Swordfish with his glasses and it was with a sigh of relief that he picked up the streaks of white ahead of them. These quickly grew into ships and they were home. Again Bill reached for his Aldis lamp, and flashed the recognition signal. As they approached, the ships turned into wind and Killer was given the signal to land. The two young officers hurried to the bridge, where the Captain, Wings and the CO awaited them.

'What kept you?' asked Lieutenant-Commander Simpson.

Bill explained how they had glimpsed the ship on the far horizon and why they decided to investigate.

'Quite right,' said the Captain, 'though I have to say we were all worried when you were overdue. What was the ship like?'

Between them Bill and Killer described the merchant-ship, with its cargo of large packing cases. The Captain was particularly interested in these and questioned Killer closely.

'Did you take photographs?' he asked.

'Yes, sir. The camera will be with the ship's photographer now,' said Bill.

'Ring through, Wings, and have the photographs brought up here immediately. And have the Navigation Officer come to the bridge.'

Whilst they waited for the photographs, Bill checked his navigation with the ship's Navigation Officer, generally known as 'Pilot'. His positions were transferred to the ship's chart.

'What course was the ship steering?' asked the Captain.

'When we arrived and when we left she was steering west,' said Bill, 'but I had a feeling that when we first sighted her she may have been steering more to the south.'

The Air Staff Officer now arrived with the photographs taken by Bill. There were five and they gave a clear picture of the ship.

'Check them up, Pilot,' said the Captain.

Killer and Bill, not having been dismissed, decided to stay on the bridge and make themselves as inconspicuous as possible.

'There's no trace of this ship in *Lloyd's Register*,' reported the Navigation Officer. 'I have a book with pictures of Italian ships. We'll consult that.'

'Compton and Hewitt, come in here and look through this with us,' he added.

Bill and Killer joined the Navigation Officer and ASO in the chart room. The Navigation Officer slowly turned over the pages of Italian ships.

'Stop,' said Bill. 'That looks like it.'

Killer agreed.

The ship was the *Triggonia,* fourteen thousand tons. A note added to the description read, 'believed to be converted into an armed merchant-cruiser'. It checked with the photo-graphs.

'Got it!' exclaimed the ASO, hurrying out with the news to the Captain. 'We think it likely,' he added, 'that the packing cases conceal large guns.'

'How soon can we get another search off, Wings?' asked the Captain.

'At present, 998 Squadron are standing by as a strike force, armed with six two-fifty-pound bombs.'

'That will shorten the range of our aircraft if we leave them on,' said the ASO. 'The *Triggonia* is already at extreme range and no doubt has altered course back to the south, away from us.'

'I suggest we send the search party off armed with only two bombs each,' said Wings. 'Even if they return with the bombs they'll still have over four hours' endurance and they may have a chance of slowing down the *Triggonia* by dropping a bomb on it.'

'Right! Have that organised,' said the Captain. 'How soon will they be ready?'

'They can be on deck, ready to take off by 1300,' Wings replied.

'Good. Now, Flags,' he said, turning to the ship's Signals Officer. 'Send a signal to *Lancashire* giving the position and estimated course and speed of *Triggonia. Lancashire is* to detach immediately and make for the last reported position of *Triggonia* at maximum speed.'

'Aye, aye, sir.'

'Simpson,' the Captain continued, turning to the CO of 999 Squadron, 'I want your aircraft to stand by with torpedoes. If we get a further sighting before 1600, you will take off and make a torpedo attack. You will just have time to return before nightfall.'

'Very good, sir.'

The Captain now turned to the Officer of the Watch.

'Have the Engineer Commander report to me on the bridge,' he instructed.

'Chief,' he said, as the Engineer Commander reported, panting, after his hurried climb up to the bridge. 'We have a problem. We've found the Italian raider, but she's at extreme range for our aircraft. What's the top speed you can give me to make it easier for them?'

'We can manage twenty-four knots for a time,' the Engineer Commander replied.

'For how long?'

'I'd think for not more than twenty-four hours. Then we must reduce to twenty again.'

'Very well. Increase speed to twenty-four knots.'

In the hangar and in the wardroom the sudden increase in speed was felt by all. Shortly afterwards it was followed by the Tannoy:

'D'you hear there? This is the Captain speaking. The Italian armed merchant-cruiser *Triggonia* has been found at maximum distance for our aircraft. *Lancashire* has been detached to intercept. 998 Squadron will take off at 1300 for an armed search. Briefing at 1200. 999 Squadron will stand by with torpedoes as striking-force. Briefing at 1400. That is all.'

'Good for Killer and Bill,' said Bolo. 'They must have found the Italian raider. It explains why they were so late back.'

After an anxious wait on the goofers' platform until the return of L-Love, the squadron officers had assembled in the wardroom. The CO was still on the bridge with the Captain.

'I think all pilots should check their own aircraft,' Bolo continued. 'Then all of us should get some lunch. It could be a long day.'

Everywhere in the ship were signs of unflustered hurry. In the engine-room, the Chief Engineer and his black gang were coaxing the engines to their fullest capacity. The last aircraft of 998 Squadron were being ranged on deck after having four of their bombs removed. The crews of 998 Squadron were in the briefing-room being briefed for the operation. 999 Squadron aircraft were being refuelled, before being armed with torpedoes.

After lunch, 999 Squadron aircraft were ranged on deck whilst the air-crews assembled in the briefing-room for briefing. Then the long wait began. At first there was eager anticipation as the squadron planned its impending attack, but as the afternoon wore on the eagerness gave way to frustration when no wireless messages were received from the searching aircraft. By 1500 the squadron began to think the Italian had escaped, and by 1600 it was decided to strike down the assembled aircraft and disarm them of their torpedoes. By 1630 the first of the search aircraft was seen approaching and by 1645 all had returned and the carrier had turned into wind to land them on. The *Triggonia* had not been sighted.

Chapter 8

The *Triggonia*

The next morning started much the same as the previous one. 999 Squadron officers were awakened early and, after a hot drink, assembled in the briefing-room. Here the Air Staff Officer addressed them.

'The situation at the moment,' he said, 'is that we have lost contact with the *Triggonia*. We believe that when it was sighted by L-Love yesterday it altered course to the west to support the identity it had given of a Dutch vessel trading between Dutch East Indies and South Africa, but, after L-Love left, it changed back to its original course, towards the Chagos Islands, and increased to its maximum speed. Our second search, yesterday afternoon, did not find it because it was beyond the range of our aircraft.

'As a precautionary measure, *Lancashire* has been dispatched at top speed to the south-east and is now eighty miles ahead of us. We believe the *Triggonia* is thirty to fifty miles ahead of *Lancashire*. Of course, we have no detailed knowledge of *Triggonia*'s movements, only a guess, so we are spreading the search as widely as possible. The parallel tracks of the search will be thirty miles apart, the absolute maximum we can allow, even in this good visibility. This is just on the limit of visual range, but *Triggonia* should be well within sight of observers using their binoculars. To make sure we do not miss the raider, I want you to do a ten-mile leg

79

to starboard when you are due to return. If you miss *Triggonia* on the outward leg you will pick her up on the homeward leg.

'If *Lancashire* is near enough to *Triggonia*, we shall leave her to the cruiser's guns. That is why *Lancashire* has been sent ahead. If we find that she has moved away from *Lancashire*'s course and is too far away for a gun action this day we shall send 998 Squadron with torpedoes as a striking-force. If you find *Triggonia*, send off an immediate first-sighting report and stay to shadow. *Lancashire* will be listening out on your frequency and will acknowledge your signals.'

When they had been given call signs and frequencies by the Signals Officer and the latest weather report by Schooley the air-crews went down to their waiting Swordfish, and at 0700 began taking off.

Bolo Hawkins settled himself comfortably in his cockpit after take-off and began climbing to the search height of three thousand feet. His observer, Lieutenant Dicky Burd, had given him his first course of forty-five miles to the east. The sea, amber in the morning sun, was like corrugated, sparkling cardboard beneath him, with the softer curve of the swell moving at an angle across the waves. He concentrated on keeping an accurate course, using sunshine and shadow, sea and cloud, to give him bearing and direction.

Following Dicky's instructions, he made the accurate turns for wind finding, and after half-an-hour's flying Dicky gave him the main course to steer, 128 degrees, to allow for wind drift. Flying was second nature to Bolo and he was able to keep a keen, searching eye ahead and on either bow.

Twenty minutes later he caught the flicker of movement on his starboard bow. He brought the mouthpiece across his face and spoke into his Gosport tubes.

'Hello, Dicky, I can see something at green three-oh.'

Dicky swung his binoculars and peered intently into the sun in that direction.

'I've got it!' he exclaimed and a minute later he added,

'I'm pretty sure it's *Lancashire*. We should pass it about twelve miles away on our starboard beam.'

As the bearing increased and the ship came abeam, Bolo was able to see clearly the high counter and the eight-inch guns of the county-class cruiser.

'I wouldn't give much for the chances of *Triggonia* if we can get *Lancashire* within range of her,' he commented.

Even at twelve miles, Bolo could see the foaming wake astern of the cruiser as she sped through the water.

Ten minutes later, Bolo spoke again. 'Smoke on the horizon, red two-five,' he said.

'It's got to be *Triggonia*!' Dicky exclaimed. 'Keep on this course until I can be sure.'

Dicky studied the smoke until he could see the tiny ship ahead of it. As the ship grew in size he was able to check it with his photograph.

'Yes, it is the *Triggonia*. Well done, Bolo!' he said. 'We should pass it eight miles away on our starboard beam. Do you want to close it?'

'No. I'll circle round it at that distance and close from the south-east. It might give them the impression that an attack is coming from that direction and cause them to turn away from us towards *Lancashire*. Get off a sighting report.'

Dicky had already done this and given the first-sighting report to his telegraphist-air-gunner, PO Mercer, to transmit. In code and call signs, interpreted it read: *To HMS Lancashire from P5K. Enemy bears 130 degrees from you, distance 30 miles. Time of origin 0830.*

Two minutes later, Mercer reported, 'Message received and acknowledged by *Lancashire*, sir.'

Meanwhile, keeping *Triggonia* at a distance of eight miles, where the ship was clearly visible to the aircraft but the aircraft was invisible to the ship, Bolo slowly circled the target. As he drew to the south-east of it he saw more smoke a further ten miles to the south-east.

81

Dicky studied the smoke through his binoculars.

'It's a cargo ship coming this way,' he reported.

'Almost certainly British, or friendly,' said Bolo. 'We must warn her of danger. I'll close her and give you a chance to signal her.'

As they approached the new vessel, Dicky could see that she was a cargo vessel of about ten thousand tons, flying a red ensign. He read the name, *Beresford*. Bolo flew past her about a quarter of a mile away, whilst Dicky slowly flashed a message on his Aldis lamp: *Enemy armed merchant-cruiser eighteen miles ahead of you. You are standing into danger.*

He received an acknowledgement from the *Beresford* and saw the ship turn to port, away from the danger area.

Bolo steered his Swordfish back towards *Triggonia*, now approaching it from the south-east. At four miles distance, shell-bursts began to appear in the sky ahead of them.

'They aren't trying to disguise themselves now,' said Dicky. 'They know they are caught.'

'Look!' exclaimed Bolo. 'They're turning away. They must think our carrier is south-east of us. They're turning towards *Lancashire*.'

Quickly Dicky coded a message to *Lancashire*, giving the new information, and passed it to Mercer. This was an interesting situation. The two ships were approaching each other at a combined speed of nearly fifty knots. In twenty minutes *Lancashire* would be within firing range.

'Message from *Lancashire*, sir,' said PO Mercer, passing a chit towards Dicky. *Will you spot for us?*

'Send an affirmative, Mercer,' said Dicky. Then, to his pilot, 'Bolo, we are going to spot for *Lancashire*. Will you take up a position four miles to the north-east of *Triggonia* and keep a height of one thousand feet?'

'Will do,' said Bolo, turning his aircraft in the right direction.

Torpedo-Spotter-Reconnaissance, TSR, thought Bolo. How seldom a Swordfish aircraft had the opportunity to spot for a shoot. And yet that was considered to be a role for the aircraft and Dicky would have been trained for it.

The first indication of firing was a long dash on the wireless, followed immediately by the fall of shot.

Six hundred yards short, signalled Dicky through his TAG.

Four enormous spouts of water had appeared ahead of the raider.

'*Lancashire's* pointing directly at her target and can only fire her forward guns,' Dicky exclaimed.

He noted movement on the raider. The camouflage of wooden cases was being removed and the big six-inch guns revealed. The raider was turning a hundred and eighty degrees away from the danger.

The wireless buzzed and another fall of shot splashed up.

Two hundred yards over, Dicky reported.

'Send a message, Mercer, plain language: *Enemy altered course to 135 degrees.*' The next fall of shot occurred where the raider would have been but for the turn. *Four hundred yards short,* Dicky reported.

Again the buzzer sounded and again the splashes could be seen.

Two hundred yards over, reported Dicky.

'They've got her bracketed,' commented Bolo.

The following shells burst one short and three over.

Straddle, reported Dicky.

Bolo could imagine the panic on the Italian ship. They were outgunned by the big cruiser and, although they were firing, their six-inch shells were falling short. A flash of flame lit up the raider as the next shells burst.

Hit, reported Dicky.

The cruiser was now firing rapidly. Two hits were recorded with the next salvo, followed by a further hit, then three hits. The raider was now burning along its length and its guns had stopped firing.

'They're hauling down their flag,' cried Bolo, and Dicky immediately reported this to *Lancashire.*

Bolo now took his Swordfish close to, and upwind of, the burning vessel. It was a shambles: guns were upended; the bridge was a mess of jagged metal; fire was spreading throughout the ship.

'Look, they're taking to the boats,' said Bolo.

Only two boats could be launched, and the Swordfish crew watched silently as men flung themselves from the burning ship into the sea and swam towards the boats. The sea was littered with wreckage and bodies, some dead, some alive, and the two boats rowing for their lives from the stricken vessel. Suddenly there was a terrible explosion in the *Triggonia,* which seemed to split in two.

'That's a magazine gone up,' cried Dicky.

The burning hulk was now going down quickly and Bolo watched with a sick feeling in his stomach as the ship slid beneath the waves, leaving behind the debris of war.

By now, *Lancashire* had arrived on the scene and had lowered boats to join in the work of rescue. It was time for K-King to return to the carrier.

Must leave you now, Dicky flashed on his Aldis lamp.

Thank you and well done was the reply.

The goofers' platform and the catwalk round the flight-deck were lined with men as Bolo flew round the carrier. It was nearly four hours since they had flown off, and all the other aircraft had already returned. *Peregrine* had picked up the wireless messages between the aircraft and the cruiser and as the battle developed, the ASO had given a running commentary on it over the Tannoy, so that the ship's company had been able to follow its progress. It was unusual for a carrier to be so closely involved in a gun battle and, as Bolo and his crew left their aircraft to report to the bridge, a spontaneous cheer went up from the watching men, which Bolo acknowledged with a grin and a wave.

Dicky had taken photographs of the closing scenes of the engagement, of the burning ship and the men taking to the boats. He had even obtained a picture of the explosion. His camera was taken down to the photographic room and, later, copies of the pictures, marked 'strictly secret', were distributed to the ship's company.

The Captain expressed his approval to the crew of K-King when they reported to him on the bridge, where the bridge party listened enthralled as Bolo recounted the events.

'And now we must get back to Mombasa and the hospital-ship,' he said, 'but first we must rejoin *Lancashire*.'

An hour later *Peregrine* met *Lancashire* coming towards her. Messages were passed from the cruiser to the carrier, giving the number of Italians rescued and the names and ranks of the officers.

We have some interesting information for you concerning the movements of the Triggonia *and a German merchant-cruiser,* Hohenlinden, the last message stated.

Captain to report aboard as soon as we anchor in Mombasa was the reply.

The ships had used much of their fuel oil in the high-speed chase after the *Triggonia*. Now it was necessary to conserve fuel, and at the economical speed of twelve knots they proceeded westwards towards Mombasa. A routine patrol of one aircraft fifteen miles ahead of the ships was maintained, and three and a half days later they dropped their anchors in the port of Mombasa.

Lieutenant Sandy Sandiford was officer of the day, with Midshipman (A) Saville as junior officer. Shortly after the ships anchored he saw a boat approaching from *Lancashire*, which was challenged by the petty officer of the watch.

The time-honoured reply came: '*Lancashire*.' That meant that the Captain of *Lancashire* was aboard it and about to pay a visit to *Peregrine*.

'Inform the Commander,' Sandy told his midshipman, 'and get back here as quickly as you can.'

As the boat drew alongside, the Commander arrived breathlessly to greet the visiting captain, and the guard, with Lieutenant Sandiford at the head, lined up to receive him. As Captain Beale ascended the gangway, the Petty Officer of the Guard sounded his bosun's pipe and petty officers and guard came to attention. Captain Beale saluted the ship as he stepped aboard and was greeted by Sandy and presented to the Commander, who escorted him down to the Captain's day-cabin.

'Well, Beale,' Captain Bentley said, welcoming his guest, 'glad to have you aboard. Come and have a drink and tell me all about it.'

His steward poured out pink gins for the two officers and retired quietly.

'Your Swordfish people did very well. The observer's reporting and spotting enabled me to make a quick kill,' said Captain Beale.

'They're a very experienced crew,' replied Captain Bentley. 'The pilot, Lieutenant Hawkins, is Senior Pilot of the squadron, and the observer, Lieutenant Burd, is a career officer.'

'I'd like to meet them before I leave. Would that be possible?'

'Yes, I'll send for them. Now, what's the interesting information you have?'

'The captain of *Triggonia* was one of the rescued men,' replied Captain Beale. 'He was in a state of shock and in a very talkative mood. I had him brought to my cabin, gave him a drink and let him talk about the action. Then he talked about his recent past, about the action at Massawa, his escape through the Gulf of Aden and his sinking of the *Coomba*. He was rather proud of that. By then he was in full flow, so I gave him another drink and encouraged him.

'He told me he was taking the ship to the Chagos Islands, where he was to rendezvous with a German armed merchant-cruiser, the *Hohenlinden*. The two ships were to make their way south of Cape Town into the South Atlantic, where they would prey on Allied shipping. Supply ships and tankers from South America would refuel them and replenish their stores and, when he met up with *Hohenlinden,* he was to be given a series of grid references for contacting the supply ships.'

'This confirms the Admiralty's suspicions,' said Captain Bentley. 'It's why we've left the Mediterranean and are being sent round the Cape. We know that once in the South Atlantic our orders are to search out and destroy a German armed merchant-cruiser. Now we know the name of it.

'There are rich pickings in the Atlantic for a German raider. At present we haven't the ships to escort convoys from Cape Town to Freetown in Sierra Leone, where they join a convoy for Gibraltar or Britain. We also have single ships making the passage from South America to South Africa. A raider in these areas could create havoc. Remember how much damage *Graf Spee* did before she was sunk. Now that we know for sure *Hohenlinden* is in the Indian Ocean it would be better for us to destroy her here, before she gets loose amongst the shipping in the Atlantic.'

'I've sent a full report to the Admiralty,' said Captain Beale. 'No doubt we'll have further orders here or in Durban.'

A knock on the door heralded the arrival of Bolo and Dicky.

'Here are the two officers you asked to see,' said Captain Bentley, 'Lieutenant Hawkins and Lieutenant Burd.'

'I'm very pleased to meet you,' said Captain Beale. 'Your reports were invaluable. We opened fire at eight miles and, at that range, whilst we could detect the line of our shot, it was difficult to tell how far short or over we were. Your spotting gave us that. And your report on the evasive turn of the *Triggonia* enabled us to correct quickly and get back

87

on target. Please give my thanks, too, to your wireless operator.'

'Petty Officer Mercer is a good hand, sir. He'll appreciate your comments.'

'What were your thoughts when you saw the *Triggonia* blow up?' Captain Beale asked.

'Frankly, sir, I felt sick,' said Bolo.

'I think we all do when we see a good ship destroyed,' said Captain Bentley. 'It's one of the horrors of this war.'

Over the drinks offered by Captain Bentley, Bolo and Dicky chatted about the action until it was time for them to leave.

Chapter 9

Mombasa

Peregrine was to stay only three days in Mombasa, and on the second day Mombasa Club organised a dance in the evening for the naval officers from *Peregrine* and the destroyers and for the nurses and doctors from *Carpathian*.

'Let's make a day of it,' Killer suggested to Bill on their first day in harbour. 'Ashore this afternoon I found a small place that hires out bicycles. Let's collect the girls and go for a cycle ride and a picnic lunch, then meet them in the evening for the dance.'

'We could make a bigger party for the dance,' Bill replied. 'Maggie and Pam are on the *Carpathian*. We could rope in Hank and Dorrie and make a party of eight. You remember we did that in Alexandria at the Carlton.'

The arrangements were soon put in hand and the next morning Killer and Bill found themselves on the jetty waiting for Janet and Ann. When the girls arrived, they all made their way to the cycle shop in a small back street of the market-place. The girls were given quite modern cycles, but the boys had to be content with rather large sit-up-and-beg machines. The girls had brought a picnic lunch and the boys two bottles of wine, and these, together with mackintosh capes, were fitted into the carrier-baskets

The four set off slowly. Ann was wobbly at first but grew steadier as she gained confidence. The route took them

89

through the town and into the forest, following a trail alongside a stream. As the town was left behind so were the trappings of Western civilisation. In town, women, dressed in cotton skirts and colourful blouses, were often to be seen, carrying parasols and sunshades. Of course it could rain, but for the present the sky was blue, the sun was shining and the trees were lush and green.

They stopped to watch a group of women washing their clothes. The method was to dip the clothes in the stream and whack them against a rock.

'Dhobeying, they call it,' said Bill.

All the women were naked to the waist and quite unembarrassed. The younger ones, some perhaps as young as thirteen or fourteen, had slim figures and firm, full breasts.

'Out here it seems so natural for them to be like that,' Bill remarked.

'I don't feel that I would be comfortable dressed like that,' said Janet.

'I like you as you are,' laughed Bill, admiring Janet's slim elegance and suntanned limbs clad in a short, white dress.

The road now became a track, which began to climb as they reached the first of the foothills. At length it became so steep that they had to push their bicycles until they came to a natural picnic spot. The stream tumbled over a rocky waterfall into a pool that looked several feet deep. A large tree gave adequate shade from the hot sun and a grassy bank provided the perfect place for their picnic.

'I'm hot. What about a swim before we eat?' said Killer.

'I haven't brought a costume,' said Janet dubiously.

'Nor have I,' added Ann.

'I haven't brought bathing-trunks, but does that matter?' said Killer. 'I have boxer shorts and they'll soon dry in the sun.'

'Well, you go in first and we'll see if we'll join you,' Janet said. 'I must say the water looks very tempting.'

The boys soon stripped to their shorts and plunged into the pool.

'Absolutely marvellous!' cried Killer, gasping with the cold.

He and Bill swam vigorously until their blood was circulating well and they began to feel less cold.

The girls had stripped to their bras and panties and stood poised on the bank.

'Come on,' shouted Killer.

Janet took the plunge, followed by Ann, and soon all four were sporting and laughing in the sparkling water. They were all good swimmers and took delight in following each other into the turbulence of the waterfall, shadow swimming in the pool and splashing each other.

Half an hour later they scrambled out and flung themselves on the grassy bank, where they lay on the turf to dry in the sun. Bill went to the bicycles, leaning against the tree, to fetch the picnic things. Janet, like Ann, lay stretched out on the grass, her eyes closed, enjoying the warmth of the sun as it began to dry out her wet clothes. Bill stood silently and let his gaze travel slowly over her body, admiring her grace and beauty, until she opened her eyes, smiled and drew him down beside her.

The picnic was a great success. The girls had made full allowance for the appetites of the boys, and the smoked salmon starter was followed by cold chicken legs and a green salad with crusty bread and butter. A trifle and then cheese concluded the meal. Killer had cooled the wine in the stream, a clear white Sancerre, and this set off the meal and left them talking and laughing together.

By mutual consent it was decided to rest after the meal. Killer tucked himself contentedly next to Ann, his head resting on her stomach, nestling against her soft breasts. Bill lay, thoughtfully, next to Janet. He could feel her limbs against his and, after a few moments, her hand reached out and found its way into his. He was happy and content to lie like this, half dozing, with visions of war chased away by the nearness of the girl.

An hour later, the silence was broken by the sound of a busy chattering and grunting. Janet looked into the green tracery of the foliage above her and saw a face peering down, then a second and a third. She woke with a gasp and grasped Bill's hand tightly, waking him, too.

'Why, they're monkeys,' he cried, laughing. 'It's a family of monkeys.'

The monkeys were quite small, mother, father and baby, and they sat on their branch chattering and gesticulating and even, Janet thought, laughing, not at the mortals but with them. It was a world of laughter and life and families, and, almost without thinking, Janet leaned over and gave Bill a big kiss. Bill did not question why, as Killer might have done. He understood Janet's feelings and he shared them. His grip tightened on her hand as he responded to the kiss.

It was time to go. All of them were dry now and able to put on their clothes. Saying goodbye to their favourite picnic spot and the monkeys who had shared it with them, the boys and girls set off down the path.

As they approached the town they came to a broader part of the river, with a dirt road alongside it and small native houses alongside the road. In the distance they could see a small boy and girl playing on the bank. Suddenly there was a shrill scream and they saw the little boy fall into the river, screaming and struggling and being carried out away from the bank. A young black woman ran from a nearby house and stood screaming on the bank.

Bill reacted first. Pushing hard on his pedals, he raced up to where the woman and little girl were standing and, slithering to a stop, he took off his shoes and plunged into the river. The little boy had disappeared. Killer and the girls raced to assist and Killer began to take off his shoes. Bill, however, had noted where the boy had gone down and had done a surface dive after him. He now emerged with the mite in his arms, limp and lifeless, and swam with him to the bank, where Killer waited to haul the boy out of the water. The black woman was wailing and the little girl was screaming. The boy had stopped breathing.

It was Janet and Ann who now took over. With all the professionalism of their experience they quickly turned the child on his stomach and whilst Janet began artificial respiration Ann made sure he did not swallow his tongue. Bill went to the woman and consoled her, whilst Killer soothed and calmed the little girl.

Anxious moments followed. Janet pumped away rhythmically until, at last, water gushed from the child's mouth and his chest began to heave. Janet continued until he was breathing properly and then gave the little boy to his mother.

'You must come to my house and I will dry your clothes,' she said to Bill, 'and I will make you all a drink.' The woman spoke good English, though with an African accent.

The four boys and girls hesitated.

'I think it would be kinder for us to accept,' said Killer. 'She needs to thank us in some way.'

They found that the small house was scrupulously clean, with simple but effective furniture. The woman, whose name was Tisha, gave Bill a blanket to wrap round himself whilst she took his clothes to dry in the hot sun.

'My husband will be home soon,' she said. 'He works at the Mombasa Club. I am sure he would like to meet you and thank you.'

Ann sat with the little boy on her knee, cuddling him and soothing him, whilst the little girl stood by her, holding her dress and staring at Bill with wide eyes.

The women had produced glasses containing a cool, fresh drink, when the door opened and young black man entered. He was about twenty-five years of age and spoke with a deep resonant voice.

'What is going on here?' he said.

Tisha ran to him and explained what had happened.

'This is my husband, Tombe,' she said.

Tombe came forwards, gripped Bill's hand and thanked him warmly. Then he went to each in turn, shaking their hands and thanking them.

The little boy deserted Ann and ran to his father, holding on to his leg.

'Are you going to the club tonight?' Tombe asked. 'A dance is organised for the visiting officers and nurses.'

'I'll be there myself,' he said when they told him they were going. 'I'll look after you.'

Bill's clothes were dry now and it was time to go. The whole family came to the door to wave to them and they all waved back as they rode slowly away.

It was seven o'clock in the evening when Bill and Killer joined Hank and Dorrie to catch the liberty boat ashore. They had soaked themselves in the bath to relax their limbs after the unaccustomed exercise on the bicycles. Midshipman Saville was cox'n of the motor boat and he was easily persuaded to divert to the *Carpathian* on his way to the jetty. The girls were waiting for them on the gangway, and it was a lively and fun-loving party that arrived ashore.

Tombe was as good as his word. He met them at the club entrance and escorted them to the special table he had reserved for them. On it was a vase of tropical flowers – from his garden, he said.

The hall was filling up and the band had arrived and soon the beat of a quickstep was enticing them on to the floor. Bill watched the others start off.

Dorrie, the musician, keeping perfect time, was dancing with Pam, a tall brunette. Pam, Bill recalled, was interested in folk music, and she and Dorrie had got on well together in Alexandria. Hank, the American, was dancing in a no-

nonsense style with Maggie, a redhead from a Devon farm. Hank's parents were ranchers in the Middle West, and the pair were soon engrossed in conversation. Killer, as always, danced pugnaciously, giving way to no one, and it was Ann's skill that kept them out of trouble.

Bill relished the moment when Janet came into his arms and began dancing. With Janet he did not have to think. The moves came instinctively, prompted by the rhythm and flow of the music, and Janet seemed to know what he was going to do almost before he knew himself. For him the quickstep was a light-hearted, gay dance, a dance to have fun with, and with Janet he was able to put sequences together and invent new steps that kept them both laughing and involved.

Laughingly, the group changed partners for the next dance, a waltz, and Bill found himself dancing with Ann. He liked Ann very much, for her warmth and compassion shown in the sick ward and for her honest and forthright morality. She was a good dancer and Bill enjoyed dancing with her. Not so tall as Janet and perhaps a little plumper, she was light on her feet and followed his long, slow steps with ease.

'This is going to be a good night,' he said as they settled into the dance.

'After the events of this afternoon, we need this to unwind,' Ann replied, 'and we've a good crowd here.'

They danced the rest of the dance in companionable silence. The next dance was a slow foxtrot, Bill's favourite dance. When he had first danced this with Janet at the Carlton in Alexandria he had had a feeling that Janet would come to mean very much to him. Now he danced dreamily and easily with her, her body just touching his, her arm resting lightly on his. The rescue of the afternoon, the war at sea, the war in the desert, all faded from his mind as he gave himself up to the present dance, with Janet.

'May I cut in, old boy?'

The suave voice cut like an icicle into his consciousness

and the hand on his shoulder felt like a heavy weight. He turned and saw the smiling face of Doctor Lovemore. Too surprised to resist, he relinquished Janet into the doctor's arms and walked slowly back to his table. He felt miserable and unhappy as he sat at the table, his head in his hands. From a mood of blissful serenity he had been thrown suddenly into one of deep despondency. How could he compete with such an accomplished man as Doctor Lovemore?

Killer had been dancing with Ann, close to Bill, when the exchange had taken place. He saw the effect it had on Bill. Ann had seen it, too.

'Look, Ann, we must do something about this,' he said. 'Would you mind?'

He steered Ann to the table and left her with Bill. Making his way through the couples, he approached Doctor Lovemore.

'My turn, old boy,' he said, mimicking the doctor's own phrase.

The doctor turned to protest, but there was little he could do. Killer took Janet from him, leaving him standing in the centre of the dance-floor. Carefully Killer steered Janet back to their table.

'Here's a wench looking for you,' he growled in Bill's ear.

Bill looked up and his whole demeanour lightened as he saw Janet waiting for him. Soon he was again lost in his dream world.

'That was nicely done, Killer,' Ann murmured as once more she joined him for their foxtrot.

The next dance was a quickstep in which the group again intended to change partners. Dorrie was going to dance with Janet. Before this could happen, however, Doctor Lovemore came to the table.

'May I have this dance, Janet?' he asked in a pleasant, but very firm, voice.

Janet looked helplessly at Dorrie and Bill, but she felt there was little she could do but accept. Doctor Lovemore was a colleague, a senior one, and she had to live with him aboard the hospital-ship.

Bill and Maggie sat with Dorrie throughout the dance and gloomily discussed the situation. It was not improved when Doctor Lovemore brought Janet back to the table.

'May I join you?' he said, drawing up an unused chair from a nearby table.

Now the life seemed to go out of the party. The group were all in their early twenties. Doctor Lovemore was thirty, and although he made an attempt to engage them in table talk no one responded, and an air of gloom settled on the table.

Doctor Lovemore was quick to take advantage of the next dance and again asked Janet to dance with him. Bill felt desolate. None of the group now felt like dancing and the evening seemed to be heading for disaster.

'Something has got to be done about this,' said Killer. 'Leave it to Doctor Compton.'

He left the table and Ann saw him approach Tombe, who was standing by the bar, and speak quietly to him. Tombe produced a pad, and Killer quickly wrote on it. He returned to the table just before Doctor Lovemore brought Janet back.

'I enjoyed that dance,' said Doctor Lovemore heartily.

Killer waited, then gave a surreptitious nod to Tombe, who approached their table.

'Who is Doctor Lovemore?' he asked, in his deep voice.

'I am,' the doctor replied. 'Why?'

'I have a message for you, sir,' Tombe said, handing him the note.

The doctor read it and asked, 'Did they say why?'

'No, sir,' said Tombe.

Doctor Lovemore pursed his lips and looked vexed.

'I'm afraid I must leave you,' he told the group round the table. 'The hospital-ship wants me back aboard – urgently.'

'Oh, bad luck!' said Killer. 'I expect it's an emergency.'

'Yes, I suppose so,' said Doctor Lovemore, taking his leave.

Once he had gone, the mood of the company brightened. Tombe came back to their table.

'Was that all right, sir?' he said to Killer.

'Perfectly!' Killer exclaimed. 'You did splendidly, Tombe.'

'Now, ladies and gentlemen, I think that calls for a glass of champagne. Would you oblige, Tombe?'

'I saw you write that note, Killer,' said Ann, when Tombe left to collect the drinks. 'What did you write in it?'

'I wrote, "Due to an emergency, Doctor Lovemore's presence is required aboard immediately".'

'Killer!' exclaimed Janet, laughing.

'Well, it was an emergency, wasn't it?' said Killer, and they all agreed.

The party now became a great success. During the interval, while supper was being served and the band was having a rest, Dorrie was persuaded to play the piano. He decided to play jazz music and as the first tune started Hank jumped up.

'Excuse me, folks!' he exclaimed. 'I can't resist this.'

He went to the band and spoke to the saxophonist, who lent him his saxophone. Soon he was playing with Dorrie, heightening the jazz with improvisations. The pair were expert players and proved irresistible to the band's drummer who resumed his place at the drums. With Dorrie leading, they were soon working well together. 'That's a Plenty', 'Royal Garden Blues', 'At the Jazz Band Ball', 'Basin Street Blues'. All followed each other in quick succession.

As the trio worked through the well-known jazz tunes, the group at the table found their feet tapping to the tunes and when Bill looked round the hall he found that everyone was responding.

'New Orleans', 'Ain't Misbehavin', 'Alligator Crawl', 'Minnie the Moocher', the lovely, slow 'Stardust'.

For half an hour the trio kept its audience enthralled and the end, with 'The Darktown Strutters' Ball', was greeted with an enthusiastic burst of clapping and cheering.

The second half of the dance was even better than the first half. Bill danced a pasodoble with Maggie, in which, straight-faced, he imitated the movements of a matador, whilst Maggie entered enthusiastically into the role of the bull, to the delight and amusement of the group. Then he danced a tango with Pam, serious and slinky. But it was with Janet and the slow foxtrot that he enjoyed himself most, lost in the sensations of the dance, a dream world, in which the girl in close proximity to him was beginning to mean so much to him.

After the dance, the four couples wandered back to the jetty, arms round each other's waists. They each found a spot in the shadows for their goodnight kisses, and the boys again persuaded the cox'n of the liberty boat to return the girls to their hospital-ship.

That night, as he lay in his berth waiting for sleep, Bill went over the events of the day: the cycle ride; the half-dressed native women dhobeying in the stream; the waterfall, swimming and the picnic; the family of monkeys sharing their pleasure; the near tragedy of the little boy and Janet concentrating on reviving him; the lovely young native family they had met; the dance and Doctor Lovemore's untimely intrusion; dancing with Janet. Most of all he thought of the moment at the picnic pool when he had gazed down at Janet, lying on the grass with her eyes closed. He could see now the soft shadows and contours beneath the white silk panties and bra, made transparent by the water from the pool. With that thought, he fell asleep.

Chapter 10

The *Hohenlinden*

The next morning *Peregrine* was astir with the activity of leaving harbour. During the night a message had been received from a Norwegian tanker, the *Thorsen Narvik*. She was being attacked by an unknown vessel twenty miles west of Cargado Carajos, an island to the east of Madagascar. The Captain had summoned to a meeting his main heads of department, the ship's Commander, Commander Flying, Chief Engineer, Air Staff Officer, Navigating Officer and the two Squadron Commanders.

'Gentlemen,' he said, looking gravely at the assembled men, 'we've been ordered to find this German raider and destroy it. If it is the *Hohenlinden*, it's the raider that's been haunting the southern Indian Ocean for more than a year, attacking our trade between Australia and South Africa. We now have some information about it. It's an ex-cargo-passenger ship of ten thousand tons, armed with six modern six-inch guns, four torpedo tubes and two aircraft. It has a top speed of eighteen knots and can remain at sea for months on end. So far it has sunk or captured nine ships, totalling sixty-six thousand tons. *Thorsen Narvik* is the tenth. This raider is believed to be one of several that left Germany at the beginning of the war. They've been attacking our ships in the North and South Atlantic and here in the Indian Ocean.

'This particular raider has not been active for three or four

100

months and we believe she may have retired to a base deep in the Southern Indian Ocean for a refit. There are several uninhabited islands in that region that would be suitable for this purpose.

'We shall leave tomorrow at dawn, escorted by *Lancashire* and *Heron*. *Carpathian* will stay in Mombasa for a further two days before proceeding to Durban with the remainder of the escort.

'Chief,' he said, turning to the Engineer Commander, 'what are your thoughts on our range and speed?'

'Well, sir, if we keep our speed down to twelve knots we can stay at sea for two and a half weeks. Any increase in that speed will cut our endurance dramatically.'

'Very well,' the Captain continued, turning to the ship's navigator. 'Pilot, how soon can we reach Cargado Carajos?'

The Navigating Officer had been briefed before the meeting and was ready with his facts.

'That island,' he said, 'is approximately eleven hundred miles to the south-east of Mombasa. At twelve knots, and allowing for flying off and on, it would take four days.'

'Very well. What about submarines or other raiders?'

'The ASO has been keeping an intelligence log of all the information we have, sir.'

The Captain turned to the Air Staff Officer.

'We know of at least one Italian submarine that escaped south, sir,' the ASO said. 'There may be others. We've no knowledge of German submarines in this area. There's also the possibility of at least two other German armed merchant-cruisers being at large in the Indian Ocean and they could be anywhere.'

'Right!' said the Captain. 'We shall need anti-submarine patrols and air-searches. Will you see to that, Wings?'

'Aye, aye, sir. Until we reach Cargado Carajos, I suggest we maintain one aircraft on anti-submarine patrol throughout the day and a parallel track search each dawn.'

The two Squadron-Commanders nodded their agreement.

'We've discussed the situation, sir,' said Lieutenant Commander Simpson, the senior of the two COs. 'On the first day 998 Squadron will carry out the search while 999 Squadron takes on the A/S patrols, and vice versa the next day, and so on. We shall share the stand-by strike force between us.'

'Very well,' the Captain replied.

'Are we all set for a dawn departure?' he continued, turning to the ship's commander.

'All laid on, sir.'

'Good! Well that's it, gentlemen. Let's hope we bring the beggar to book.'

Janet and Ann were on the afterdeck of *Carpathian,* watching the aircraft-carrier take its departure. They spotted Killer and Bill on *Peregrine's* quarterdeck as she passed close by them and they waved to the two boys.

'Will we ever see them again?' mused Janet sadly, as she watched the great ship steam past. She felt more and more drawn to Bill. Each time they parted she longed for their next meeting. Was she in love? she wondered. They had known each other for only six months and, apart from Bill's spell in hospital, had met less than a dozen times. But in wartime each meeting was significant. Where would it end?

On *Peregrine,* the two officers waved back to Janet and Ann.

'It will be nice to see the girls again when we finish this little jaunt,' said Killer. 'I'm getting fond of Ann and I think she is beginning to like me.'

'Come on. Let's go up to the goofers' platform and watch the search party take off,' said Bill.

His feeling for Janet was too deep and too uncertain for him to talk about it, even too deep to think about it. It was safer to take refuge in the familiar routine.

*   *   *

Day after day, the routine anti-submarine patrols continued and the search parties searched the endless sea. The weather was kind, the flying easy, and when they were not flying the crews relaxed in the sunshine on the goofers' platform, or on the quarterdeck in the shade beneath the overhanging flight-deck. Each pilot and observer had a daily flight of three hours, either on search or on A/S patrol.

On the third day, the search aircraft on the extreme right came within sight of the coast of Madagascar. And still the carrier continued on its course of 130 degrees, turning into wind every three hours to fly off and land on aircraft.

By the end of the fourth day nothing had been sighted and no signals of distress had been received. Unlike the Mediterranean, this sea was vast and without boundaries. The raider could be anywhere; it could even be making for the Atlantic.

The next morning, an hour before dawn, the silence was again broken by a distress call. A freighter from Malaya on its way to England via Cape Town, with a valuable cargo of rubber, was being attacked by an unknown ship, fifty miles south-east of Mauritius. The final message came, 'Abandoning ...' and then broke off in mid-sentence.

Immediately the Captain ordered a change of course to the south to intercept and an increase in speed to twenty knots. The mood aboard the carrier changed, became less relaxed, more purposeful. There would be more flying: the dawn search would be followed by one in the late afternoon; the anti-submarine patrols would continue. The squadrons would take it in turns to fly the searches and share the patrols, and this meant that some crews flew twice a day, once on a search and once on a patrol.

The weather, too, was becoming more demanding. As the ships made their way south, into the southern winter, the air grew colder, the wind stronger and the waves higher. Taking off and landing on became more difficult, requiring fine judgement to gauge the rise and fall of the flight-deck. Flight was bumpier. It was more difficult for the pilot to fly a steady course and for the observer to handle his navigational instruments. The broken sea required more effort from everyone in the aircraft. They were looking not only for the raider but also for lifeboats from the stricken freighter.

The dawn search sighted nothing. It would be up to 999 Squadron to find the lifeboats, if any, before darkness set in. With this in mind, a five-aircraft search party was ordered to take off at 1600 and fly up to a hundred and fifty miles ahead of the ships. The Captain did not want to alert the enemy raider, so wireless silence must not be broken. Any aircraft spotting the lifeboats was to return immediately and inform the carrier so that help could be sent.

The deck-control party had difficulty in handling the aircraft in the rising westerly wind and the buffeting sea. The aircraft had a tendency to fall over sideways as the wind abeam caught them and the ship rolled heavily to port. Squadron personnel doubled up with the deck-party, adding their weight, and eventually the five aircraft were lined up, with wings unfolded, ready for take-off.

In G-George, Hank Phipps and Dorrie Dorrington were keen and eager to carry out the search. Since he had joined the carrier, Hank had become an experienced pilot and he was confident in his observer's navigation. With the strong wind blowing across their track, careful navigation was essential, particularly in finding and applying the wind at the search height of one thousand feet. Having settled the aircraft on its correct course and speed, Dorrie and his TAG, Leading Airman Kirk, concentrated on searching ahead and abeam, leaving Hank to concentrate solely on flying the Swordfish.

An hour and a half later, having passed Mauritius to

starboard, Dorrie was searching ahead with his binoculars when he spotted the two boats.

'I've got them,' he called triumphantly to his pilot, 'red one-oh, about ten miles away.'

Hank immediately turned on to the required course and opened his throttle to the full. Six minutes later he was circling the two boats. Lashed together, they each contained about ten men, some of them clearly in a distressed condition, wounded or sick, others cheering madly.

Whilst Hank circled the boats, Dorrie carefully and slowly flashed a message on his Aldis lamp.

Raise arm if you understand.

Two men in the leading boat raised their arms and Dorrie flashed again.

Help arriving in four hours.

He saw an arm raised after each word and then a general waving of arms when he had finished. They had got the message. It was time to go.

An hour later Hank was circling the carrier, flashing the news of the boats and their position. A few minutes later he saw *Heron* detach itself from the group and, with a great bow wave, surge ahead at her maximum speed. She would reach the lifeboats in three hours.

G-George was ordered to patrol round the carrier and cruiser until the remaining aircraft returned. An hour later all aircraft had landed safely and Hank and Dorrie were making their way to the bridge to report to the Captain.

When *Heron* rejoined *Peregrine* she brought with her the survivors of *Lymington Star* the British merchantman destroyed by the raider, and the officers and wounded were transferred to *Peregrine*. Whilst the sick men were being settled in the sickbay and the officers in the Midshipman's Flat, Captain Bentley sent for the First Officer for his report on what had happened. From him he learned that the raider was a vessel of about ten thousand tons with a single funnel and with two derricks forward and two aft of the bridge. She was sailing under a Dutch flag and her name was *Zuyder Zee*. The Captain of *Lymington Star* had survived, but had been taken prisoner by the Germans.

'What were her tactics of attack?' the Captain asked.

'Well, sir,' the First Officer replied, 'she approached us from astern until she was a quarter of a mile on our starboard beam. We thought she was a friendly ship, wanting a chat halfway across the Indian Ocean. However, suddenly she spoke to us over her loudspeaker. "This is a German raider," she said. "Stop your engines. Do not attempt to transmit on your wireless or we'll open fire."

'Our Captain wasn't standing for that and he ordered Sparks to send an SOS. As soon as we began transmitting she opened fire and destroyed our aerial, but not before Sparks sent off his message. Then she ordered us to abandon ship. She was going to put a torpedo into us.

'She didn't attempt to interfere with us as we took to the boats except to order our Captain to go alongside. He was taken aboard the raider and we were ordered to stand clear. Then she put a torpedo into the old *Lymington*. She was a fine ship. It nearly made me weep to see her go down.'

'What happened then?'

'The raider disappeared eastwards, towards the island of Rodriguez, and that was that. I can't tell you what it meant to us when your aircraft appeared. We thought we hadn't much chance of survival and suddenly we knew from the old Stringbag that there was a British aircraft-carrier around. When the Swordfish flashed us that help was coming we were really chuffed.'

After consulting with his Chief Engineer and Navigating Officer, Captain Bentley decided to pursue his enemy, and altered course to the east, to the island of Rodriguez. On the Chief's advice, he reduced speed to sixteen knots, to conserve fuel. He also decided to cancel the anti-submarine patrols. It was unlikely that submarines would be in this area and, if they were, at sixteen knots in the present weather the ships would be impossible targets for submarines. All their efforts would be on catching and destroying the raider. To this end there would be dawn and late-afternoon searches, with the non-searching squadron standing by with torpedoes as striking-force.

The weather was presenting an increasing problem. Not only were the big seas presenting difficulties for the aircraft taking off and landing on, but there was also the effect of the strong wind on the aircraft's endurance. With the gale blowing from the west, aircraft returning from the search would have their speed over the sea cut down from ninety to fifty knots, almost halving it. Aircraft would therefore have to turn for home earlier than they would have done with a moderate wind and this would cut down the area of search.

998 Squadron had the dawn search. Wings watched anxiously from the bridge as the deck-handling party rolled the aircraft on the pitching deck from the lift to the starting-positions. Again extra hands were used to hold down the aircraft. Once given the green, it was the Deck Control Officer's task to time the take-off so that the plunging ship was coming up to the horizontal at the moment of take-off. If the aircraft took off at the bottom of the downroll it would fly into the sea. If it took off at the top of the uproll it would most likely stall and crash.

Nothing was sighted by the search party, but anxiety showed again when the aircraft returned. Most of 999 Squadron were on the goofers' platform to watch. This was one way they could learn from the experience of others. It was the Deck-Landing Control Officer's task to bring the aircraft down safely. With his bats he could tell the approaching pilot if he were too high or too low, too fast or too slow. A new factor was the rise and fall of the carrier's stern by forty feet or more. The DLCO must judge whether to bring the aircraft in and give the pilot the signal to land or to wave him round for another try. An error of judgement could be disastrous.

One such error occurred with the third aircraft landing on. The pilot seemed to be perfectly placed for a good landing when a freak wave hit the ship and caused the carrier's stern to rise even higher than usual. The DLCO had already signalled the pilot to cut his engine. The officers watched with horror as the wheels of the Swordfish struck the round-down, tipping the aircraft on to its nose and sending it slithering into the island. Almost before it stopped, the observer and air-gunner were scrambling out, but the pilot was slumped forward in his cockpit, unconscious.

The watchers saw the flicker of flame, then the flash as the aircraft caught fire. Clumsy figures, clad completely in asbestos suits, were moving forwards, some with extinguishers, but two making for the cockpit. They saw the rescuers pull the pilot, already alight, out of his cockpit, onto the deck where others were waiting to wrap him in an asbestos blanket. The fire was quickly brought under control and the injured pilot carried away on a stretcher.

In the meantime, the remaining aircraft of the squadron were circling the carrier, waiting to land. The Deck Control Officer looked up at the bridge and received a nod from Wings. He knew what to do. The watchers saw the deck party manhandle the smouldering aircraft to a position aft of the island, where the crane was already swinging into position. Within five minutes of the crash it had hoisted the wreckage outboard and dropped it over the side into the sea.

'Our turn this afternoon, chaps. What can we learn from this morning's experience?'

Lieutenant-Commander Simpson eyed the young men in front of him.

'Borrow an asbestos suit before we take off,' said Killer quickly.

The others laughed.

'Seriously, sir,' said Bolo, 'there is something we can do. These conditions are exceptional. The danger is with the rise and fall of the round-down, at the after end of the ship. Towards the middle of the flight-deck you haven't the same amount of movement. I think we should ignore the first two arrester wires and aim to pick up the third or even the fourth. In that way we would be well past the danger of hitting the round-down.'

'What about overshooting?' said Biddy Bidwell.

'To be on the safe side, our airspeed for landing is, say, seventy knots in this wind. Take off forty knots for the wind and fifteen knots for the ship's speed and we are travelling at only fifteen knots over the flight-deck. We should be able to catch one of the last three wires easily.'

'That makes sense,' said the CO. 'It would be best to come in high over the round-down and sink quickly onto the flight-deck once you are past it. After lunch, I want all pilots to meet in the guest-room and we'll have a discussion with Bats.'

Just before midday another signal was received, from *Devonian*, a fast passenger liner that was being used to transport Australian troops to Africa. *Am being attacked by unknown merchant ship in position 23 degrees south, 67 degrees 40 minutes east.*

'That's three hundred miles south-east of Rodriguez,' said the ship's navigation officer, plotting rapidly on his chart.

'Give us a course to that position, Pilot,' said the Captain.

'118 degrees. Distance 300 miles, sir.'

'Good. Officer of the Watch, steer 118 degrees.' The bridge was now tense with activity as the ship prepared to meet this new threat.

'Another signal from *Devonian*, sir,' said the signals officer, handing a chit to the Captain.

The Captain read: *From SS* Devonian. *Have been shelled at a range of six miles by unknown ship. We escaped at high speed to the north. Attacker did not follow but continued eastwards. Ship had one funnel and derricks forward and aft of the bridge. Time of origin – 1210.*

'No reply,' said the Captain. 'Maintain wireless silence. The Captain of *Devonian is* a good man. He is warning any ships in the vicinity of the danger and giving a description of the raider.'

'It is, of course, the German raider that attacked *Lymington Star,*' said Wings.

'Not much doubt about it!'

The sense of urgency communicated itself to the flying-crews and throughout the ship, particularly when the Captain addressed the ship's company over the Tannoy and gave them a picture of the developing situation. The hangar crews put their backs into maintenance and refuelling, making light work of the backbreaking task of moving the aircraft along the rolling and pitching deck.

999 Squadron was detailed for the afternoon search and for the dawn search on the following morning. This would leave 998 Squadron as stand-by strike force for the two searches and save the need for moving the torpedoes from one squadron to the other.

Bolo Hawkins thought that he had never flown in such weather as this as he took off for the afternoon search. The sky was grey and overcast, with black clouds racing across at about two thousand feet. The search was at one thousand feet and at that height the surging, wind-wracked sea looked dangerous, even menacing. His aircraft was buffeted by the turbulence.

'First course, 190 degrees,' came Dicky Burd's calm voice, and Bolo settled down grimly to his task of steering an exact course over the storm-ridden waste below.

The searching aircraft sighted nothing and the crews were very weary as they circled the carrier. The CO was last to return. He was farthest east in the search and had to steer straight into the forty-knot wind on his return leg.

The tactics for landing on, discussed with Bats, worked well and there was only one mishap. All the aircraft picked up an arrester wire safely, but Midshipman Cartwright, the latest addition to the squadron, in H-Howe, hit the deck rather heavily and broke his tail-wheel. His aircraft slewed to the right but was pulled up short of the island by the arrester wire.

It was a subdued meal in the wardroom that evening, and most of the flying crews were glad to get their heads down early. Bolo decided to check the aircraft before going to bed. As he expected, the hangar was alive with activity. In the bright arc lights mechanics and riggers were working on their aeroplanes, checking engines and airframes, refuelling and, in the case of H-Howe, changing the tail-wheel. Chiefy, alert and energetic, walked round the hangar with Bolo, who had a word with each group of men, listening to their comments, encouraging them and, when asked, telling them what he knew of the enemy raider. He retired to his cabin, knowing that the aircraft would be on top line in the morning.

'999 Squadron range nine aircraft.'

The message on the Tannoy awakened Bolo from his deep sleep. He looked at his watch. The time was 0600, time to get up. In the wardroom he met the remainder of the squadron, subdued and quiet. There was considerable movement in the ship as they sipped their drinks. The storm had not abated. They were in for a rough ride.

Sub Lieutenant 'Bing' Crosby, pilot of M-Mike, and his observer, Sub Lieutenant 'Harold' Lloyd, pushed their way, heads down, against the thrusting wind as they made their

111

way to their aircraft. At one point Harold almost lost the holdall containing his Bigsworth chartboard and navigating instruments as a swirling gust caught it, and even their aircraft was rocking on its wheels as the mechanics fought to hold it steady. They were on the extreme right of the search and, as they sat waiting to take off, Harold told Bing what their tracks would be, due south for seventy miles, then south-east until it was time to return.

Crosby and Lloyd were short-service-commission officers who had joined the Royal Navy Air Branch before the war. They had joined *Peregrine* just as Italy was entering the war and had served throughout her spell in the Mediterranean as pilot and observer of M-Mike. On their first mission, a dawn attack on Tobruk, they had been damaged by Italian flak, and Bing Crosby had brought his Swordfish home to the carrier with part of the lower mainplane missing. Bolo had nursed him through that difficult flight. Many subsequent operations had developed the skills of all three occupants and formed them into a reliable team.

'Time to turn on to the second leg,' Harold said into his Gosport tubes. 'Steer 150 degrees.'

'150 degrees,' Bing repeated, making sure he had heard correctly. He noted that Harold had allowed fifteen degrees for the wind drift.

They were now on their second leg and Harold and his TAG, Leading Airman Davey, concentrated on searching the sea ahead and on either bow. Nearly an hour later, as they were nearing the point where they must turn back to the carrier, through his binoculars Harold detected a faint shadow that was not caused by the sea, about fifteen miles away on his starboard bow.

'It's almost time to turn home, Bing,' he said, 'but I've just caught sight of something about fifteen miles away on the starboard bow. Do you think we should go and have a look at it?'

112

'I think we must,' Bing replied.

'It'll make us late returning to the carrier,' said Harold, 'but I agree with you. Steer 180 degrees.'

Ten minutes later the Swordfish was approaching the vessel, which was plunging heavily into the storm-tossed sea.

'It doesn't look like the *Hohenlinden*,' Bing said.

Harold noted the details on his pad – about ten thousand tons, two funnels, a single derrick fore and aft of the bridge. Course 260 degrees. Speed about ten knots.

What ship? Harold flashed.

From the bridge came the answering response: Woollongong – *Australian – Sydney to Cape Town.*

'It's Australian,' said Harold.

They could see the Australians, in their large slouch hats, lounging on the upper deck, waving to them. A large Australian flag was flying astern. Bing circled the ship whilst Harold exchanged signals.

'I'll just take a few photographs,' said Harold, 'for the record.'

He took his pictures from both beams and from ahead and astern of the ship, a dozen in all.

'Right! That's it!' he exclaimed. 'Let's get back to the carrier.'

Bing made a last fly-past over the ship and waggled his wings. The men on the bridge waved back. Harold took a last photograph from almost overhead.

They were half an hour late when they arrived back over the carrier and all the other aircraft had already landed on. The light was going early in the murky weather and Bing flashed the recognition signals as they approached. He was glad to see the ships turn into wind immediately and even more pleased when he had landed safely and the aircraft was being taken to the forward lift to be stowed in the hangar. Bing and Harold hurried to the bridge, Harold taking his camera and chartboard with him.

The Captain was waiting for him, with Wings, the ASO, the Navigation Officer and his CO. Harold explained how they had seen the ship at the outward end of their course and described the ship, its appearance, its flag and the Australian crew. He indicated that he had taken a number of photographs and the Captain asked for these to be developed immediately.

The ASO, after thumbing through *Lloyd's Register*, had a puzzled frown on his face.

'It says here that the *Woollongong* is a small cargo ship of four thousand tons,' he said.

'Are you sure it was ten thousand tons, Lloyd?' the Captain asked Harold.

'Certain, sir, give or take a thousand tons. Also, aft of the bridge was a large, boxlike structure.'

'What about you, Crosby?'

'I'm sure it was bigger than four thousand tons, sir. More like ten thousand.'

The Captain turned to his Officer of the Watch and said, 'Ring through to the photographic-room and have those photographs developed as quickly as possible and brought up here. In the meantime,' he continued, turning to Harold, 'check your navigation with the Navigating Officer.' And then, 'Pilot, transfer *Lloyd's* positions to the ship's chart.'

As the officers hurried to carry out his instructions he turned once more to Bing. 'Crosby,' he said, 'tell me a bit more about this Australian merchant ship.'

'She had a very large Australian flag, sir, and some of the men were wearing Aussie hats. The bridge party all waved to us when we took departure.'

'Did you see anything suspicious at all?'

'Not really, sir. She seemed a normal Australian ship, though perhaps the big construction astern of the bridge was a bit odd. It seemed out of proportion and I couldn't see the point of it.'

'Could it have been a hangar?'

Bing thought for a moment, and then said slowly, 'Yes, it could, sir. It had big doors facing aft, big enough to let an aircraft through.'

By now the photographs had been developed and brought to the bridge. The Air Staff Officer produced a magnifying glass and studied them intently.

'There is something odd about the after funnel,' he said. 'This shadow, at the base, is different from that in the forward funnel. It could be a dummy.'

When they came to the final picture taken by Harold from overhead there could be no doubt about it. Through the magnifying glass they could see the wooden battens inside the funnel that were part of its construction.

'Gentlemen,' said the ASO, 'we've found the *Hohenlinden*.'

'Give us a course to where *Hohenlinden* will be at 0700 tomorrow morning, allowing for her course eastwards at ten knots,' said the Captain.

Peregrine's course was adjusted accordingly to make an interception.

'We shall have an armed search at dawn tomorrow, Simpson,' the Captain told the CO of 999 Squadron. 'Arm your aircraft with four two-fifty-pound bombs. Arrange the details with Wings and the ASO.'

Through the night the ship steamed, whilst maintenance crews toiled to service and arm the aircraft. After dinner, the CO called a briefing meeting in the briefing-room. There the pilots learned that they were to fly in line abreast ten miles apart, to cover an area ninety miles wide. Observers were told that if they sighted the enemy they were to send a signal giving position, course and speed, and stay to shadow. The other aircraft were to close *Hohenlinden* immediately and link up with the CO, so that they could make a concerted attack on the enemy. 998 Squadron would provide a follow-up torpedo striking-force.

The next morning conditions had deteriorated still further. The wind was gusting to storm force and the sea, as a result of the constant gale, had built up even more than the day before. The stern was rising and falling by fifty feet. Normally, flying would be cancelled in such conditions, but the Captain knew how vital it was that the *Hohenlinden* should be caught. How many more Allied ships would she sink if she escaped now? He gave the order to proceed.

At 0700 they began to take off, labouring over the cavorting deck and sinking almost into the waves as they rolled off the bows of the carrier. Bolo looked at the spindrift beneath him and at the black storm clouds overhead. Visibility was not good, but he thought that at ten miles apart the aircraft would establish a visual overlap. Killer Compton and Bill Hewitt, in L-Love, were to starboard of him and Bing Crosby and Harold Lloyd, in M-Mike, to port. He had arranged that if they did not find the enemy raider, L-Love and M-Mike would close up on him for the return flight. He knew that the other sub-flight leaders had the same plan. In the appalling conditions there was safety in numbers.

By 0900 they had reached the end of the outward leg. No W/T message had come through. The German raider had escaped. Bolo dropped a smoke-float and circled it, waiting for his sub-flight to form up on him and, ten minutes later, with Lovel and Mike on either side, he set off for the carrier.

From time to time Bolo glanced at the aircraft of his sub-flight. They were flying in open formation and Bolo saw the aircraft bouncing up and down like yo-yos. Survival was now the key thought. Landing was going to be very difficult. Should they ditch the bombs? Bolo decided against it. Bombs were in short supply and should they continue the searches they would need every bomb they possessed. The nearest supply was at Simonstown, near Cape Town.

At length they found themselves circling the carrier with all the other aircraft. Bolo watched as the CO landed,

116

followed by Holy Temple. Given the ferocious up-and- down motion of *Peregrine,* they made good landings. Hatters Dunne was not so fortunate. He hit the deck heavily, and Bolo saw his undercarriage crumple. The aircraft was manhandled on trolleys to the forward lift and lowered into the hangar. Biddy Bidwell was next. He landed safely. Midshipman Cartwright, following him, hit the deck hard and his tailwheel shattered. His aircraft was safe, however, and was wheeled below.

How long, Bolo thought, before we have a fatal accident? Then the ship began flashing, catching the attention of each aircraft in turn.

'Proceed one mile to port and jettison your bombs.'

'Thank God,' said Dicky Burd, and Bolo echoed that sentiment.

There were no more accidents and by eleven o'clock all aircraft had been struck down in the hangar. The wind was force ten. Flying was cancelled. The search was abandoned. *Peregrine,* herself, now had problems. Against the strong wind and violent sea she was using extra quantities of fuel. There was scarcely enough to reach Durban.

After two more days of battling against the elements, the wind abated and the sea subsided. Everyone was glad to see the opening into Durban harbour, the Chief Engineer more than anybody.

Chapter 11

Durban

As the taxi drew up at the Edward Hotel, in Marine Parade, Durban, the huge major-domo, a Zulu dressed in immaculate costume, stepped forward with a beaming smile to open the door.

'Welcome, masters and misses,' he said in a deep voice, and led the way up the steps through the swing doors into a palatial foyer, with huge ornamental columns and twin curved stairways leading up to the upper floors. All four of the visitors were dressed in uniform: Bill and Killer as sub lieutenants in number fives, the normal English uniform, worn now because of the cool evening of the South African winter; Janet and Ann in their VADs uniform. They had been advised to wear uniform. *Peregrine* had called at Durban on its way to the Mediterranean from the Far East, and the ship's officers had been shown great hospitality in the town.

'You have to be recognised as serving officers, though,' Dicky Burd had told them, 'so wear your uniforms.'

The value of this advice soon became apparent. They had no sooner sat down at a table in the dining room than the Asian waiter approached with a note.

'Would you care to join us for dinner?' It was signed 'Frank Pettigrew'.

Killer had read the message aloud and now they all looked to where the waiter was indicating. At a table laid for six, a

118

man and woman in their late fifties were smiling a welcome at them.

'Shall we?' Killer asked, and when his friends nodded their consent he led them over to the table and introduced them.

The man shook hands with each of them and then introduced his wife, Mary. He was the owner and managing director of a large sugar plantation just north of Durban. His office was in the docks area and he had watched *Peregrine* and *Carpathian* enter harbour.

Under the influence of the South African wine, the four young people soon relaxed and began to chat to the older couple. Over soup, the girls explained what VAD meant and described their lives in hospital and aboard the hospital-ship. Over fish, Killer described what flying from a carrier was like, whilst Bill explained the role of an observer in the Fleet Air Arm, both carefully avoiding any reference to recent operations. Over the meat course, the boys and girls told of how they had met in hospital when Killer was wounded and how their friendship had developed. Frank Pettigrew and Mary were gentle in their probing, but there was no doubt of their approval of their young companions. Over the sweet, Frank invited the four to visit his house for the weekend. His son and daughter, who were of a similar age, would be at home to entertain them.

Alas! Killer and Ann were both on duty, but Bill and Janet were both free and would be delighted to accept.

'What a delightful couple!' Janet said, after they had taken their leave. They had decided to walk back to their ships and enjoy the exercise after the splendid meal.

'Just my luck, to be on duty!' Killer exclaimed ruefully. 'I bet you'll have a whale of a time up in them there hills.'

'Never mind, Killer!' said Janet. 'I'm sure if we stay here long enough you'll get an invitation.'

'I heard we are here for only four days,' said Killer. 'It's Friday today, so I expect we'll be off on Monday.'

'You enjoy your weekend away,' said Ann, 'and tell us all about it when you return.'

The next morning a taxi was waiting on the quay to take Bill and Janet to the Pettigrews' home, Vanderley, about ten miles north of Durban. As they climbed the hills above Durban, Bill saw that they were entering an area of large houses, surrounded by gracious grounds and gardens. Vanderley was approached by a long drive, lined with trees. The house was a two-storey mansion, built in English style, with a gravelled forecourt and steps going up to the threshold. At the top of the steps, with smiling faces, Frank and Mary were waiting to greet their visitors.

'Welcome to Vanderley,' said Mary. 'I hope you enjoy your visit. And here are Joel and Laura to greet you.'

Janet watched as the young man, perhaps a year or two older than they, shook hands perfunctorily with Bill and came towards her.

'What a beauty we have here!' he said, taking her arm possessively. 'Come inside, and I'll get you a drink.'

He ignored Bill. His voice, unlike that of his parents who had very English accents, had a trace of South African. He reminded her of Doctor Lovemore. Handsome and confident, he showed the same touch of arrogance in both appearance and speech. She felt she was being hurried away from Bill.

In the meantime Laura, a year or two younger than her brother, after a casual 'Hiyah' to Janet, had gone up to Bill, taken both of his arms in hers and greeted him with a resounding kiss on his lips, exclaiming, 'My hero!'

'Here, not so fast,' laughed Bill, disentangling himself and casting an anxious eye after Janet.

'You must excuse our children,' said Mary indulgently. 'I think we spoil them too much. They are used to having their own way.'

Bill glanced at the girl, who had now taken his arm and was leading him into a morning room. She was certainly attractive, with golden tresses and blue eyes, now sparkling with mischief as she regarded him. She led him to a table, where a coal-black girl dressed in white was serving drinks.

'Let's take our drinks onto the terrace,' Laura said, taking Bill's hand and leading him out through the french windows to the terrace, where Janet and Joel were gazing at the view. Bill noted that Joel had his arm round Janet's waist.

The garden still had plenty of colour, but what attracted Bill was the swimming pool, surrounded by a Cupressus hedge to protect it from the wind, with its own paved terrace. Loungers and low tables were set invitingly alongside the pool. Bill noted that Joel was talking earnestly to Janet and would like to have known what was being said.

'Do you ride?' Joel was asking Janet.

'Yes, I do. I love riding, but I'm afraid I haven't had an opportunity since I left England.'

'We can remedy that this afternoon. Father keeps a good stud here and we've a mare that would suit you perfectly.'

'But I have no riding clothes,' said Janet.

'That's all right. Laura can lend you some breeches and a shirt. You are much of a height. So that's taken care of.'

Again Janet felt she was being rushed into something.

'Won't Bill and Laura be coming with us?' she said questioningly.

'If you like,' replied Joel in a non-committal tone. 'Let's ask them.'

'I'm sorry, Janet,' Bill said when the invitation was put to him. 'I've never ridden in my life. I wouldn't know how to start.'

'That's all right,' Laura interjected quickly. 'Bill can come swimming with me while you go for a ride with Joel, Janet. You do swim?' she said, turning to Bill.

'Yes, of course, but I haven't any bathing trunks with me.'

121

'You don't need them in our pool,' said Laura, but when she saw the look on Bill's face she added, 'Joel will lend you some.'

Mrs Pettigrew had now come to the door and was calling to them.

'Lunch in half an hour. Can you show Bill and Janet their rooms and give them an opportunity to freshen up?'

Bill found his room was next to Janet's with Joel's room on the other side of Janet. Laura had the room next to him. Joel showed him into his room, and almost immediately came back with a pair of swimming trunks. In a similar manner, Laura provided riding kit for Janet.

After lunch, Bill changed into his borrowed trunks to join Laura by the swimming pool, whilst Janet went up to her room to change into her borrowed riding habit. Very attractive she looked as she came down the stairs in jodhpurs and open-necked shirt and riding hat. Joel, too, had changed and was waiting to greet her.

'Hello, my lovely. You look delicious,' he exclaimed.

Janet blushed and did not know whether to laugh or protest. She recognised the male chauvinism. She had met it in Doctor Lovemore.

Joel took her arm firmly and led her to the stables, where the stableboy was waiting with two horses, a stallion for Joel and a mare for Janet. Janet took to the mare at once. She was docile and friendly and nuzzled her head against Janet's shoulders as she stroked the mare. The mare's name was Trudy.

'Come on then. Let's get started.'

Joel had no time for sentiment and was eager to set off. He led Janet out of the garden on to a bridle path that took them up the hillside to the summit of the low hills. The mare followed willingly. From the path, Janet could see the distant sea, bleached white in the sparkling sunshine, and the Umgeni River flowing seawards below them. Joel brought his horse alongside Janet's and gave a running commentary on the scene below.

It was a glorious day. The air was warm and fresh and Janet breathed deeply, beginning almost to like Joel and responding to his small talk. She looked at him again and noted the proud set of his head and the arrogance in his face, and reserved her opinion.

'See that bluff a mile ahead, by the edge of the wood,' Joel cried. 'There's a magnificent view there. Come on. I'll race you to it.'

With that he urged his horse into a gallop and raced ahead. The mare followed and Janet found herself exhilarated by the ride. The pounding of the hooves, the wind and sun on her face, the feel of the mare beneath her, all made her flushed and excited and set her blood racing.

Joel pulled up his horse in a dramatic stop, rearing on its hind legs, and turned to greet Janet. Janet could see that he was excited. Leaping down, he hobbled the two horses and helped Janet down from hers, staring at her with blazing eyes. A flicker of fear ran through her. No other person was within miles of them and she was totally unsure about Joel. She wished Bill were present.

Joel guided her forcefully to the edge of the bluff and, throwing out a dramatic arm, he declared, 'This is our country – my country. Aren't you glad to be here, girl? This is what we came for.'

Swinging Janet round to face him, he pressed close against her and sought to kiss her on the lips. Janet arched backwards, crying, 'No, Joel, no!'

Joel laughed. He was used to having his way and expected Janet's resistance to crumble. He enjoyed a little fight before he settled down to the serious business of seduction.

Janet began to perceive how serious her predicament was. There was no holding Joel. He was excited by the ride, expecting her to give way to his charm. Resistance could easily turn into rape. She let herself go limp and stood passively, allowing him to kiss her. This he did, hungrily, exciting himself even more. When Joel began to undo the buttons of her shirt, Janet became really alarmed.

'No, Joel,' she said again. 'Please, Joel, no.'

She struggled silently, trying, without success, to prevent Joel from pulling the shirt from her shoulders.

'Joel, please. Not now. Tonight! Come to my room tonight.'

This was her last defence. She had no way of restricting Joel. He was too strong for her. And his mood was savage and dangerous.

She had got through to him. He leaned away from her, gazing into her eyes and she saw the wildness leave him.

'All right, my lovely,' he breathed. 'Tonight. I'll come to your door at midnight. We'll make a glorious match.'

Janet eased from him, buttoning her shirt and breathing heavily. She made her way back to the mare, mounting quickly and waiting for Joel to join her. She was silent on the ride back, wondering how to deal with the situation. Joel thought she was contemplating the coming night's amours.

In the meantime, back at the pool, Bill was having his own problems. Laura's method of seduction was more gentle, more subtle, than that of her brother. She lay on her lounger, wearing the skimpiest of bathing briefs and top and, handing him her sun-lotion, she invited him to apply it to her beautiful body. It was indeed beautiful, the suntanned limbs lithe and seductive. She lay on her front whilst he rubbed in the oil. Then she turned onto her back, inviting him to apply the oil to her front. Bill was quite out of his depth. The cleavage of her breasts was exposed invitingly to him as he gingerly rubbed in the oil.

'Now my legs,' she commanded, when he had finished

oiling her midriff. Bill started to apply the oil to Laura's shins, slowly working upwards.

'I am particularly vulnerable to the sun at the top of my thighs,' Laura said, as Bill's efforts began to peter out.

Willy-nilly, Bill found himself massaging the soft flesh below the briefs. 'A bit higher, Bill. I'll take the briefs off if it would help.'

'No you won't, Laura, not if I have anything to say about it,' Bill said, drawing away and laughing.

Laura was laughing, too, her eyes full of mischief. She had realised that Bill was an essentially shy man and she was deliberately teasing him and enjoying herself immensely.

'Now I'll rub you,' she said, jumping up and seizing the bottle of oil.

'No you won't,' Bill said, backing off hastily. 'I don't need oil.'

Laura noted with approval the flat stomach, slim hips and tanned, muscular body. This was a man, she thought hungrily.

For a while they lay in the sunshine on their loungers, talking desultorily. Laura was intrigued with the scar on Bill's leg and wanted to know how he came by it. Slowly, and with a great deal of effort and perseverance, she drew the story from him, how he was shot down and wounded in the Western Desert and, with his pilot, Holy Temple, was taken prisoner; how the Italians looked after him and attended to his wounds; how the prisoner convoy was attacked by a long-range British armoured patrol and how, in the mêlée, Holy Temple and he hid under the sand, using their Gosport tubes as air pipes. Bill told her of the long, torturous walk across the desert; they discovered a burnt-out vehicle and raided its radiator for water; they were found by another patrol and flown back to Alexandria and hospital. Bill did not tell her how he met Janet. Janet belonged to his private world, a world that Laura would never know.

Laura was intrigued by Bill's story, so much so that for a while she stopped teasing him. This did not last for long, however.

'Come on,' she cried, jumping up. 'Time for a swim. Let's see how well you do it.'

Paradoxically, Bill felt he would be on safer ground in the water and, diving in at one end of the pool, he swam vigorously to the other end with an excellent crawl. Laura was impressed and even more determined.

'I'm coming in now,' she called and plunged cleanly into the water.

Bill trod water, waiting for her to emerge. The water had been soaking up the sunshine and was passably warm. Where was Laura?

Suddenly, he felt hands grasping his feet, running up his legs, thighs and chest, and circling his neck. Laura clung to him closely, her lips against his, but he was having none of it. As they went under together, he broke away and swam hard for the other end of the pool, with Laura following him, laughing.

Bill laughed, too. Suddenly he could see the funny side of the situation. Instead of boy chasing girl, it was girl chasing boy, literally. He entered into the fun of it, playing with Laura, escaping from her clutches, diving under her and heaving her out of the water, racing her to the steps. Laura loved it. So, Bill thought, did he, as long as he could keep it at the playful level.

After half an hour's swimming, Laura pulled Bill onto the grass, by the pool's terrace.

'Let's lie out in the sun,' she said gaily.

Bill's thought was 'rest at last', an escape from Laura's tricks. Not a bit of it. No sooner were they lying side by side than Laura sat up and pulled Bill's head onto her lap. Bill could feel the smooth, wet flatness beneath his head and then Laura was bending over him, her breasts just brushing his face, the nipples hard and firm.

126

'Get out of this,' cried Laura, laughing.

Bill gave up. He lay there supinely, eyes closed, pretending to sleep, and allowed Laura to stroke his hair and think her thoughts.

Throughout dinner that evening Janet was very quiet, pecking at her food and allowing the conversation to drift over her. Laura was gay and lively, with a fund of amusing stories. The meal was excellent, the best food and wine that South Africa could offer. Bill enjoyed every minute of it, except for one difficulty. After each course was finished he could feel Laura's knee rubbing against his and her hand under the table on his thigh, stroking him, as she told another funny story. Each time he removed her hand, laughing with her as she laughed, but wondering what the others would think if they knew what was happening.

When his eyes rested on Janet, Bill knew instinctively that something was wrong. She seemed distant and anxious, and Bill wondered and worried about what might have happened during the afternoon. As they left the table, Janet joined Bill for a moment and whispered in his ear.

'Come up to my room before you go to bed, Bill. I must have a word.'

At ten o'clock, Mrs Pettigrew, who had noticed how quiet Janet had been, said, 'Janet, my dear, you are looking tired. Are you feeling well?'

'I am tired,' said Janet. 'I think it must be the fresh air and unaccustomed exercise. Would you think me ungracious if I retired to bed?'

'Not at all, dear. We want you to have a good rest and enjoy yourself tomorrow.'

Janet kissed Mrs Pettigrew and said goodnight to the others.

A few minutes later Bill said, 'With your permission, Mary, I'd like to go up too. All this fresh air and exercise is too much for me,' he added, looking at Laura.

Making sure that no one was watching her, Laura closed one eye in a broad wink. Bill shook his head and went out of the room, laughing.

Janet was waiting for Bill in her room, by the window, looking out over the garden. She turned as Bill knocked and entered and he could see that she was deeply disturbed. He went over to her quickly and took her hands in his. They were very cold.

'What's wrong, Janet?' Bill asked.

In a rush, Janet poured out her story of the afternoon's episode with Joel.

'I'm sure he would have taken advantage of me... I stopped him only by pretending that I'd be available tonight. Bill, I'm so worried and frightened. I don't know what to do.'

She paused and looked anxiously at Bill. Bill looked into her face and thought for a moment.

'Would you like me to stay in your room tonight?' he said.

'Oh, Bill. Would you? There are two beds in the room and you can sleep in the other one.'

'All right, Janet. You take the bed by the window and I'll have the one nearer the door. I'll go and get changed now. I'll come back, if it's all clear, at eleven o'clock.'

When Bill returned to Janet's room, she was sitting up in bed, with a dressing gown over her nightdress. She looked cold and apprehensive, holding her gown up to her chin.

'Try to relax, Janet,' Bill said, slipping into his own bed, still wearing his dressing gown over pyjamas. 'I'll deal with Joel if he comes.'

He lay back on his pillow and noted, with approval, that Janet had lain down and tucked herself under the bedclothes. They could hear a clock chiming the quarters. For Janet the wait seemed interminable. She was filled with an undefined dread as she recalled the moments on the bluff.

As the notes of midnight died away she heard a gentle tapping on her door. Bill had left the key in the lock.

'Open up, darling,' Joel's voice whispered. 'This is Joel. Remember? We have a date.'

When Janet did not answer the voice became more insistent.

'I'm coming in, Janet, whether you agree or not. You can't play me up like this. I have my own key to this room.'

Unfortunately, Bill had left the key in the upright position and now it clattered to the floor as Joel inserted his own key. The sound of the lock turning was loud and terrifying, and Janet watched with horror as the door handle turned and the door slowly opened.

By this time, however, Bill had jumped out of bed and was standing four square in the doorway. The door opened fully to reveal Joel, grimacing lasciviously.

'Well, mister! And what do you want?'

Janet had never heard Bill's voice so low, determined and forceful. She saw Joel's jaw drop open with astonishment.

'I'm … I'm sorry. I made a mistake,' he said, stuttering with his sense of frustration and ignomy.

'Get out of here! And don't come back or you'll really have something to be sorry about.'

Bill closed the door and locked it, half-turning the key so that it could not be pushed through. He turned to Janet.

'You can sleep now, Janet. Would you like me to stay the night in case he returns?'

Dumbly, Janet nodded. She had slipped out of bed and shed her dressing gown. Silhouetted against the full moon shining through the window, Bill could see her figure outlined clearly through the shimmering silk of her night-dress, and then she slipped into bed.

Bill went to her and tucked the bedclothes in carefully. Then he leaned over her and brushed his lips lightly against hers, saying, 'Goodnight, my dear. Sleep tight.'

'Dear Bill,' Janet whispered, reaching up to him and kissing him firmly. 'Thank you, Bill.'

For a moment Bill gazed at the girl. The fear had gone from her face, which was now in a state of repose, her eyes following him as he took off his dressing gown and climbed into his own bed.

He watched her silently as her eyes closed and she drifted into sleep. He now knew that he loved this girl. If she wanted him he would cherish her throughout his life. He would never let harm come to her, nor would he betray her in any way. With that thought in mind he fell asleep, dreaming of Janet.

His dreams merged into reality as he felt the gentle shaking of his shoulder and the soft brush of lips on his own.

'It's six o'clock, Bill. I don't think anything will happen now.'

He opened his eyes and there was Janet's face above him, looking serene and relaxed.

'Did you sleep well, Janet?'

'Yes, thanks to you.'

'It's time for me to return to my own room. Make sure you lock the door securely after I leave.'

With a quick kiss, he left her room and heard the lock click behind him. His own room looked cold and uninviting, but he was soon asleep again.

By eight o'clock, Janet and Bill were in the dining room, helping themselves to breakfast from the sideboard. Frank and Mary Pettigrew were already seated at the table.

'I hope you slept well,' Mrs Pettigrew said as they sat down.

Janet glanced at Bill.

'Yes, thank you, Mrs Pettigrew. Very well indeed.'

'Good. Now Frank and I like to go to Sunday communion at the Protestant church. Are you interested?'

'I'd love to go, Mrs Pettigrew,' said Janet.

Mrs Pettigrew looked at Bill.

'I'd love to take communion this morning with Janet,' said Bill.

'That's good,' said Mrs Pettigrew, looking at her husband. 'I wish our children felt the same. They never attend church now.'

'I don't suppose you'll see them until we return,' growled her husband. 'They never get up for breakfast on Sunday.'

The walk to the church was along a leafy lane. The older couple were ahead, and Bill and Janet followed hand in hand.

'I don't know how such a lovely couple could have a son like Joel,' Janet said.

'I wouldn't think too harshly of him,' Bill replied. 'He has probably grown up having his own way with girls. Droits de seigneur and all that. No doubt he didn't realise how offensive he was being.'

'I don't think there's any excuse for a man to force himself on a woman,' said Janet.

'A pity we haven't retained the ideal of medieval chivalry,' said Bill. 'In those days the knights considered it their duty to protect women, not molest them. At least the nice ones did.'

'I remember my Chaucer,' said Janet. 'Bill, you are my "verray parfit, gentil knight".'

'Not such a perfect, gentle knight yesterday afternoon,' said Bill, laughing. 'I spent most of it evading Laura. She's fun, but she's a man-killer. I'm sure she came to my room last night. It must have been a shock to her when she found it empty. You see, Janet dear,' he concluded, laughing, 'it was you saving me from the clutches of a beautiful woman, rather than the other way round.'

Janet turned and looked at Bill, laughing with him. Nevertheless she grasped his hand more tightly.

By now the group had reached the small church, where they were welcomed by the vicar. The church was quite full, but most of the congregation were middle-aged. As Bill

131

followed Janet to the altar and received the bread and wine he silently renewed his vow that he would love and cherish the girl next to him throughout his life.

Laura was waiting to greet them on their return. She greeted them gaily and led the way to the terrace, where drinks awaited them. She told them that Joel had been called away unexpectedly and would not be in to lunch. When she saw Janet talking earnestly to her parents she came close to Bill and whispered to him.

'I came to your room last night. You weren't there. Where were you?'

Then her eyes widened as the significance of the night dawned on her. She looked quickly at Janet and then back at Bill.

'Bill you weren't … you couldn't …'

Again she looked at Janet, this time, Bill could see, with approval. Janet had gone up in her estimation. She was not a jealous girl.

'Ah well,' she said, smiling, 'you win some and you lose some. Janet's a lucky girl.'

Bill laughed. Laura would never get beyond sex in her understanding of love.

At lunch, Bill sat between Janet and Laura. The talk was gay and lively, and Mr and Mrs Pettigrew were delighted with their guests. Janet was vivacious and exciting, and Laura, if it were possible, more subdued.

At least, Bill thought, laughing within himself, Laura did not spend most of the meal trying to stroke his leg.

Chapter 12

Cape Town

Janet and Ann stood at their usual off-duty position, at the stern of *Carpathian,* leaning against the taffrail. It was eleven o'clock on a fine Monday morning and they were watching the Swordfish ranged on the carrier astern and to port of them, wondering if Killer and Bill were the crew. They stood in companionable silence for a while, observing the manoeuvres of the plane taking off and the one landing on. Then Ann turned to Janet.

'You've been very quiet about your weekend, Janet,' she said. 'What happened?'

Janet regarded Ann seriously. Janet was an only child and had never had a sister to confide in or a brother to tumble with. She had always had a best friend at school, and since leaving school and joining the VADs Ann had become her best friend, a friendship established and strengthened by their relationships with Killer and Bill.

'I had a difficult time at Vanderley,' she said slowly.

And then she knew she wanted to confide in Ann. She told Ann how she felt she was being separated from Bill and about the ride with Joel.

'I met the usual boys at parties and during school holidays and after I left school, but really we were children in those days. I've dealt with plenty of men in hospital, but they were patients. Bill's the first man I have met and thought of as a

133

man, and he's so gentle. I've never met anyone like Joel and I didn't know how to deal with him. I was frightened.'

'Of him raping you?' Ann asked.

'I'm not sure,' Janet replied honestly. 'At the time I was more frightened of the unknown and of the violence.'

'What happened then?' Ann asked.

'After he began stripping off my shirt, I struggled with him and protested, but that only seemed to make him more determined. I believe he thought I was more experienced than I am and he expected me to give way to him. We were miles from anywhere and there wasn't a soul in sight. I could think of only one way of stopping him; I promised to be ready for him in my room after everyone had gone to bed. I felt terrible, Ann. I knew I was only putting off the evil moment and I didn't know what to do about it.'

'How awful for you!' Ann exclaimed. 'What happened?'

'Bill happened. Bill was marvellous. I told him about Joel and he offered to stay in my room and deal with him. There were two beds in my room and Bill took the other bed. When Joel came, Bill faced him. I said that Bill was gentle; he is with me, but with Joel he was forceful. He spoke to him quietly but very firmly and he had Joel cringing. Then he offered to stay with me all night, in case Joel returned, and I accepted.'

'So you had a man in your bedroom all night,' Ann said gently. 'Did you sleep with him?'

'No. He was very, very gentle with me. He tucked me up and kissed me goodnight and went to his own bed. I think one part of me wanted him to comfort me like that, like a child, particularly after the traumas of the day; another part of me wanted him like a woman.'

'Are you in love with him?'

'I don't know,' said Janet slowly. 'I think I may be, but I'm not sure what love is. I don't think girls in our situation ever know much about men and love and sex. Of course I heard the usual tales at school, but I wasn't very interested. In a vague sort of way, I suppose, I thought I'd one day meet a man and fall in love with him, but my thoughts never really went on to the sexual side of things.'

'What is Bill's attitude to you?' Ann asked.

'I think he may be falling in love with me. I know when we dance together he is physically excited, but I think, like me, he probably feels that love is more than just jumping into bed. When I first met Bill we were both very young, very immature.'

'Yes, I remember that first party at the Carlton Hotel in Alexandria,' said Ann. 'Bill was so shy and reserved. He let Killer do most of the talking and the ordering.'

'I felt then,' said Janet, 'that it was me bringing Bill on; it was only when we danced together that he took the lead.'

'A year has made a lot of difference to us all,' said Ann. 'The war is making us grow up fast; it's all those experiences concentrated in a small space of time.'

The two girls stood for some moments in silence, observing the ship's wake tumbling astern.

Then Ann said quietly to Janet, 'Would you sleep with Bill if he asked you?'

Janet thought for a long while. Then she said slowly, 'I'm not sure, Ann. My upbringing tells me, no, but after this last weekend I think it could be possible for my flesh to say yes. My natural inclination is not to have sex until after marriage. I'm not sure whether that is because I've been conditioned to thinking that way, or perhaps that I am not a sexually active person. I know I was revolted by Joel, but with Bill it could be very different. Since meeting Bill I've always enjoyed his company and now I find he's in my thoughts a lot of the time when I'm not with him.'

Janet pressed her friend's hand. Ann was good for her. She had made her look honestly at her disturbed thoughts and feelings and she knew that the answers to Ann's questions still lay in the future. But what of Ann? Janet had been so

135

taken up with her own problems that she hadn't given a thought to Ann.

'What about you and Killer?' she said suddenly. 'How's your romance?'

'Coming along nicely,' said Ann, smiling. 'I'm pretty sure I love Killer and I think he loves me, but we are both content to let things develop at their own pace. I know that at some future date Killer is going to take over his father's medical practice and that will suit me. I'd love to be a doctor's wife.'

'So when will you get married?'

'Killer thinks life's too precarious for a Fleet Air Arm pilot to marry. He always puts it that if he survives the war he'll become a doctor. He's a realist about the possibility of being killed.'

'Would you like to marry him, in spite of that?'

'Yes, I would. I'd like him to give me a baby so that if he died I'd have something of him left.'

Janet was amazed at her friend's response. Ann was far more down to earth than she was. Janet realised that she herself was still living in an adolescent half-world compared to the real world that Ann inhabited.

'Would you sleep with Killer?'

Ann answered without hesitation.

'Yes, of course, if he wanted me. I haven't your inhibitions about sex, Janet. I love Killer. I think sex is the crowning act of love, the physical expression of a deep emotion. I think I have been ready for it for some time. Unfortunately, like your Bill, Killer is very much a gentleman and he doesn't want to hurt me. Sooner or later, when he finally accepts that he loves me, he'll want me, and I'll go to him. If we can be married beforehand, so much the better.'

Janet realised how different Ann was from herself and the knowledge of this difference made her love her friend all the more. She thought how fortunate she was to have such friends as Ann and Killer and such a young man as Bill to take care of her. She breathed a sigh of sheer happiness as they left the taffrail and made their way below.

Meanwhile, aboard *Peregrine,* Bill and Killer were relaxing in the sunshine on the goofers' platform. They were not flying; in fact their squadron was on stand-by for the day and this meant a day of relaxation once they had attended to their squadron duties. Bill was thinking about Janet. Unlike Janet, he had no intention of discussing his thoughts with anyone, and Killer did not press him. Bill was fond of Ann; she was Killer's girl and Janet's friend. Bill thought how lucky he was to have such friends.

Janet was something else. He now knew that he loved Janet deeply, so much that he no longer worried about her parents or their wealth. When Janet had turned to him for protection she had touched a vein of chivalry that was natural to him. Janet was young and had to be protected, but she was growing older and he could foresee a time when they would naturally come together. So far he had avoided forcing himself on her, but Cape Town was coming nearer and he believed that at Cape Town their paths would diverge. He could not bear the thought of losing Janet, but he still felt too unsure of himself to speak of his love. At times he had thought that Janet might – just might – love him, but he was afraid of risking all by declaring his own love. If a situation presented itself at Cape Town he must speak out. He must contrive to have Janet alone with himself for long enough for the moment to present itself. With a sigh Bill closed the book on his thoughts and gave his attention to the Swordfish approaching to land-on.

The passage to Cape Town was an easy one for the squadron. No real danger from either enemy warships or enemy submarines was expected in these waters. Somewhere ahead was *Hohenlinden.* It was generally assumed that she had made her way far south of Cape Town into the wastes of the South Atlantic, where it was known that supply ships and a tanker awaited her. After Cape Town, Bill knew they would be searching the endless sea for the elusive raider. Janet, he was fairly sure, would accompany her patients homewards to England.

On the day after the small convoy arrived at Cape Town it was learned that *Carpathian,* which had been held up at Suez and had had engine trouble again at Mombasa, had a serious engine defect and would have to go into dry dock for repairs. All her patients, together with medical staff, were to be accommodated in hospitals in Cape Town. The naval patients, with Sister Harvey and the VADs, were to go to the Naval Hospital, and this made it easier for Bill and Killer to arrange to meet their girl friends. Janet and Ann worked regular hours in the hospital, with regular days off, and it was on Janet's first free day that Bill organised his day's outing with her.

As the carrier entered harbour he had been fascinated by Table Mountain, rising almost straight up from the outskirts of the town, its top hidden by mist. When he made enquiries, he discovered that there was a trail that he and Janet would be able to follow that would take them to the top of Chapman Peak, at the southern end of the Table Mountain Range. From this vantage point they would be able to see both the Atlantic and the Indian Oceans, on either side of Cape Peninsular. Schooley gave Bill a good weather forecast. A high-pressure system was developing and the weather would be clear, bright and warm for late May, South Africa's autumn; and, more importantly, they could expect Table Mountain to be free of clouds.

Janet had a free day on the Monday after they docked and early on that morning Bill collected her at the hospital. The taxi took them south to Clovelly and then through Sun Valley to the southern foothills of Chapman Peak. They were already at some altitude when the taxi deposited them so that they had about two thousand feet to climb to the peak, along a trail outlined on his map. His knapsack contained sandwiches, fruit, a bottle of water, a compass and a groundsheet, and they were both in a cheerful mood as they set off along the path, looking forward to their climb and their picnic lunch.

The path climbed slowly at first, through wiry grassland dotted with autumn flowers. It meandered in and out of the rocks, giving them tantalising glimpses of the sea. Sometimes they were forced to clamber up a small rock cluster and Bill, who was leading, stopped to give Janet a hand. On one such occasion, with the path broadening so that they could walk side by side Bill retained Janet's hand in his and she did not attempt to withdraw it. On another, as a spectacular view of mountain and sea opened up, Bill stopped to admire the spectacle, holding Janet in front of him. She leaned against him and he was aware of the softness and fragrance of her hair against his face. On yet another occasion, Janet had to jump down four feet from a rock. Bill opened his arms and Janet jumped into them, laughing. Each of these incidents set Bill's blood tingling and made him extraordinarily aware of Janet's presence.

It was very quiet in the upland air and their voices when they spoke to each other were low, sometimes breathless with effort, sometimes vibrant with the joy of living. They talked of the flowers they saw, of the gulls and other seabirds flying below them, of themselves. Most of all, they talked of themselves, revealing more of their lives to each other and discussing their beliefs and their attitudes. Their talk ranged over their experiences of war, religion and literature. They were both well read and had many books in common; in fact they discovered an agreeable similarity of tastes and interests and it was in this spirit of harmony that they reached the summit.

The views were spectacular. To the west was the Atlantic, to the east the Indian Ocean; southwards stretched Cape Peninsula as far as Cape Point, the Cape of Good Hope itself, beyond which the two oceans meet. Bill spread his goundsheet in a sheltered spot, out of the wind, where the sun warmed them. Around them was the silence of great rocks and, far beneath them, the sea. They were in a world of their own, far away from any other living person.

'I'm hungry,' said Janet, opening Bill's packages, meat and cheese sandwiches, tomatoes, lettuce and apples. 'Your steward has done well.'

'The food's plain and simple,' said Bill, 'but I thought with the climb ahead of us I'd keep the weight down. Otherwise I'd have put a bottle of wine in the package.'

Talk continued along these lines, bordering on the mundane, as though both of them were putting off the time when something momentous would happen. It was out of keeping with the dramatic landscape, the backcloth to what was happening.

Bill was aware that by keeping the conversation at this level he was avoiding the real issue, but now that the moment had arrived, he felt extraordinarily shy, unsure of himself. Janet meant so much to him that he feared to put his proposal to her; he feared that their relationship might suffer irreparable damage.

'Do you mind sharing this bottle of water with me?' he asked. 'I didn't put glasses or cups in the pack.'

'Of course not,' Janet replied, stretching out her hand for the bottle.

Bill felt that the act of sharing the bottle was symbolic. He watched as Janet cleared away the picnic remains and sat looking at him intently.

The blood rushed to his head as he leaned back against the warm rocks and, stretching out his hands, he said, 'Come here, Janet.'

Without a word Janet slid across the groundsheet and

nestled in Bill's arms. Again he could feel the softness of her body against his and smell the fragrance of her hair. Again the blood rushed to his head.

'Janet,' he said simply, 'will you marry me?'

The pause that followed seemed an eternity and Bill's heart stopped beating while he waited. The rock was hard and warm beneath him; the sky was a cerulean blue above him; far below him two seas met and he thought that this symbolised the meeting of his and Janet's spirits. His senses were excruciatingly alert. Time stood still.

'Bill, dear,' Janet said at length, 'I've been wanting you and not wanting you to ask that question. I now know the answer. It is yes, yes, yes.'

Bill leaned over her and kissed her lips, gently at first and then with deep passion as the full significance of Janet's reply burst upon him.

'Darling,' he breathed. His hands reached upwards to her breasts and through the thin cotton he felt her nipples harden. He lay there for some moments, savouring the sensation and letting his love pass physically by the touch of his hands through to Janet. His right hand moved slowly downwards over her skirt and came to rest lightly between her thighs. Janet gave a small gasp.

Under Bill's hands she felt her breasts swelling and her womb seeming to open to receive Bill. Involuntarily her own hand moved down over Bill's body and came to rest on the swelling beneath his shorts. It felt huge and powerful and pulsating with a life of its own.

'Bill,' she said, in a small voice, 'I want you so much.'

She knew now how the savage power of a man could bring out the deepest instincts in herself. She was no longer afraid. In Joel the power had been uncontrolled, lustful. Bill's power was infinitely stronger, but it was gentle, giving rather than taking. Bill, she realised, was no longer shy with her, nor she with him. If he wanted her now she was ready to go to him.

141

Bill turned her in his arms and looked steadily into her eyes.

'You know I want you, too, Janet dearest, but not now, not like this. When we come together, finally, it will be with the blessing of your church and your family. I love you so much, Janet, that I can wait for that time to come.'

Janet grasped Bill's hands in hers and held them firmly against her breasts. She wanted Bill to take her now and ease the ache in her loins and the yearning in her heart, but at the same time she knew Bill was right, and she loved him for it.

By now both she and Bill were emotionally exhausted. The two youngsters had for the first time felt the powerful pull of sexual love. They had dealt with it in their own way, working out for themselves, as youngsters have had to do throughout the ages, the parameters they would find acceptable. Loving was spiritual and emotional and sexual. They would explore each other using all five senses, the sound of each other's voices, the sight of each other's bodies, the taste of each other's lips, her fragrance and his masculinity, but most of all the touch and the feel of each other, her softness against his hardness. The sixth sense, discovered in the sexual act, they would leave until after they were married.

And they would further explore each other's minds and emotions. Already they had discovered common interests and ideals. But Janet was a woman and Bill was a man and their opposite polarities would pull them together. Bill would use his strength to protect and defend Janet; Janet would use her sympathy and understanding to cherish Bill.

These thoughts and many others ran through Janet's mind as she lay contented and serene in Bill's arms. Her thoughts drifted to the day they would be married when their love would be consummated. Vaguely, in a half dream, she thought beyond that to having a family of Bill's children, of their future home. It was easier at present to think of Bill. His presence was etched sharply on her mind. She thought her mother and father would love Bill, who would be like a son to them. And her thoughts turned full circle and came back to giving Bill a son and sharing the home he would provide. With these thoughts she fell asleep, smiling.

Bill looked at and felt the girl sleeping in his arms. Power surged through him and he felt strong and unafraid of the future. He did not regret not having intercourse with Janet. Janet was a long way from home and his role was to cherish and protect her. They had all their lives before them to develop and consummate their love. What of the future? It would be for Bill to provide for Janet and their family. How big a family? At least three children, Bill thought, though the idea of a larger family did not frighten him, but he would like to delay having a family so that he could enjoy Janet for herself.

Man was different from all other creatures, Bill thought. Unlike animals, he could plan ahead and think about the future. There was a divine spark in him that enabled him to appreciate beautiful things, to raise his sights above mere instincts, to love and cherish his wife. But what brought two people together? Bill had met many girls and danced with them and chatted to them and enjoyed their company. With Janet, he now knew, it had always been different. Why had he been so attracted to Janet from the moment they had first met? And by what strange, divine quirk did Janet return that love? Was it just chance? Or was it that their two spirits were destined to join each other, like the waters of two streams, converging to form a large river? With Janet in his arms, he had felt at peace with himself, whether it was dancing a slow foxtrot or, as now, lying in the sun with Janet asleep on his breast. He felt very tender towards her, wholly protective. He remembered his vow in church. He would cherish and protect her all the days of his life. All the days of his life. Unlike Killer he did not visualise his own death. He was immortal, or loving Janet had made him so. And with that thought, with Janet in his arms, in the warm sun, at the top of a marvellous mountain, he too slept.

Janet's next free time was on the following Thursday evening. Ann was also free, and Bill and Killer arranged to collect the girls for an evening at the Mount Nelson Hotel for dinner and dancing. Once again the boys were in mess-undress, bow ties and short white jackets with black epaulettes, over black trousers and cummerbunds; the girls were in long evening gowns, Ann in dusky-pink satin with a lacy stole, and Janet in a flowing ivory-coloured silk with a small black cape. An immaculately dressed Zulu, in uniform and epaulettes that Killer thought made him at least a colonel, greeted them on the steps of the hotel and opened the swing doors for them. They were all impressed with the wealth and luxury of this famous hotel, reflected in the glittering jewels of the ladies and the evening-dress of the men. The headwaiter led them to a table by the dance-floor, a privileged position Bill realised.

Smiles greeted them from people sitting at nearby tables, emphasising the welcome given them by the people of Cape Town. Killer was his usual ebullient self and both Ann and Janet responded to his humour. Janet looked beautiful. Her evening gown set off her golden tresses; her face was slightly flushed and her eyes sparkled with excitement, suggesting a depth and quality that Ann had never noticed before. Ann looked quizzically at her friend and then at Bill who seemed to be quiet and a little restrained. He recovered during the meal and the small party was lively and gay, enjoying the excellent food and wine, the quiet, soft background music, and the wit and banter of their conversation. One or two couples took to the dance-floor, but by common consent Killer's group kept to their table, savouring their food and wine and the atmosphere of the hotel's restaurant.

Eventually, Killer pushed his chair back and invited Ann to

dance with him. Bill watched them start off. Killer had improved, Bill noted, and was steering easily through the other couples. Maybe Ann had given him some lessons.

'Shall we dance, Janet?' he said, drawing her chair back.

Janet smiled and slipped easily and comfortably into Bill's arms. It was a slow, hesitant waltz, Janet's favourite dance, although she knew that Bill preferred the foxtrot. The familiar position, Bill's arm round her waist, her arm resting on his, her hand on his shoulder, their bodies just touching, seemed to have taken on a new meaning for her. She felt warm and comfortable in Bill's arms, as though she belonged there, and as she responded to the long, slow steps, the dancers around her became a background of dimly seen figures and faces, a dreamy half-world. Only Bill was real, and she could feel his love for her expressed in the languorous rhythm of the dance. The dance itself had taken on a new meaning; it meant home and security, excitement and adventure, and the promise of future bliss; it meant Bill. Janet felt that she was dancing on air, her eyes half closed, her body floating through space and time. The dance could go on for ever.

And then it was ended. Movement stopped; she heard the burst of applause; she opened her eyes and found she had landed and was back on earth, in Bill's arms, with people all round her laughing and talking and walking back to their tables.

'Shall we go out to the terrace?' Bill was saying to her, and she nodded her agreement.

Pausing only for Janet to retrieve her cape, Bill led her through the swing doors on to the terrace and down to the garden. The scene was illuminated by a nearly full moon and discreet garden lamps. Bill guided Janet past a flower-bed of late gazanias into the rose garden where he found a garden seat. The fragrance of the roses added to the sense of beauty, and Table Mountain, lit by the same moon, provided a magnificent backcloth. Bill fumbled in his pocket.

'Darling Janet,' he said, 'I brought you out here because I wanted to give you this.'

Janet gazed at the black velvet box and then at Bill. She opened it slowly and took out the ring, a single diamond set against a cluster of small diamonds on platinum. Bill took it from her and put it on her engagement finger. It fitted perfectly.

'I measured your finger against mine last Monday, while you were asleep,' Bill said. 'I bought it this morning in Cape Town. I hope you like it.'

'Dearest Bill, it's wonderful. Thank you very, very, very much.'

Their figures merged as Janet leaned towards him and gave him a long, long kiss. They sat quietly, Janet leaning against Bill, savouring the splendid beauty all around them, totally in love with each other.

At length, Bill sighed and said, 'I think we should go back to the dance, Janet. Killer and Ann will be wondering what has happened to us.'

'I haven't told Ann yet about our engagement,' said Janet. 'She's my dearest friend and I want her to be the first to know.'

When they returned to their table Janet was astonished to find that everything was as they had left it. The band was playing; couples were dancing; and Killer and Ann were sitting at their table, regarding them expectantly.

'Well, children, and what have you been doing?' Killer asked.

In answer to the question, Janet held out her left hand to Ann.

'Janet! Congratulations!' Ann jumped up to kiss her friend and then Bill.

'What's all this about, then?' said Killer, clearly mystified.

'Janet and Bill are engaged,' cried Ann.

'Well, blow me down!' exclaimed Killer.

He, too, rose to pump his friend's hand and kiss Janet.

'This calls for champagne,' he said.

The maître d'hôtel, having noticed the slight disturbance at Killer's table, had come across to investigate, and when told of the engagement that had just taken place immediately provided a bottle of champagne on the house. He then had a word with the dance-band leader and the dance-band played the new Fleet Air Arm tune, 'Wings over the Navy'.

Dancers in the restaurant looked mystified at these proceedings. The maître d'hôtel whispered in Killer's ear. Killer nodded and waited while a microphone was brought over to him. Then he stood up and addressed the crowd of diners.

'Ladies and gentlemen, you may be puzzled by what has just happened. It is my pleasure to tell you that my friend, Sub Lieutenant Bill Hewitt, of the Fleet Air Arm, has just this minute become engaged to Miss Janet Hall, a VAD from the hospital-ship in the harbour. I ask you to drink to their happiness.'

He paused for glasses to be charged.

'To Janet and Bill,' he exclaimed, raising his glass.

'Janet and Bill,' echoed the crowd.

This was followed by a round of applause. Then the maître d'hôtel took the microphone.

'I ask Sub Lieutenant Hewitt and Miss Hall to lead the next dance, which will be a quickstep.'

Janet and Bill had been startled by the toast to them, but had responded warmly to it. Now Bill rose and led Janet to the dance-floor, accompanied by clapping from everyone. A crowd followed them and stood around the edge of the dance-floor, waiting for them to begin. They soon realised that they were witnessing something unusual and, rather than join in the dance, they remained on the edge of the floor, watching.

Bill was inspired. He led Janet with long, quick steps,

147

delicate chassés, twinkling running steps, turns and reverse turns, and many steps invented and adapted to the music. Janet followed all of them. They danced as one, using the full scope of the floor and quite unconscious of the crowd absorbed by the display. They floated over the floor, their feet scarcely seeming to touch the ground, and the band responded with a virtuoso performance seldom heard.

As the dance finished with a series of eight consecutive turns, the applause broke out and people hurried forwards to congratulate them. Goodwill was shown to Bill and his companions all evening. Bill and Janet danced many dances, sometimes Bill with Ann and Janet with Killer, but mostly together, jazzy quicksteps, slow foxtrots, gay old-fashioned waltzes, a rhumba (with much laughter), a tango (serious and solemn), until it came to the last waltz.

The lights were lowered and Bill took Janet into his arms for the last dance. It might well be the last dance they would have together before they met up again in England, for they both knew that *Peregrine* might leave at any time to search the Atlantic for the German raider, and Janet had been told that she would be accompanying a contingent of naval wounded home to England. It was a poignant moment for them and Bill held Janet very close to him as they performed the slow movements of the waltz. They came almost to a standstill in the near darkness as his lips sought those of Janet.

And then the dance was over and they were joining hands with everyone for 'Auld Lang Syne'.

Chapter 13

The Southern Ocean

A long blast on *Peregrine's* siren wakened Bill from his deep sleep. He heard the low whine of machinery, felt the vibration in the ship and knew they were leaving harbour. It was eight o'clock on Sunday, the first of June. Thoughts of the previous night came rushing back to him.

He had invited Janet, accompanied by Ann, to dinner in the wardroom to celebrate their engagement. The meal was a huge success. Most of the squadron officers had already met the girls several times and quickly gathered round them in the anteroom. Janet and Bill were subjected to some humour, but it was gentle, not ribald, and Bill's friends were quick to offer their congratulations. Many times Bill was told he was a lucky man and his hand was shaken warmly. Even more warmly the younger officers queued up to kiss Janet, and some of them, for good measure, kissed Ann, too.

Ann herself took a back seat, with Killer, enjoying her friend's popularity. It was a happy group of officers that escorted Janet and Bill into the wardroom for dinner, a meal marked by lively conversation and much laughter. Towards the end of it, after the last plate had been cleared away, the port passed round and the Loyal Toast drunk, the ship's Commander rose and called for silence.

'Ladies and gentlemen,' he said, 'I have known our guests, Janet and Ann, for some time.'

He paused while the oohs and ahs died away.

'And it gives me great pleasure now to propose a toast. Will you please rise?'

Janet and Bill remained seated while everyone else stood.

'To Janet and Bill and their future happiness.'

'Janet and Bill,' they all echoed.

Bill smiled to himself as he remembered the scene, and then he remembered how he and Killer had taken the girls into the hangar, where naval airmen Bailey and Riggs, their fitter and rigger, with other squadron maintenance crews, were glad of the opportunity to meet the girls. Both girls were popular with the men, whom they had met after the previous dinner-party in *Peregrine,* and they were encouraged to pose for photographs in front of L-Love, Bill with Janet, Ann with Killer, all four together and, at a laughing request from Bailey, Bailey and Riggs with the girls and the officers.

Then Bill had taken Janet up to the goofers' platform for a last farewell. He did not tell Janet that the ship was leaving next day. Janet, however, was able to tell him that she expected to be leaving for England with naval wounded in a few days' time in the *Empire Star,* a passenger-cargo ship. Bill knew that convoys were not usually organised between Cape Town and Freetown and he guessed that *Empire Star* would be travelling alone.

Although their farewells were sad, both Janet and Bill were full of hope and optimism for the future. Their wedding would take place soon after Bill returned to England, whenever that would be.

'D'ye hear there? 999 Squadron range two aircraft.'

The bald announcement broke into Bill's thoughts. The romance of Table Mountain was over. The routine of searching the endless sea had begun. When would he see Janet again?

Bill washed and dressed and hurried to the quarterdeck to see Cape Town receding into the distant mist. The only ship accompanying them was HMS *Daventry*, a light cruiser. Their course, he noted, was westerly.

At ten o'clock he joined the remainder of the squadron in the wardroom to listen to the Captain's broadcast.

'D'ye hear there? This is the Captain speaking. We are proceeding westwards towards Tristan da Cunha in search of the German raider *Hohenlinden*. From what we learned from the Captain of *Triggonia*, we believe that *Hohenlinden* is making for the South Atlantic to rendezvous with a tanker south-west of Tristan. She will then be in a position to raid our commerce between South America and South Africa and up the west coast of Africa. Our task is to seek her out and destroy her. Our only escort will be the *Daventry*, so we shall mainly be relying on our aircraft for offence and defence.

'To enable us to remain at sea beyond our normal endurance, a rendezvous with a British tanker has been arranged. We shall follow our normal practice of dawn and dusk searches, with single Swordfish anti-submarine patrols throughout the day. That is all.'

'Into the guest-room, chaps,' said Lieutenant Commander Simpson, when the broadcast ended. 'We must have a little chat about this.'

When all of them were seated, with only Holy Temple and Midshipman Saville absent, on anti-submarine patrol, he addressed them seriously.

'This is going to be no pushover,' he said. 'Initially we shall send up searches of five aircraft in the morning and regular A/S patrols. The squadrons will alternate, carrying out searches one day and anti-submarine patrols the next. This means that most of us will fly once a day. Once we are past Tristan da Cunha we'll have morning and afternoon searches of eight aircraft to cover as wide a spread as possible. The squadrons will each cover a search every day and share the anti-submarine patrols. This means that everyone will fly at least once a day, some twice.

'It's not going to be easy. We're going into some of the emptiest ocean in the world, and the dreariest. At this time of the year it will be cold, often wet and sometimes murky. You'll need all your concentration to survive. I advise you to get in as much rest as you can when you aren't flying, and wear your Sidcot suits with kapok linings when you are. You may feel warm enough on deck, but at three thousand feet in an open cockpit, the cold will penetrate, and that's when you make mistakes.'

Turning to Bolo, he asked his senior pilot if the aircraft were on top line.

'I think so, sir,' Bolo replied. 'The morale of the maintenance crews is good at present. They've put their backs into their work, particularly in dealing with damaged aircraft and making them operational again. In this way they feel part of the operation and share in the success we've had over the past few months.

'However, we are now in for a period of endless searching with probably little to show for our searches. This is where morale may weaken and effort decline, so I'd like flying-crews to put in appearances in the hangar and encourage the men.'

'The point is well made,' echoed the CO. 'If you are miles from the carrier and your engine fails, you are just as dead as if you were shot down by enemy gunfire.'

'What's the drill if we sight the raider?' Killer asked.

'The usual. The aircraft sighting stops to shadow; the remainder return to the carrier to arm with bombs or torpedoes. The non-search squadron will be on stand-by, ready to arm up for a torpedo attack.'

'Will there be any night-flying?'

'Some. The *Hohenlinden* is probably well-armed with ack-ack guns, so our best chance is a night-attack. We'll try to time the attack so that we land in daylight, though, as Bolo and Killer have already proved, night-landings are not impossible.'

At length the questions dried up and the CO dismissed his squadron.

Steadily, the carrier ploughed its way south of west, through the mounting seas, towards the roaring forties. Monotonously the Swordfish searched the ocean; patrol followed patrol; search followed search. The air grew colder, the wind stronger, the skies cloudier. No enemy ships were sighted, but this period was not without incident.

On Tuesday afternoon Hank Phipps and Dorrie Dorrington, in G-George, were on anti-submarine patrol, immediately after lunch. In the morning the clouds had cleared, leaving a blue sky with very good visibility. Keeping *Peregrine* within visual range, Hank had gradually increased his distance until he was thirty miles ahead of the carrier. Dorrie was aware that the range had increased but not by how much. As was customary on A/S patrol, he had left the navigation to Hank whilst he scanned the horizon with his binoculars. Navigation was visual, and so long as Hank kept within sight of the carrier and doubled back on his course every fifteen miles, Dorrie did not worry. What he had not appreciated was that in clear air distances were deceptive.

When he picked up a wisp of smoke at visibility range to the west, the way the ships were heading, he decided to investigate. He thought the smoke was about fifteen miles away. It would be a simple matter to investigate, return on a reciprocal course, pick up the carrier and resume his patrol. They had three-quarters of an hour of their patrol left. He did not even plot his navigation, though he was careful to log his relative position from the carrier, the time he set off to investigate and the compass course to the target.

After half an hour's flying the target was still several miles away. Dorrie had failed to realise that visibility distance was more than thirty miles, not fifteen as he had thought, and the westerly wind into which he was heading had increased to thirty knots. He was still not too worried as visibility was very

153

good and on a reciprocal course he would be bound to close the carrier.

Five minutes later they were circling the ship, which Dorrie flashed with his Aldis lamp. Slowly he obtained the information he was seeking; the ship was Argentinian, bound for Cape Town. Hank made two more passes up-sun of the vessel so that Dorrie could take photographs. The whole operation had taken fifteen minutes. They were now nearly an hour's flying away from the carrier and, what Dorrie had not noticed while they were circling the target, the weather was deteriorating; clouds now blotted out the sun and visibility was decreasing rapidly.

He gave Hank an easterly course to take them back to the carrier and in normal circumstances this would have been good enough. On the way back, he checked the wind, and on his course and speed calculator applied it to his past and present courses. Using his original estimated distance of fifteen miles from the carrier as his starting point, he plotted his resultant tracks and the carrier's movements on his chartboard. He then gave a corrected course for his pilot to steer to bring them back to the carrier.

At 1615, after nearly four hours in the air, they arrived at his estimated position of the carrier. All that he could see were the bleak, storm-tossed waves; not a ship was in sight.

Dorrie's mouth was dry. This was the worst situation for a navigator: little more than half an hour's petrol remaining and not knowing which way to turn. He knew that some months previously Andy Andrews and Hampers Hampden had been lost in a similar situation.

'I can't think what has happened, Hank,' he said to his pilot. 'I've checked my navigation and this is where the ships should be.'

'Should we call up the carrier and ask for a bearing?' said Hank.

'I think not,' Dorrie replied. 'The German raider might be

in the area and a wireless signal would reveal the presence of a carrier.'

'I guess then we'll just have to stick it out. If we have to ditch, let's hope the carrier will send out a search party to look for us. I haven't too much fuel left.'

The Navy had prepared him for this situation and Dorrie immediately started the routine of a square search, ten miles north, ten miles east, twenty miles south, twenty miles west.

Anxiously all three of the crew scanned the sea, trying to penetrate the murk. Visibility was little more than seven miles. Dorrie had the taste of iron in his mouth, the taste of fear. He ticked off the courses, ten miles north, ten miles east, twenty miles south. Then, just as he was about to give the order to turn onto the westerly course, the last course they would have fuel for, his TAG. cried out, 'I think I can see them, sir, green two-oh.'

Dorrie peered through the murk to starboard and saw the outlines of the two ships, only six miles away. They were steering south, not west as they should have been.

'Send an emergency signal,' cried Hank. 'I don't think I'll have enough petrol to go round again.'

At four miles distance Dorrie fired a red Verey cartridge and had the satisfaction of seeing the ships begin an immediate turn into wind. By the time Hank reached the carrier, Bats was in position, signalling them in. There was no time for finesse. Bats brought the aircraft in high so that it would not hit the round-down that was rising and falling twenty feet. Hank touched down hard, halfway along the carrier, breaking an oleo leg. His hook had caught the last arrester wire, however, and the aircraft slewed to a halt.

Hank and Dorrie hurried to the bridge to report to the Captain, whilst the camera was taken down to the photographic department for the film to be developed. Dorrie explained how they had investigated suspicious smoke on the horizon and how they had started a square search when they found the ships missing on their return.

'I suppose you are wondering what happened to the ships,' said the Captain. 'About an hour ago, one of the lookouts reported a suspected submarine periscope to starboard. I ordered an immediate turn to port away from the danger and we've been steering south ever since. We had no intention of breaking wireless silence and I must compliment you on doing the same. However, we were preparing a search northwards to where you might have ditched and *Daventry* was ready to go and pick you up.'

In the operations room, whilst waiting for the photographs, Dorrie discussed with the ASO and his Senior Observer, Sandy Sandiford, what had gone wrong with his own navigation and why he had almost failed to find the ship.

He had underestimated the visibility in the unusual atmospheric conditions and had consequently under-estimated the distance of both ships from him when he first sighted the stranger. He had underestimated the wind's strength and therefore the time it would take him to reach the merchant-ship. He had failed to note the deteriorating weather and visibility. He had done well in starting a plot soon after leaving the merchant-ship, ascertaining the wind and correcting his navigation; his square search was perfectly correct and proper procedure. By far the biggest factor contributing to the near loss was the unreported change of course of the carrier.

As Sandy said to him, 'When it comes to the safety of the ship and the success of the mission, I am afraid that we, the air-crews, are expendable.'

Dorrie's final thought as they returned to the bridge was that they had been lucky and that he himself was a wiser and better observer for the experience.

A photographic technician had arrived with the photographs and these were eagerly studied and compared with *Lloyd's Register* and a book containing pictures of South American merchant-ships. It was soon ascertained that the ship was what she said she was, a merchant cargo vessel operating under the Argentinian flag.

Although no one aboard *Peregrine* was to know it, the Captain's caution on wireless transmitting was to be justified very shortly. That same night, in the early hours of the morning, the *Hohenlinden* crossed the track four miles astern of *Peregrine*. *Peregrine* was silhouetted against the half-moon, whilst *Hohenlinden* was on the dark side of the carrier. Gun sights on the German raider were trained on *Peregrine* and German guns followed the gun sights.

For some moments the German Captain stared thought-fully at the carrier and at the cruiser accompanying it. The target was tempting. Then he shook his head. Their task was to sink Allied shipping, not engage warships. He had successfully rendezvoused with a tanker and supply ship from Argentina and was now prepared for several months at sea, attacking enemy shipping. He gave the order to continue on their way north-eastwards to the shipping lanes along the African coast.

A few hours later, at 0800, five aircraft from 999 Squadron took off for a parallel track search to the west, looking for *Hohenlinden*. Hank Phipps and Dorrie Dorrington, in G-George, were again flying, this time on the starboard leg of their search. The weather had again improved and visibility was up to fifteen miles. An hour and a half after setting off, as they neared the end of their outward leg, Hank drew Dorrie's attention to the bank of clouds ahead of them and slightly to starboard. Dorrie stared through his binoculars.

'I think it's Tristan da Cunha,' he said. 'We should see it at the end of the leg.'

Ten minutes later they were flying over one of the loneliest inhabited islands of the world. Surrounded by a cluster of smaller uninhabited islands, the main island rose to a peak of eight thousand feet, an extinct volcano, around which the clouds had gathered. At the base of the volcano was the main village with little over a hundred inhabitants. Hank was flying at one thousand feet and he could clearly see the people below waving to him. Enthusiastically he waggled his wings in reply.

'Gosh! Dorrie,' he exclaimed, 'it takes guts to live in a place like that. I don't think I could do it.'

'No doubt it has its attractions,' said Dorrie. 'At least they've escaped from the horrors of modem warfare.'

Sixty miles to the south of them, in L-Love, Bill Hewitt was scanning the sea through his binoculars. Suddenly a movement caught his eye, several miles away on the port bow.

'There's something at red four-five,' he said urgently into his Gosport tubes. 'Killer, it could be a submarine.'

Killer was already turning his aircraft on to the bearing given by Bill.

'It could be a sub on the surface,' he said. 'It's big enough. Pity we haven't any bombs or depth charges.'

'Let's have a look at it,' said Bill. 'If it's a sub, I'll send off a sighting report.'

None of the crew could really make out what the object was until they were quite close.

'Blow me down!' exclaimed Killer. 'It's a whale.'

The huge creature, seventy feet in length, lay on the surface, sunning itself. Suddenly it emitted a fountain of water through its blowhole.

'That's what I must have seen when I first sighted it,' exclaimed Bill. 'I'd like to take a photo. Would you go down a bit and fly over it?'

Killer took his aircraft down to three hundred feet, whilst Bill took photographs. On the second run he had a dramatic picture for, no doubt disturbed by the noise of the aircraft, the huge creature flicked its tail and submerged with a mighty swirl.

'One for the line-book!' cried Killer, climbing back to a thousand feet to resume the search.

Searches and patrols continued the next day and the next with the weather again deteriorating, with gale force winds and huge, lumpy seas. Accidents occurred. An aircraft of 998 Squadron was thrown into the island when the ship corkscrewed suddenly as the pilot was about to lift off. Hatters Dunn, in C-Charlie, slewed to the left when his undercarriage broke, finishing up with his tail in the air and his nose buried in the catwalk. Only his hook, caught on an arrester wire, saved him from being thrown into the sea. Bing Crosby hit the round-down, bounced into the air, caught the last wire and slewed into the island, damaging his wing tip. Twice tail-wheels were damaged and once an aircraft finished on its nose, bending the propeller.

Maintenance crews worked hard, replacing broken parts, repairing the damage and keeping the planes flying. They worked in difficult conditions, on a floor that was never still, with a stench of oil and petrol, dope and sometimes vomit. In addition to the work they did in the hangar they had to add their strength to that of the deck-handling party in order to prevent aircraft sliding into the sea off the rolling and pitching deck. They did not have the successful operations of the past to sustain them, only the searching of the endless sea morning and dusk, and the weary patrols throughout the day, sighting nothing but an occasional whale.

One thing that broke the monotony was the first sight of the albatross, astern of the carrier, soaring, wheeling and swooping, its great wings twelve feet across scarcely moving as it used the heat of the carrier to give it uplift. Far out to sea it followed them, day after day, feeding off the sea itself and scavenging scraps from the carrier's garbage.

Bill was fascinated by the great bird, by its sense of life and freedom. He thought about Coleridge's poem *The Ancient*

Mariner and wondered how anyone could ever bring himself to kill an albatross. Often he stood on the quarterdeck with Killer, watching it, admiring it and half envying it.

Six days out of Cape Town, on longitude twenty-four degrees west, it was time to turn north for the rendezvous with the tanker. With the wind now on the beam, the roll of the ship was even more disconcerting than the pitching earlier. Fiddles were put up on the wardroom tables, but even with these there were several minor disasters when crockery and food finished up in a heap.

Gradually, as they drew north, the wind eased and the sun appeared more often. The weather became warmer and the officers were able to dispense with their battledress and leather Irvine jackets, and once more wear the easygoing khaki slacks and bush shirts they had first adopted in the Western Desert.

The Southern Cross was large and luminous in the southern sky, and often Bill found himself quietly contemplating it and enjoying the peace of a calm night, thinking of Janet and of their future together, remembering the past and their growing love for each other, wondering if her ship had already left Cape Town for England.

Flying was easy and regular and there were no minor mishaps. When they were not flying, pilots and observers were often to be found on C deck or the goofers' platform, relaxing in the warm sunshine. Frayed nerves mended; tired bodies relaxed; the squadron unwound.

Flying fish now began to appear, whole shoals of them, leaping from the sea with a flutter of fins to fly several yards before flopping back. Bill loved to spend time on the fo'c'sle, watching the strange creatures. He formed the impression that flying was their means of escaping their enemies, the deep-sea predators.

On Tuesday, the ninth of June, they were due to meet up with their oil tanker, in position twenty-four degrees south, twenty-four degrees west. The dawn search soon revealed the tanker and by eight o'clock it was making its approach. *Peregrine* was moving just enough to keep steerageway, whilst the oil tanker approached forty feet away on its starboard side. Slowly the low side of the tanker crept along the high side of the carrier until the fuel pipe coiled on the tanker was opposite the jumbo crane on the carrier. The two ships now proceeded at the same speed. A line was shot from the carrier to the tanker, fed onto a larger one from the tanker and this was fastened to the oil pipe, which was hauled aboard the carrier and clipped onto the fuel intake valve. A bridle was lowered from the crane and made fast round the oil pipe and the crane turned outboard to provide support for the oil pipe, which might otherwise have sagged under the heavy weight of fuel.

All was ready. The life-giving fuel was turned on and *Peregrine* began filling her tanks. It only remained for the Officers of the Watch on each ship to maintain station and distance, not an easy matter with large vessels in such close proximity.

Refuelling would take several hours. Holy Temple had noticed several sharks on the port side of the quarterdeck, nosing forward just below the surface and turning away. He decided to organise shark fishing to while away the time and soon had several of 999 squadron officers to assist him. Hunks of rotten meat were obtained from the galley, together with old tins of corned beef. A six-inch hook was quickly made in the squadron workshop and a pulley run outboard to the outer end of the flight-deck overhang. A working rig ensured that the line rove through the pulley would haul the fish out of the water, and the pulley itself, with the fishing-line and shark, could then be hauled inboard.

The bait was lowered and the group of officers on the quarterdeck watched expectantly. Bill was intrigued to see how the shark operated. Some distance from the meat, the

161

first shark opened its mouth and released half a dozen pilot fish that had been harbouring inside it. These formed a cordon ahead of the shark and guided it to the meat. The shark followed its guides to the bait, nudged it once with its snout – and turned away.

'They aren't hungry,' said Bing.

'It's not that. It's the smell of the rotten meat, enough to put off even a shark,' commented Killer.

Holy, experienced shark hunter that he was becoming, had another trick up his sleeve.

'There's only one thing for it,' he said. 'We must tempt him. Hank, I want you to draw the bait up slowly until it is out of the water and then lower it gently back again.'

Hank did as he was told and a third shark, the largest yet, some sixteen feet long, nosed forwards and gazed at the slowly receding bait. Still he did not take it. The onlookers watched expectantly.

'Dunk it,' cried Holy. 'Dunk it, Hank.'

Hank did as he was bidden and dunked the bait in and out of the water. There was a great flash of movement, startling everyone, and the coiled rope was screaming away through the pulley as the shark made off with the bait and hook.

There was no finesse about their fishing.

'Stop!' cried Holy, and Hank took a turn round a bollard.

The shark had now gone mad and was thrashing and breaking surface in a desperate attempt to lose the hook.

'Pull in,' commanded Holy.

The team took up the strain and hauled steadily at the rope. Slowly the great fish was brought home and then out of the water until it was dangling, all sixteen feet of it, below the overhang.

'Haul in,' called Holy.

The second rope was now pulled in and the shark was hauled inboard. Its mouth was open, revealing the wicked teeth. Its great weight made it difficult for the shark to thrash wildly, but great tremors ran through its body as it struggled to free itself.

'All yours, Killer,' said Holy.

No one wanted the shark to suffer longer than necessary. Killer walked to the taffrail and put three bullets into its mouth. In all, three sharks were caught, when the Paymaster Commander decided that he had enough meat for the whole ship's company, and with that the operation was brought to a close.

As soon as *Peregrine* had completed refuelling, she was replaced by *Daventry* whilst *Peregrine* circled at high speed, guarded by three of her Swordfish. At length *Daventry* had finished refuelling and the two warships resumed their journey northwards and the search for *Hohenlinden*.

The next morning, Killer and Bill with other officers of the squadron were having breakfast in the wardroom when they felt an increased throb in the engines and a slight heeling of the ship as she made a rapid turn.

'Hello! Something's up!' exclaimed Killer.

A short while later the Tannoy stilled conversation.

'D'ye hear there? This is the Captain speaking. We have just received an SOS from the *Empire Star*. She has been shelled by an armed raider and is abandoning ship. She has given her position and, as she was carrying wounded naval personnel home to England, I have decided to alter course and search for survivors. That is all.'

'My God!' exclaimed Bill. 'Janet's on that ship. And Ann, Killer. Ann's with Janet.'

Bill's anguished remarks had been overheard by several other officers, who briefly came to console Bill and offer sympathy. Janet and Ann were popular with the squadron officers who had all attended the engagement party of Janet and Bill.

The Commander came over to them to offer a consoling and helpful word of advice.

'We know that this raider's captain does not interfere with those abandoning ship. In fact on more than one occasion he has been most helpful to them. If they managed to get away safely, there's a good chance we'll find them and pick them up, if they've not already been rescued.'

Bill was comforted by these words, but he felt the need to do something.

'Come on, Killer,' he said. 'Let's find the ASO and see what's happening.'

They found the Air Staff Officer in the operations room and he was able to give them more information. Fuel requirements for crossing the Atlantic meant that the ship's speed must be kept to sixteen knots. The sinking was approximately seven hundred miles to the east, and at sixteen knots, allowing for taking off and landing on, that would take four to five days.

'Janet and Ann have got to survive five days,' Bill said, as they left the ops room.

'They can do it, Bill. They are both nurses and in their own way they are tough cookies. They'll survive, Bill. You'll see.'

Chapter 14

Abandon Ship

'Does anyone want anything more before we go and get our own breakfast?'

'No thank you, Janet.'

'You're looking after us very well.'

'You're doing us proud.'

'I'm happy!'

'Go and get your breakfast.'

The chorus of replies came from the four wounded men in the big cabin. These had been severely wounded in the Mediterranean, but had slowly been recovering on the way south in the hospital-ship.

Lieutenant Ken Riley, from *Warspite*, had a chest wound from an exploding shell in the Western Desert. Internally his wound had healed, but the big scar across his chest still showed signs of weeping and needed careful attention. Sub Lieutenant Harry Tucker had been hit by shrapnel in the lower leg, and his skin and some of the bone had been chipped away. This was taking a long time to recover and he was still confined to bed. Ben Brown, another sub lieutenant, also had a leg injury, in his thigh. His leg had been saved, but he had had to relearn how to use it as the severed nerves began to mend. Tom Watkins, a midshipman, the youngest of the party, had suffered severe injuries to his face and was slowly recovering.

Janet and Ann were responsible for these and six other wounded navy men taking passage in *Empire Star* to Freetown, where they were to pick up a convoy. The naval party was en route to England for further treatment.

The girls enjoyed their work. They were both caring and professional in looking after their patients and were popular with the officers and men. The three cabins occupied by the patients, as well as their own cabins, were on the boat-deck abaft the bridge, and they stepped out onto the boat-deck and stood for a moment, leaning against the taffrail, enjoying the warm sunshine. This was their fourth day out of Cape Town and the weather was already turning warmer as they made their way northwards. The ship was making the passage alone, using its speed of sixteen knots to avoid enemy submarines.

'What's that ship doing?' said Ann, indicating a large ship, about three miles away, approaching them from the port beam. 'It seems to be steering straight for us.'

Janet looked up at the bridge and saw a group of officers and men, including the Captain, gathered on the port side to observe the approaching ship.

'I don't like the look of this, Mister,' the Captain was saying to Second Officer Wray, the Officer of the Watch. 'Get Sparks along here at the double.'

The strange ship was edging closer, now two miles away, matching their speed and remaining on a constant bearing on the beam.

'Sparks,' the Captain said, 'prepare to send off an SOS: "Am being attacked by an armed raider, position so-and-so." Get the position from the Navigator. Quickly, lad. I'll let you know if I want it sent.'

The wireless operator hurried across the bridge to where the Navigator was already plotting his up-to-date position.

The Captain watched the approaching ship. He saw a passenger-cargo vessel with one funnel and a large boxlike structure aft of the bridge. Closer the ship came until it was only five hundred yards away, when canvas covers were thrown back and three large guns were revealed. Their guns turned until they were pointing directly at the *Empire Star.*

A megaphone blared from the ship.

'This is a German armed merchant-ship. Do not – repeat not – use your transmitter or we will fire on you.'

'Get that message off, Sparks,' cried the Captain.

The W/T office was at the after end of the bridge and Sparks was waiting in the doorway for the Captain's order. Now, he hurried into his office and began transmitting.

Janet and Ann had watched with horror as the German vessel had approached and given its message. Now they saw flashes of flame and smoke from the muzzles of the raider's guns and almost immediately heard a crash and rending sound on the bridge, which disappeared in an explosion of flame and smoke. The bridge was destroyed and all personnel on it were killed instantly, including the wireless operator, but not before he had sent his message.

A fragment from the bridge caught Ann a glancing blow on the side of her head and she went down, pole-axed.

'Ann!' cried Janet, bending over her friend.

'Listen carefully.'

It was the enemy ship again.

'Abandon ship immediately. I intend to put a torpedo into you.'

The incipient panic aboard the *Empire Star* was brought under control by the Chief Mate. He had obtained a megaphone and was calling through it.

'Go to your boat-stations. We are abandoning ship. Go to your boat-stations.'

Janet was close to number one boat, her abandon-ship station, and she was soon joined by the members of the naval party, who were all on the same station. Some of them were limping, assisted by their less wounded colleagues.

Ken Riley joined Janet and with her carefully lifted Ann into the lifeboat. Slowly and painfully the remainder of the wounded party clambered aboard.

The Chief Mate appeared with a small party of men.

'You should have had the Second Mate in this boat,' he said, 'but I'm afraid he is dead. I'm the only surviving deck-officer and I must stay to see everyone away. Can you manage?'

'Yes, sir, we can manage. We'll be all right,' Ken replied.

'Right then! Lower away.'

He spoke to the men on the falls, who lowered the boat into the water. As it settled, Harry Tucker in the bows and Ken Riley in the stern, released the ropes attaching them to the ship. Ken started the engine and steered away out of the line of fire, for their boat was on the same side as the German raider. Janet could see figures mustering on the other side of the ship, as two other lifeboats prepared to take off the ship's company. She could also see the twisted metal of the shattered bridge, on fire, with flames and smoke eating it up. The ship's engines had stopped and it was lying stationary in the water. There was a pause as the other two boats made their escape on the further side of the ship.

'There's the torpedo!' cried Ken.

He had been watching and had seen the launch of the torpedo. Another huge explosion occurred, immediately below the bridge, and the *Empire Star* began to settle. Ken Riley turned off his engine and they watched the drama from a safe distance. Slowly the ship sank as its lower decks flooded until, almost with a sigh, it put its nose down and slid gently beneath the waves.

They were alone. The German raider was disappearing westwards; the other two lifeboats were already three miles away from them. Janet surveyed the scene in their own boat. She was sitting in the bows with Ann's head cradled in her lap. Ann looked pale and ill and Janet feared for her life. Ken

Riley was sitting on the stern thwart, slumped over the tiller. Between them were nine other men, all wounded, some seriously. Janet was the only unwounded person aboard the boat. She lowered Ann gently onto the bottom boards and propped her head against a life jacket. Then she crawled aft to discuss the situation with Ken Riley.

'We won't try to join the other boats,' he said. 'They seem to be making for land. But land is a hundred and fifty miles away and we have fuel for less than a hundred. I think our best chance is to stay put and rely on a rescue. The Chief Mate, when he gave me our position, told me that the ship had sent off an SOS, so I'm sure we shall be picked up.'

Janet was happy to leave this kind of decision to Ken. He was a professional sailor. Her task was to keep these men and Ann alive for as long as it took to be rescued. Noticing Ken's drawn face and slumped body, she thought she had better start with him.

'Let me have a look at your chest,' she said.

Carefully she undid and pulled back his pyjama top. The bandages were stained red.

'It happened when we lifted Ann,' he said. 'I think I must have strained my chest and opened up the wound.'

Janet searched for the first-aid box and found that it contained bandages, sticking plaster, lint, iodine, disinfectant, morphine tablets and a pair of scissors. Quickly she cleaned Ken's wound and rebandaged it. Then she turned to the others.

Ann was her first priority. Gently she bathed Ann's head. A bruise extended from above Ann's left ear to her eye which was sunk beneath the black swelling. Where the object had hit, the skin was broken and bleeding. Janet bathed the wound in sea water and cleaned it with disinfectant. Then she applied iodine, lint and a sticking plaster. Ann's breathing was unsteady and her heartbeat irregular. She was

169

in the full glare of the sun and Janet thought it was essential to provide some shade.

She crawled back to Ken and had a word with him. He spoke to Simpson and Manders, two leading hands with less severe injuries, who were fairly mobile, and asked them to rig the short mast, lying along the thwarts, and the foresail as an awning. This was a big improvement. In the heat of the day the sail could be used as an awning; at night-time it would serve as a cover, for warmth. Harry Tucker had brought a blanket with him and Janet thought this could also be used.

Next, Janet inspected the water supply, roughly four gallons in a cask. If she allowed each person a half-pint per day it would last for five days. If they were not picked up in five days, then heaven help them. She also found some biscuits and chocolate, not much to keep twelve adults alive, but she knew that thirst, rather than hunger, would be the bigger problem.

Now she crawled round to each patient, arranging them comfortably on the bottom boards, low down in the boat, with their backs against the sides, using life jackets as cushions. In this way it was possible to walk down the centre of the boat, stepping over the men's legs. She left Ann in the bows where she herself would retire for the night. She also had Simpson and Manders rig an oar as a spar across the mast. On this she could hang the blanket to give the girls privacy when they needed it. At night-time the blanket would be used for protection against the cold, leaving the men to share the sail.

Janet made a last round of the men, checking bandages and offering words of encouragement. Then she returned to the after thwart and sat down beside Ken, to whom she whispered for a few minutes.

'I'd better tell them the worst,' she concluded.

'Can I have your attention?' Ken called in a loud voice. 'Janet wants to have a word with you.'

'I've checked the water and food supplies,' said Janet, 'and I think we've enough for five days if we ration them carefully. It will mean two biscuits each per day, which I'll issue in the morning, and a half-pint of water each, that is a quarter of a pint in the morning and the same in the evening. I don't think hunger will worry us too much. You've been feeding well on *Empire Star* and you've all had a good breakfast. You'll not be active, so conserve your energy. That'll save the need for food. Thirst is going to be much more difficult. In this hot, salty atmosphere, your throats will become dry and you'll get very thirsty. Under no circumstances must you even sip salt water. That would add to your thirst.

'I'll make my rounds each morning and evening. If you have any problems, particularly with your wounds, you must let me know and I'll see what I can do. I have a certain amount of kit in the first-aid box.'

She looked at Ken. He marvelled that this slip of a girl, whom he had always thought of as gentle and patient, could wield so much authority. The men, he knew, would respond to her.

'Well, men,' he said, 'you've heard what Matron has said.'

Janet and the men laughed.

'Now, as to our present situation. Sparks managed to get off an SOS before the bridge was hit. In fact, that was why Jerry opened fire. It cost Sparks his life, and that of all those on the bridge. The Mate and the other boats have obviously decided to try and make a landfall. I know these boats and I know we would not have enough fuel to make it. Even if we did, it's a treacherous coast and there's no way we could be sure of surviving. I think our best bet is to remain stationary. If our SOS and position did get through we should be picked up, but it may take a few days. There aren't many ships on this route these days and they may have to send a ship from Cape Town. Fortunately, the weather is calm. I'll use the engine only to keep our head to wind if the wind gets up.

171

'Now, we are a ship's company, even if our ship is only a boat, so we'll start a system of watch-keeping, in three watches. Mr Watkins and Stoker Black will be excused because of their injuries. The other officers will take turns on the tiller and you men will share lookout duties, two hours on and four off. You're the senior hand, Leading-Seaman Simpson. Will you arrange the watch-keeping roster?'

'Aye, aye, sir.'

'If you see anything, particularly an aircraft, shout. We have flares in the locker under the stern thwart.

'And remember what Matron says,' he concluded. 'Stay out of the sunshine and conserve your energy as much as you can.'

Slowly the day wore on and the sun sank low, a huge orange disc. Janet had given out the evening ration of water. Now she sat with Ken, looking at the men. They seemed dejected, dispirited.

What about a sing-song?' she called and, without waiting, began singing in a sweet, clear voice.

'Roll out the barrel.'

First one and then another joined in until all were singing heartily.

'Run, rabbit, run' was followed by 'I'll be hanging out the washing on the Siegfried Line'.

Half an hour later the sun had slipped below the horizon and the twilight was going fast. It was time to stop. With cheerful 'goodnights' for the men as she passed them, Janet made her way back to the bows.

Ann was still unconscious, but her breathing was more regular and her pulse steadier. Janet settled Ann on the kapok-filled life jackets supplied by some of the men, tucked the blanket round both of them and then lay back herself, her eyes open, staring at the firmament above her. The stars were very bright, particularly the Southern Cross. She thought of Ann and Killer and wondered where Bill was and what he was doing, and with that thought she fell into an exhausted sleep.

The next morning she woke with the sun hot on her face, startled by the unaccustomed motion. As her eyes took in the slumbering men along the boat the full significance of the situation hit her and just for a moment her fortitude faltered. Then her eyes turned to Ann, who was awake and staring at her, and the adrenalin began to flow.

'Ann, you're awake at last. Thank goodness.'

'What's happened? Where are we?' Ann said feebly.

Janet told her about abandoning ship and how they were in the lifeboat with all their patients.

'I feel very weak,' said Ann. 'What happened to me?'

'You were hit by a metal splinter and concussed,' said Janet.

As she spoke, Janet was wiping her friend's face with a cloth, dampened in sea water. Her pulse was weak but regular and some colour had returned to her face. Her lips were very dry and, cradling Ann's head in her arms, Janet carefully offered her her first drink, a quarter of a pint of drinking water.

Then Janet made her way aft with biscuits and water, giving each man his allotted share, and attending where necessary to their wounds.

'So far so good,' she said when she reached Ken Riley. 'Most of them have slept surprisingly well and they seem refreshed.'

'I expect they were exhausted by yesterday's events,' Ken replied. 'I know I was. It's going to be more difficult today, particularly if nothing turns up.'

'Do you expect anything?'

'Not really. Not today.'

Most of the men were buoyed up by the thought of rescue and spent much of the day looking for imaginary ships or aircraft. The sun was very hot and, even with their awnings,

173

was blistering on their faces and arms and dazzling to their eyes from its reflection on the water. Simpson and Manders had rerigged the blanket so that it could be used for shade or as a curtain, whatever the girls wished. Janet was very glad to have the shade. Three times during the day she made her rounds and each round took more than an hour to complete. Again, after the final round with its issue of water, she had them singing, and again the boat's company settled for the night in good heart.

On the third day the men began to show signs of deterioration. Thirst was now acute and the two most serious cases had become hot and feverish. Black, who was giving Janet cause for worry, a stoker from a destroyer, had been in the engine-room when his ship was torpedoed and had suffered severe burns and scalding. Now he had developed a temperature and at times began to ramble wildly. Janet bathed his face gently and took his hands in hers. Under her influence the anguish left him and he became calmer, talking rationally and calmly about his young wife and child.

Her other worry was young Tom Watkins. He was only seventeen years old and had been a midshipman in the same destroyer as the stoker-mechanic. He, too, had suffered burns, to his face, and these were now weeping in the hot sun. He was very dry and running a temperature. Janet stayed with him, talking to him about his home and his mother and father. The boy seemed to want to talk.

Indeed, all the men seemed to want to talk to Janet, even Ken Riley, a lieutenant, regular Royal Navy, Dartmouth trained. He was married, with no children. He talked to Janet about his wife, about his ship, *Warspite,* and about his prospects. Janet was patient with him as she was with all the men, listening to them and prompting them, instinctively giving them something they craved in their lowered conditions, a woman's company. She was all women to all men, a mother to one, a wife to another, a sweetheart to a

174

third. Perhaps even more than dressing their wounds, Janet's presence and companionship helped to keep up morale. No one felt he could let her down.

Again, after her evening rounds, Janet held her sing-song. It was hard, this time, to get them involved, but she succeeded, at last, in encouraging everyone to sing, however feebly.

The night was very cold and the two girls were glad of each other's warmth. Although Ann was still weak, Janet drew comfort from her. She felt stimulated and revived by the presence of another woman, particularly her friend, Ann. As she stared into the night sky, she again thought of Bill. She recalled the evening on the roof of the Red Sea Hotel with Bill and Ann and Killer, when they had gazed at the stars. That had been Bill's bedroom, she recalled, just as this boat was her bedroom now. Thinking of Bill, she again fell asleep.

The next day was a scorcher. Right from the start, Janet knew it was going to be difficult. As she stood up to walk past the men she saw the shape, a triangular fin, weaving backwards and forwards across the stern of the boat.

'It joined us at dusk yesterday,' Ken told her. 'We've enough problems on our hands, so I decided to keep quiet about it.'

Janet could see the huge creature, just below the surface, about twelve feet in length. More than the shark itself, it was the fin, stark and threatening, cutting through the water with evil menace, that put fear into her.

Some of the men were now in a bad way. Stoker Black was awake and talking endlessly, rambling on about his home, his wife and his daughter. Janet bathed his perspiring face and sought to soothe him and calm him, talking quietly to reassure him.

Midshipman Watkins was too far gone to talk. Janet took his hands in hers and talked to him about his family and his home, feeling his response in the slight pressure of his fingers on her hands. She felt very sad. She was losing Tom Watkins and there was nothing more she could do about it.

Ken Riley, too, looked worn out. His face was shrunken like that of an old man and he sat slumped in his seat, unable to sit up. His voice was a croak. His chest was giving him more trouble. Janet changed the dressing, talking to him quietly, giving him some of her own strength, using up a little more of her own.

Only Leading Seamen Simpson and Manders had any real life in them and they did what they could to encourage their companions, but it was Janet, going from one man to another, dressing their wounds, talking to them, who kept alive the spark of endurance in them. Some were so listless they did not want to eat. Black and Watkins were too far gone to drink the small cup of water that Janet offered them and it was only by patiently nursing them and feeding the water to them that Janet persuaded them to drink.

The sing-song that evening was feeble. Ann joined Janet in the well-known tunes, and Simpson and Manders did their best. The remainder came in, one by one, with harsh, croaking voices. Even Tom Watkins' lips moved, though no sound came forth.

As the sun went down that night, Janet could see the symbol of death astern of the boat, weaving from side to side, patiently, endlessly. The next day would be their fifth day. The water was almost exhausted. Some of the men, she knew, would not survive the day, perhaps not the present night.

Ann was asleep when Janet resumed her place in the bows. She looked up at the stars, huge and bright, perhaps for the last time. Her thoughts returned to her own life, to Bill. She remembered how Bill had proposed to her on the sheltered ledge above Cape Town, how she had wanted Bill then, physically, completely. She had agreed then with Bill that it would be better for them to wait until after they were married. Now, she thought sadly, she would never know Bill

176

in that way, never know the ultimate ecstasy of love. Her thoughts wandered over the incidents of their knowing each other, particularly Bill's coming to her rescue from Joel, her 'verray parfit gentil knight'. She smiled at the thought and with that thought fell asleep.

She was still smiling when she woke abruptly. The sun was well up. Bill was looking at her, waving to her. She thought this must be a hallucination, part of her dream. Then she heard Simpson and Manders cheering. It was indeed Bill waving to her as the Swordfish swept low over the boat for the second time. Tears were in Janet's eyes as the boat slowly came awake and men realised they had survived the night.

Even Ken Riley was sitting straighter. On the third run, at fifty feet, Janet watched as Bill threw out a small tin box from his cockpit. Ken Riley started the engine and motored to it, leaving Leading Seaman Simpson to retrieve it. Janet joined Ken Riley in the stern of the boat and listened as Ken announced in a surprisingly clear voice:

'Listen, men.'

He waited until he had the men's attention.

'Here's a message from the aircraft; "We must leave you to get help. A rescue ship will be with you in six hours. Another aircraft will return in two hours. Keep your spirits up."'

A feeble cheer greeted the news and Janet noted the reviving spirits.

'Here's a note for you, Janet,' Ken said.

'Darling,' she read, 'this is the most wonderful moment of my life, to find you alive. Longing to hold you in my arms again. Killer sends his love to Ann. All my love, Bill.'

Janet choked back her emotion and waved to Bill as they came round for a final pass. She waved, too, to Killer, who was waving to them, a broad grin on his face. With a final waggle of his wings, Killer took the aircraft southwards.

Now it was time for Janet to check her patients and to share out the remaining water and biscuits. Once more she

177

made her rounds, stopping where needed, giving encouragement, rejoicing with the men at their rescue. She stopped longest with Tom Watkins. He was still alive, but only just. She topped up his share of the water with some of her own, desperate to prolong his life until help came. Then she returned to the bows to share her talk with Ann, about Killer and Bill.

Chapter 15

Recovery

999 Squadron air-crews sat in the briefing-room, listening to the Air Staff Officer's briefing.

'At 0700,' he was saying, 'we'll be in the position where *Empire Star* was torpedoed. We know that if the German raider were the *Hohenlinden*, then the crew and passengers would have been allowed to take to their boats before the ship was sunk. It is now five days since the sinking and no trace has been picked up of any survivors.

'However, we are now in the Benguela Current, which flows northwards at about two knots, and the survivors can be up to two hundred miles north of here. We'll follow the current northwards, with air-searches ahead of the carrier. You will form the first search at 0700, following parallel tracks, twenty miles apart. When you reach the end of your search leg, make a dogleg course to the west of ten miles and then return to the carrier by 1030. A second search will be sent off at 1500.'

Sandy Sandiford gave the crews their exact tracks and Schooley briefed them on the weather, which was calm, with light winds from the southeast and good visibility.

The crews were grim-faced as they made their way to their aircraft, none more so than Bill and Killer. Killer was worried, but hopeful, and optimistic about Ann; Bill was in a state of anguish about Janet. All the crews knew about Bill's

179

engagement to Janet and that Janet and Ann, with a party of naval wounded, had been passengers on *Empire Star.* They had a personal involvement in the search and they were determined, if possible, to make it successful.

For the fiftieth time Bill began to sweep the horizon through his binoculars. They had been flying for nearly two hours and it would soon be time to return to the carrier. He felt desolate. He peered through the glasses, willing them to reveal the missing boats. He had been backed up in the search by Killer and L/A Gibbons who had maintained a continuous lookout of the seas nearer their track. Desperately Bill searched the horizon. Then he paused, and moved his glasses back a few degrees. Had he caught sight of a speck on the ocean? He removed the glasses and wiped his eyes. Then he focussed them again on the spot. Yes.

'Green three-oh,' he shouted. 'Green three-oh. I am sure it's a boat.'

Immediately Killer turned on to the bearing. He could see nothing with the naked eye. Bill was peering through his binoculars over Killer's shoulder.

'Yes. It is a boat, seven or eight miles ahead.'

Then Killer saw it. He opened his throttle and pushed his stick forward, building up speed. They passed over the boat, about five hundred feet above it, and Bill's heart stopped as he saw the lifeless figures. No one moved. They were all dead. He could clearly see the two girls in the bows of the boat, Janet and Ann, lying inert.

Killer was descending now, in a tight turn, to sea level. Miraculously, Bill saw two men and then Janet sit up and start waving. Then others were waving, some feebly.

'I'll drop them a note, Killer,' Bill said, 'and then we must get back to the carrier to start a rescue operation.'

'Right, Bill! I'll pass them at fifty feet, a few yards away. Give Ann my love.'

Bill emptied a tin containing an aluminium dust-marker, wrote his note and a note to Janet and placed them in the tin. The tight-fitting lid made it watertight. Bill watched as the boat's engine started and it moved the few yards to where the tin was floating. He saw the sailor in the boat retrieve the tin and pass it astern. He saw Janet reading his note.

'Time to go, Killer. Let's go and set the rescue in motion.'

As soon as they returned to the carrier and reported to the bridge, they had the satisfaction of seeing the ship's speed increase to twenty-four knots and a Swordfish flown off with water and food for the survivors.

Six hours later the decks of *Peregrine* and *Daventry* were lined with men as they drew near the lifeboat. Killer and Bill were on the flight-deck, watching the rescue. In the boat, most of the occupants were slumped out on the bottom boards. Only four figures seemed to be alive, two sailors, Leading Seamen Simpson and Manders, and the two girls.

The Captain brought the carrier round until it formed a lee for the boat, protecting it from the wind and creating a patch of calm water from which to operate. *Peregrine*'s Commander was in charge of the rescue operation. Through a megaphone he addressed the sailors in the boat.

'Can you bring your boat alongside?'

Leading Seaman Simpson waved an affirmative, started the engine and brought the boat round to where the Commander was standing, by the ship's crane.

'These people are too weak to climb aboard. I intend to hoist the boat with all its occupants on the ship's crane,' the Commander announced to his working party.

'We shall lower slings to you. Can you hook on?' the Commander called.

Simpson and Manders waved their acknowledgement, and Manders moved to the bows and Simpson to the stern. The crane swivelled outboard and the slings were lowered and hooked on by the two men.

'Hoist away. Handsomely, now,' called the Commander, and Bill watched anxiously as the boat was slowly raised from the sea until it was clear of the flight-deck. The crane was swivelled round until the boat was over the deck and, with the help of the deck-party, gently lowered onto the flight-deck.

Janet waited in the boat until all her patients had been evacuated and placed on stretchers. Then she stepped out.

'Bill,' she breathed.

Her legs gave way under her and she collapsed into Bill's arms.

'Stretcher-party!' called the PMO, taking over. 'Take her and Nurse Woods to cabin twenty-two.'

This was Bill's and Killer's cabin. Apart from the beds in the sickbay, there was no spare accommodation in the carrier and they had offered their cabin for use by the girls. They themselves would keep their kit in the midshipman's flat and sleep on the quarterdeck.

Janet was lifted carefully onto the stretcher and, with the others, taken to the after lift and lowered to the hangar deck. From here the men were taken to the sickbay and the girls to cabin twenty-two.

The two girls changed into pyjamas left by the boys, Killer's for Ann and Bill's for Janet. Ann, who was now the stronger of the two, found that she had to help Janet with her pyjamas and into the lower berth. Ann took over the upper berth, above Janet's.

When the PMO came to examine the girls, Janet was in a coma. He had just finished his examination when there was a knock on the door and Bill entered.

'I came to find out how Janet is, sir,' he said.

The PMO knew of Bill's engagement to Janet and he had a good deal of sympathy for the young man. Now he took him aside and regarded him gravely.

'I'm afraid your young lady is in a very serious way,' he said.

'From what I've heard from the men, she must have taxed herself beyond her endurance to look after her patients, and probably gave up some of her own water ration to them. She's now suffering from dehydration and a total collapse of her mental and physical powers. It's as if she called on all her resources to see her patients through their ordeal and when she saw them safely aboard this ship she was unable to look after herself She will need all the loving care we can give her if she is to survive.'

'I'll stay with her, if I can,' Bill said. 'Will you ask if I can be excused flying duties, at least for a day or two?'

'Yes, I'll certainly do that.

The PMO closed the door quietly behind him and Bill went over to Janet's bed. He could scarcely believe the figure before him was his beloved Janet. The girl's face was thin and gaunt, with deep red patches of burnt skin and puffy blisters. In startling contrast to the red burns, her skin had a deathly pallor. Her eyes, now closed, were sunken, black hollows.

Bill's heart went out to her. Through the ugliness of disfigurement shone a beauty of spirit that touched him deeply. With a damp flannel he wiped her brow, and sat quietly beside her, watching her intently.

Ann's soft voice came to him from the bunk above. He had forgotten all about her. 'How is she, Bill?'

'Not too good at present, Ann, but I shall nurse her back to health.'

'I'll be able to help in a day or so. Janet saved my life and I feel better by the minute. I'll nurse her.'

Bill stood up and squeezed Ann's hand.

'Killer will be along to see you shortly,' he said.

That evening the PMO paid his last visit of the day to Janet. Her pulse had become feeble and erratic; her breathing was shallow.

'How is she, sir? What are her chances?' Bill asked.

'Tonight is critical. Just before dawn will be the danger

time, when spirits are naturally low. If she survives that, I think she'll live. But I fear you must be prepared for the worst.'

Through the night Bill sat at Janet's bedside, wiping her face, willing her to live. At three o'clock in the morning he thought he was losing her. He could scarcely feel her pulse and her breathing was very shallow.

In the bunk above, Ann shared Bill's feelings. Then, not wanting to listen, she heard Bill talk to Janet in a low, clear voice. She heard him tell Janet of their first meeting at the Carlton Hotel in Alexandria with Killer and herself. He told Janet how he was attracted to her from their first dance, when he had first held her in his arms.

'Darling Janet, let me keep you alive,' he whispered.

He lingered over his account of their outing at Mombasa. He told her that this was where he knew he was in love with her. He reminded her of the climb to the top of Chapman Peak and of the intimate and loving moments of his proposal to her.

Ann held her breath as Bill bared his soul and sought to reach out to Janet. She loved these two people and she felt privileged to share their secret life. Never would she reveal what she overheard.

It was nearing five o'clock in the morning. Bill could feel Janet slipping away from him. Her body was becoming colder, her flesh even more pale. He gathered her in his arms, pressing her to himself.

'Don't leave me, Janet, darling. I cannot live without you.'

He pressed his lips gently against hers. He felt the faintest response.

That night Bill fought death – and won. He had reached through to Janet. His voice had kept her alive, but it was the touch of his lips that brought back strength. Her heart steadied; her breathing became less shallow.

Taking off his shoes, Bill quietly entered Janet's bed,

holding her close to him, passing strength from his body to hers, warming her and making her live.

Ann knew what was happening, and she knew it was right and that Janet would now live. At last she herself could relax and sleep. She was awakened two hours later by knocking on the cabin door and the entrance of the PMO. Bill was sitting next to Janet's bed, holding her hand. Janet herself was sleeping peacefully.

'Remarkable,' the doctor said, taking Janet's pulse. 'You are really very fortunate, young man. I did not expect your fiancée to last the night.'

Bill stayed with Janet until she awoke, two hours later, her scarred face tranquil, a smile spreading to her lips and eyes as she recognised Bill. Bill leaned over and kissed her gently, feeling her lips responding to his.

'What's happened?' Janet murmured. 'Where have I been? Where am I?'

'You're aboard *Peregrine,* in Killer's and my cabin, with Ann in the bunk above you. You've been on a long, long journey, but you've come back to us. We thought we had lost you.'

'Dear Bill. I sensed you were near me. I thought I could hear you talking to me in a dream. I tried very hard to come back to you.'

'Time for you to go and rest now, Bill,' said Ann, swinging her legs over the upper berth. 'I must tidy Janet up.'

Ann was well again, the professional nurse, looking after her patient and dealing with the visitor. Bill was very tired and was glad to find his bed in the midshipman's flat where he could get the rest he needed.

The recovery of both girls was soon under way. They were both young and healthy and determined. Ann quickly left behind the effects of concussion. She had rested in the boat, nursed by Janet, and the graze on her head was already healing. She was able to devote her time to Janet, who was much weaker and had to remain in bed longer. The PMO and other doctors visited her regularly and were able to tell her that all her patients, even Midshipman Watkins, were recovering well. This knowledge boosted her recovery, but it was Bill's visits she looked forward to most, and Ann sometimes left them alone together to enjoy each other's company whilst she joined Killer on C deck.

Peregrine had sent a search party to look for other survivors, without success, but two days later they received a wireless message saying that the survivors had been discovered by fishing boats and taken to Benguela Harbour. The carrier and cruiser also received a message instructing them to meet a convoy making its way from Cape Town to Freetown. After the sinking of *Empire Star*, the Admiralty had decided that all ships moving along the West African Coast must travel in convoy.

Four days after being rescued, Janet was permitted by the doctor to go up on deck. It was a great moment for her when Bill came to escort her to the goofers' platform, where they were joined by Ann and Killer and a crowd of Fleet Air Arm officers.

Bolo Hawkins greeted them, with a smile. 'We hereby appoint you honorary goofers and give you the freedom of the goofers' platform.'

Bill settled her in the lounger that had been provided next to Ann's, and the officers crowded round to welcome her and compliment her on her recovery. This was to be the favourite place for Janet and Ann as their convoy made its way at twelve knots towards Freetown.

Janet looked at the ships surrounding them. *Peregrine,* with *Daventry* forward of her and another cruiser, *Drake,* astern of her, was the centre of five columns, each containing six ships. Ahead of the convoy, five destroyers formed a broad vic, protecting the convoy from lurking submarines. The carrier and cruisers were the convoy's defence against attack by an armed raider.

At twelve knots, high up on the goofers' platform, Janet was scarcely conscious of the ship's movement. The wind was light, the sea calm and the sun shining. Putting aside thoughts of war and her recent experience, Janet allowed herself to relax, soaking up the warmth and peace. Even the routine of air searches and patrols added to her sense of peace and security.

Each morning, in bed, she had heard the Tannoy, setting in motion the morning search, and the clang of the lift as aircraft were taken up to the flight-deck. Each afternoon she was allowed by the doctor to go up to her favourite position on the goofers' platform. There she watched the A/S patrols take off and land on and the search party take off. She found this routine soothing. These were easy conditions for the experienced aircrews and none of them had difficulty in completing their operations. The Swordfish, circling the fleet at five miles, was a regular feature of the routine, and Janet drew comfort from the defensive force so that she was able to put the terror of the German raider's attack to the back of her mind.

She watched Killer and Bill take off and, with Ann, waited for their return. If they were not flying in the afternoon Killer and Bill joined the girls to give them a running commentary on the operations. Often she and Bill sat in silence, basking in each other's company. Sometimes they talked in low voices, about themselves, about their pasts, about their future, exploring each other's minds and memories and liking what they discovered.

At times, when Killer and Bill were flying, other members of the squadron joined them and talked to them, for the girls were very popular with the young officers and drew them like queen bees.

As Janet regained her strength and required Ann less, Ann was able to offer her services in the sickbay to help with her former patients. She spent two hours each morning tending to their needs and providing them with that indefinable feminine sympathy and support that were beyond the scope of the male nurses. The PMO was sure that her influence aided the men's recovery.

Three days before they arrived at Freetown, Janet was deemed to be well enough to visit the men in the sickbay. She was greeted by a small cheer and an involuntary handclap, and this did much for her own morale. These men knew that they owed their lives to Janet's indomitable spirit during their trial in the boat and they were now eager to meet her and talk to her, assuring her of their recovery. She spent rather more time with Midshipman Tom Watkins and Stoker Black, letting them talk through their ordeal and encouraging them to think of the future. Both were still strict bed, but their burns were again under control and their spirits were mending. She also talked at length to Ken Riley who had been a source of strength in the boat until his own wound had laid him low. Ken was now recovering well.

Now, both Janet and Ann were able to eat in the ward-room, always the centre of a group of officers, but it was after dinner that Janet loved most. Then she would go with Bill to the quarterdeck and stand by the taffrail, looking astern at the phosphorescence stirred up by the wake of the ship. The moon rose, large and luminous, and each night the Southern Cross dropped lower to the south. They talked in quiet voices. Bill told Janet of his life in southern waters, of whales and flying fish, of the albatross, of being nearly lost, of the endless search of wind-tossed seas. Janet told Bill of her experience in the boat, of the water rationing, of the weeping wounds she needed to dress, of their thirst and the deterioration of her patients. She described her feelings when she thought she was going to lose two of them, and finally her thoughts on what she expected to be the last evening of her life. She told Bill how sad she had felt that she would never know him intimately.

Bill listened in silence, his arm round her shoulders, and let her talk, and Janet was able to push the nightmare out of her system, not back into her subconscious mind. This helped in the recovery of her spirits so that by the time the ship entered Freetown, ten days after her rescue, Janet was almost restored to full health.

Chapter 16

Freetown

Monkeys chattered in the trees high above the road as Bill and Killer walked up to the Naval Rest House. The sun was pouring down an intense heat and the air was humid and sticky. This was very different from East Africa, where the air had been hot and dry. Wearing only khaki shorts and bush shirts and protected by khaki sun helmets, the two officers, nevertheless, felt overdressed. The narrow, winding road climbed steeply up the Sugar Loaf Mountain to the Rest House, which was at an altitude of two thousand feet.

They had arrived in Freetown two days before and the girls and the naval patients had been transferred to the Rest House to complete their convalescence and wait for a suitable convoy to take them home to England. At the foot of the hill, the road had taken them past small, neat, brick houses. An old man, working in his garden, whom they had stopped to talk to, had told them with pride that he was descended from a freed slave.

'This town,' he told them, 'is called Freetown to mark the freeing of the slaves.'

He was grateful to the British for the freedom they had bestowed, but he hoped that at some future date Sierra Leone would become an independent country.

Killer and Bill had refused the offer of a taxi from the harbour, both preferring to enjoy the exercise that a walk would give them. By the time they reached the Rest House they were regretting their decision for both of them were bathed in sweat after the five-mile uphill walk.

Janet and Ann greeted them with cool orange drinks, sipped on a shady verandah overlooking the valley. At two thousand feet the air was refreshingly cooler than in the town, and Killer and Bill were able to sit back on the loungers and relax and feel virtuous after their exercise.

Both girls had recovered well after their ordeal and looked tanned and fit. The deep hollows had disappeared from Janet's eyes and her cheeks had filled out. She still retained a thoughtful, even haunted look, although her conversation was brisk and cheerful.

The graze on Ann's head had disappeared and she was very much her old self, thoughtful, patient and helpful. Both girls were helping with their patients. Although most of them were no longer bed patients, their wounds still needed attention. The Rest House was run by a naval doctor with the help of naval sick-berth attendants and, with the influx of the ten patients, the VADs were a welcome addition to the nursing staff. The girls were considered to be semi-convalescent so their duties were light and they were given much free time to relax and recuperate.

The boys had set off early and had arrived at ten o'clock and planned to take the girls down to explore the town and swim off the large, golden beach. A jeep was made available and Killer drove them down to the market-square. The colourful market was laid out in lines of stalls, beneath a thatched roof, open at the sides. The stalls were small and covered with produce, grown locally around the town, brightly coloured clothes, shoes and leather goods and local craft products. The girls were particularly interested in buying themselves swimming costumes and clothes to replace those lost on the *Empire Star*, and all four enjoyed the good-humoured bargaining before the purchase was completed. Killer was particularly good at this, making an absurdly low offer for what the girls chose and allowing himself to be persuaded reluctantly upwards. Neither Janet nor Ann had much stomach for bargaining and nor did Bill, but they were amused by Killer's technique and both girls were satisfied with their bargains.

The men in the market, on the whole, wore Western-style clothes, khaki slacks and bush shirts, but the women went in for the brightest colours, red and orange predominating, and Janet and Ann thought that what might have been garish in England looked right in the fierce African sunshine. They particularly liked the women walking about the town in their flowing dresses, colourful parasols and beaming smiles on coal-black faces. It seemed to them all a happy town and they found this mood infectious.

'Hello, gorgeous!' Killer greeted Ann as the girls emerged in their new swimming costumes from behind the sand-dune where they had changed.

Seizing their hands, the boys ran the laughing girls down the beach and into the sea, non-stop until they were properly submerged. The sea was cool to the skin and they swam briskly until their blood had warmed. Then they sported in the shallows, splashing each other, racing each other, and having a mock fight with the girls on the boys' shoulders. The terror of the sinking and the ordeal in the boat were completely forgotten and all four were happy and relaxed as they threw themselves on the beach to dry in the warm sunshine.

'Hello! What's this?' exclaimed Killer as the old woman approached them. She was carrying a branch with hands of bananas on it, which she was offering to sell them. 'How much?' Killer asked, ever ready to bargain.

'Five for a penny,' he was told and even Killer was speechless.

'We'll have twopennyworth,' said Bill, offering the two pence and taking the ten excellent bananas.

192

'To think some children in England have never seen a banana,' Ann said, 'and here we are eating ten between us at a cost of twopence. You have the third one, Killer.'

'No, we'll share it,' said Killer.

And that is what they did, Killer sharing with Ann and Bill with Janet, each taking a bite until the bananas were finished. Bill thought it was particularly intimate, sharing his banana in this way with Janet.

By one o'clock they were hungry and sun-satisfied, so they made their way to the Harbour Hotel. Local fish were being served, and Hank and Dorrie, who were at the bar, were invited to join them. The mood was light-hearted as they described to each other their experiences in the market and on the beach. Janet and Bill were well content with their day as they kissed each other goodbye on the verandah at the Rest House.

The next day was a red-letter day for both squadrons on the *Peregrine*. The latest convoy had brought new equipment for them and specialist engineers to install it. Fog, mist and darkness had always been a prime enemy of Fleet Air Arm crews and had caused the loss of more than one aircraft. Dead reckoning is reliable only up to a point and that point is passed by a sudden, unexpected wind change, or by an unforeseen alteration of course by the carrier. If this is combined with a decline in visibility the situation can become very grave, as when Hank and Dorrie were nearly lost.

The new equipment consisted of the latest aircraft radar sets, known as ASVs. By later standards these were primitive, but to the crews of 999 Squadron they were miraculous. The newly arrived electrical engineer, with his team of technicians, spent two days installing the sets in the aircraft and a further two days in training observers in how to use them and the squadron electricians in how to maintain them. At the same time, R/T, radiotelephony, sets were installed, push-button crystal tuned, with a range of up to ten miles, enabling pilots of different aircraft to speak to each other or to converse directly with the carrier. The R/T set also provided internal communication in the aircraft and replaced the Gosport tubes.

The mood of the squadron was excited and optimistic as *Peregrine,* with three screening destroyers, left harbour for a training run. 999 Squadron was briefed for aircraft to fly in different directions from the carrier for a distance of thirty miles, then switch on their ASVs and return to home in on the carrier. They would also have some practice with their R/T sets.

Killer and Bill left on a course of 270 degrees. Bill plotted the navigation carefully, for he was by no means sure that the ASV set would work, and he had no intention of losing the carrier. Twenty minutes later he instructed Killer to turn on to a course of 090 degrees. All three crew found that the new equipment was superior to the old Gosport tubes. The ASV deprived Bill of much of his legroom. It consisted of a large metal box, with a screen, fitted in the forward part of the observer's cockpit where Bill's legs would have stretched. Now he found his position somewhat cramped, but he was prepared to accept this if the ASV was as good as the electrical engineer claimed.

Bill switched on and watched the screen come slowly alive with a green glow. He could see the vertical line promised by the engineer, but the screen itself was covered by a mush of interference. Carefully he turned the tuning knob until the mush disappeared and the vertical line became sharp. He had three ranges to choose from, forty miles, fifteen miles and five miles. He selected the forty-mile range. They were now twenty-five five miles away from the carrier by dead reckoning.

'Nothing on the screen, Killer,' he told his pilot.

Leading Airman Gibbons, his air gunner, was watching over his shoulder.

'We're still probably out of range at this height, sir,' he said. 'We're flying at one thousand feet. If we were higher we might do better.'

'We'll stay at this height for the time being and see what happens,' said Bill. 'Later we can try different heights.'

Suddenly Bill spotted a slight blip on the right of the vertical line.

'I've got something,' he said triumphantly, 'at twenty-one miles. The blip is to the right, so if it is the ship then that will be to the right of us. Turn slowly to the right, Killer, until I stop you.'

Killer eased his aircraft gently to starboard.

'Stop,' Bill cried.

The blip was now central at fifteen miles. Bill transferred to the larger fifteen-mile scale. On this, the blip was larger and clearer, altogether more definite. Three other smaller blips had now appeared on the screen. They had moved to the right again.

'Turn to the right again, slowly,' Bill instructed. 'The ship must be moving across our course. I can also see the destroyers.'

Again the blips became central, moving slowly down the scale of miles. At five miles Bill switched on to his five-mile range and saw all four blips clearly now, again moving to the right. For the last time, he gave his instruction.

'Turn slowly to the right, Killer. Stop. The carrier is four miles dead ahead of you.'

Throughout the exercise Bill's head had remained inside the cockpit underneath the ASV's visor. Now he looked up over his pilot's shoulder. There was the carrier, four miles ahead, moving across them.

'Miraculous!' exclaimed Killer. 'I've had the carrier in sight for the last fifteen miles and every instruction you gave was spot on. The only problem I've got now is all the other aircraft converging on *Peregrine*.'

'Hello, Ilford Aircraft, this is Ilford Leader. Do you read me? Tell off. Over.'

Bill was startled by the loudness of Sandy's voice. This was the new jargon of R/T they had been learning up. Ilford was the squadron call sign. Sandy Sandiford, the senior observer, was asking each observer to report the strength of the voice signal he was receiving. He listened with interest to the replies.

At the end of the exercise, Sandy called, 'Hello, Ilford Aircraft, this is Leader. Receiving you all loud and clear. Form up on me. I will drop a smoke-float two miles on the starboard quarter of the carrier. Out.'

Killer immediately turned his aircraft towards the position indicated and shortly afterwards saw the smoke-float in the sea. From various directions aircraft were converging on the CO who was circling the smoke-float.

Another voice broke in on the R/T, from the carrier.

'Hello, Ilford aircraft, this is Mother. When you have formed up you will carry out a second exercise on the same tracks as your first exercise. This time you are to test your equipment at different heights. Ilford Leader will give the order to start the exercise. Is the message received and understood? Acknowledge. Over.'

'Did you hear that, Killer? That was *Peregrine*, telling us to repeat the exercise.'

'Yes, understood,' said Killer.

Bill listened to the replies.

'This is Ilford Leader. Wilco. Over.'

'This is Ilford Baker. Wilco. Over.'

And finally, 'This is Ilford Mike. Wilco. Out.'

By now Killer had formed up on Bolo and the third sub-flight was converging on the CO. When all the aircraft were in formation the CO gave his order.

'Hello, Ilford aircraft, break off and carry out exercise. Go, go.'

At the word 'go', Killer broke away and turned to a course of 270 degrees.

'I like the new communication system,' he said, as they flew on the outward leg.

'Yes. It sounds a bit stilted,' Bill replied, 'but at least we understand the jargon. It'll be useful if reception is poor.'

'Better than waggling wings!' was Killer's comment.

Killer, at Bill's request, had taken his aircraft up to four thousand feet. Thirty miles from the carrier he turned to 090 degrees and, to Bill's amazement, he saw a blip at twenty-nine miles.

'Start to descend,' he told Killer.

At two thousand feet and twenty-five miles away the blip disappeared.

'Circle round and climb to three thousand. I'll drop an aluminium dust marker.'

As Killer came back on course towards the carrier at three thousand feet the blip reappeared at twenty-five miles.

'Come down to one thousand,' Bill instructed.

At twelve hundred feet the blip again disappeared, at a range of twenty-two miles. It reappeared at twenty-one miles.

'There's no doubt about it,' said Bill, 'more altitude means a better range. Come down to sea level.'

The blip disappeared at two hundred feet, even though the aircraft was only fifteen miles from the carrier. Once more, Bill made an approach to the carrier, tracking it on his ASV, and successfully brought Killer home to it.

In the wardroom that evening, as the ships returned to harbour, the crews were jubilant.

'I won't have to rely on your dead reckoning, Dorrie,' said Hank.

'Nor will I,' laughed Dorrie.

'I wonder if it means that we can search at night-time,' said Bing Crosby.

'I'm sure it does,' said Bolo. 'What do you think, Sandy?'

'Well, we'll be able to detect the position of enemy ships or subs on the surface at night-time, using the ASV, even though we can't see them. We can also return to the carrier safely. I think it might mean lots of practice in landing on at night.'

'We'll have to brush up on our night-landing technique,' said Bolo.

'You can say that again!' exclaimed Killer. 'The only night-landing I made on a carrier nearly killed me.'

'I would think,' said Sandy seriously, 'that it might be possible to shadow an enemy ship at night-time using ASV.'

'And also in daytime, using the clouds for cover,' echoed Snowball Kennedy.

The advent of ASV had made a big impact on the flying crews of both squadrons, and this was echoed in the wardroom party that night when Dorrie Dorrington introduced the new song he had written, quickly picked up by the flying crews:

No more relying on dead reckoning,
No more being lost at sea,
No more doing square searches,
We've now got the ASV.

No more missing the target;
Fog is covering the sea.
We can see through fog, or cloud, or smog.
We've now got the ASV.

Now we'll start night-flying, lads,
Night searches over the sea.
We can see through the dark without a spark.
We've now got the ASV.

Now we can talk to one another,
Using our new R/T.
We can talk to our ship when we find her
With the help of our ASV.

Chapter 17

Fire

The next day, Bill had planned to call on Janet at the Naval Rest Home. However, just after daylight an SOS had been received from a British merchant ship three hundred miles north of Cape Town. *Hohenlinden* was active again. All leave was cancelled. Bill tried to telephone Janet, but was told that no telephone calls ashore were being allowed. He felt most unhappy, fearing that Janet might leave on a convoy to Britain whilst *Peregrine* was searching for *Hohenlinden.*

Routine soon established itself and the two squadrons followed their usual pattern, one squadron searching while the other stood by as striking-force, and sharing the submarine patrols. The only ship accompanying *Peregrine* was *Daventry.* The two ships expected to spend at least a month on the search, refuelling at sea from a tanker.

'We are making for St Helena,' the Captain informed the ship's company in his first broadcast, 'where we shall await developments. *Hohenlinden* might have gone north or west after the sinking. We shall wait to see if any other ships are engaged. In the meantime, special care must be taken by ship's lookouts and anti-submarine patrols. Submarines are known to be in this area and we have no escorting destroyers. Our Swordfish are our first line of defence.'

His words were to come true the next day. Biddy Bidwell

199

and Wes Weston in F-Fox were on first outer anti-submarine patrol, fifteen miles ahead of the ships, with Hank Phipps and Dorrie Dorrington in G-George on inner patrol. Both aircraft were ranged on deck in darkness and took off just before dawn, as the sky was brightening in the east.

'This is just a routine A/S patrol,' Biddy said. 'I'll fly out to visibility distance, probably ten miles in this light, and patrol across a fifteen-mile line ahead of *Peregrine*. As the light improves I'll open the distance to fifteen miles.'

'OK, Biddy,' his observer, Wes Weston, replied. 'I'll make a sweep with the ASV.'

The crew, including PO Jarman, the TAG, was very experienced, having been with the ship since it left the China Station more than a year before. Biddy Bidwell was a Royal Navy regular officer who had transferred to the Fleet Air Arm in 1938 and Wes Weston was a short-service-commission officer who had joined the Fleet Air Arm at the beginning of 1939. Both had survived many operations in the Mediterranean and Red Sea and, with PO Jarman, had participated in numerous operational searches and anti-submarine patrols. The new feature in this patrol was the ASV.

As soon as the screen came alight Wes knew that he had a contact, only ten miles ahead and slightly to starboard.

'I've got a contact, Biddy, only ten miles away.'

Both his pilot and his TAG sat up, alert and expectant.

'Turn to starboard slowly, Biddy.'

Biddy eased the stick across.

'Stop. Target eight miles ahead.'

'I'm going straight in,' Biddy exclaimed, putting his nose down to build up speed. He could see nothing ahead. A pre-dawn light was flooding the area, but this was pale and shadowy.

'Get an R/T message off to the carrier, Jarman,' said Wes. *'Enemy contact green two-oh, twelve miles from you.'* He heard

Jarman call up the ship whilst he concentrated on the screen and, when Jarman finished giving his report, on keeping his pilot informed.

'Target five miles ahead.'

He switched over to the five-mile range.

'Target four miles – three miles – two miles – one mile.'

'Got it!' exclaimed Biddy.

He could just see the oblong box of the conning tower in the dim light. His Swordfish was now travelling at a hundred and thirty knots, skimming the sea at fifty feet. He carried two depth-charges, which he set to go off at the shallowest depth, aiming ahead of the target. He realised that they had caught the submarine unawares, on the surface, probably charging its batteries, and this was a golden opportunity to achieve a kill. Not a shot was fired at them as they approached the submarine and dropped the depth charges.

Unfortunately, in the semi-darkness, Biddy had failed to notice that the U-boat was stationary. The depth-charges dropped ahead of the U-boat and exploded where, apart from shaking it up, they had little effect.

As Biddy brought his aircraft round in a tight turn, Wes saw the bubbles rising from the submarine as it crash-dived.

'Drop a flame-float where it disappeared, Biddy,' he said. 'G-George can have a go.'

G-George had flown off the carrier with them for the inner patrol. Switching on his R/T, he called up the other aircraft.

'Hello Ilford George, this is Fox. Have dropped a flame-float to mark a U-boat position. It was heading north-west. Over.'

'Hello Fox, this is George. I can see your flame-float. Am attacking now.' This time they could hear the voice of Hank Phipps, the pilot of G-George.

Wes watched as the shadowy outline of the Swordfish appeared and lined itself up with the flame-float in the direction he had indicated. A few seconds after George passed the flame-float the water erupted as the two depth-charges exploded.

Both aircraft circled the area, their crews watching intently. They saw nothing. Wes felt sure that the U-boat had escaped. They must return to the carrier for instructions.

Biddy called G-George on his R/T.

'Hello George. Form up on me. Am returning to Mother. Over.'

'Hello Fox, this is George. Wilco. Out.'

Wes gave Biddy a course to steer to rejoin *Peregrine,* but as they climbed to a thousand feet he was not surprised to see the blip on his screen showing the two ships at a distance of eighteen miles. They had turned away from the enemy on receiving his first-sighting report.

He conned Biddy towards the carrier and at five miles he called up the ship to ask for instructions.

'Hello Ilford Fox, this is Mother. Both aircraft prepare to land on. Am now turning into wind.'

Wes watched as the two ships turned. He could see two Swordfish, with wings unfolded, lined up on deck and, as the wisp of smoke at the fore end of the flight-deck lined up with the carrier, the first aircraft took off, followed by the second. As the second aircraft left the deck Biddy was already approaching from astern and in short time both aircraft had landed and the flying crews were reporting to the Captain. Biddy was unhappy at reporting his miss but both crews were sure that the U-boat had escaped.

'Never mind, Bidwell,' the Captain said. 'Your warning alerted us and enabled us to turn away from the danger, and your attack put the submarine out of a position from which he could attack us. How did you manage to spot it?'

Wes described the ASV contact and their controlled approach until Biddy was in visual range at one mile. The story quickly spread round the ship, and the squadrons were heartened and encouraged by this proof of the value of their new equipment.

Three days later 999 Squadron was involved in the afternoon search. The two ships had made their way southwards at fifteen knots, with regular searches for the German raider and regular patrols looking for U-boats. Nothing had been sighted. During the day, when they were not flying, officers relaxed on C deck, lounging in the sun, or on the goofers' platform to watch landings and take-offs and deck-hockey. At night many of them sought coolness on the quarterdeck, under the overhang, having camp-beds made up for them by their stewards.

This was a time, too, for writing letters. Bill found it extraordinarily difficult to put his thoughts into words. He thought his letter to Janet was stilted, not expressing his deep feelings. These he felt were best expressed by close contact and in speech. He had discovered that love was a complex experience, a compound of sensuous feelings, emotions, and a joining of spirits, that he found hard to describe. Essentially, by instinct and upbringing, he was a religious man and religion, he was sure, played some part in his love for Janet. Loving was both earthy and spiritual; a man's love for a woman, he thought, was probably the best thing he was capable of. Some of these thoughts he tried to put on paper, but even as he tried he knew that words were too limiting; his thoughts were best felt, not expressed.

Bolo, too, spent some of his time writing – to Joyce. Joyce would now be finishing at Cambridge and soon would be starting as a Wren officer, at the Admiralty, for which she had been recruited whilst at Cambridge. Bolo wrote to her, encouraging her in her new role, describing life in harbour and aboard ship, circumscribed only by the need to avoid classified information. He told her of the engagement of his young protégé, Bill Hewitt, to Janet Hall, and of the dinner aboard ship to mark their engagement. He told her simply and directly of his love for her and of his hopes for the future.

Bolo was thinking of Joyce and his letter to her now as he flew south. The sea was calm, textured like beaten brass, the wind light and the sky blue, uncluttered by clouds, except for a strange cluster on the horizon. Bolo had been watching this phenomenon for some time. Now he spoke to his observer.

'How far are we from St Helena, Dicky?'

Dicky Burd, his observer, consulted his chart.

'About fifteen miles,' he said. 'St Helena is just to starboard of our course.'

'I think I can see it,' said Bolo. 'At least I can see clouds covering it.'

Almost inevitably the first indication of an island is the appearance of clouds above it, and this was no exception. Through his binoculars, Dicky could just make out the island rising majestically to nearly three thousand feet, with towering cliffs over a thousand feet high. These grew plainer as they neared the island and soon Bolo could see the central mountain with its extinct volcano. So this was where Napoleon was imprisoned, Bolo thought, as they flew close by the island. The settlement, Jamestown, on the north-west coast of the island, looked small and desolate in the towering wilderness, something, Bolo thought, he might write to Joyce about, without naming it or giving away the ship's position.

That night, after darkness had fallen, the two ships crept into the anchorage just outside the small harbour. They were protected from the south-west wind by the island itself, and where they anchored was only a gentle swell. The soundings were very deep and a great length of chain was used to anchor them.

In the morning the ship's company awoke to the calls of local traders in small boats coming alongside to sell their wares. Bill bought a present for Janet, a belt made of pomegranate seeds, coloured brown and red. Bolo bought

Joyce a small bag, or purse, made in the same way. The bumboatmen were very different from those at Aden. These were much quieter, offering their wares and waiting patiently for purchasers. They did a good trade.

The ship was on full alert, so no one, other than the Paymaster and cooks, was allowed ashore. The Paymaster made purchases of locally grown fruit and vegetables for the wardroom and for the ship's company.

Holy Temple again proved his worth as a fisherman. At first he tried surface fishing, but when no fish appeared he decided to fish off the bottom. This was forty fathoms down, so he prepared a line of two hundred and fifty feet. He soon had his first fish and very strange it was. Brilliantly striped, it was about a foot long with a bloated body.

It's bloated because the pressure at two hundred and forty feet is very great so that as the fish comes to the surface, where the pressure is much less, its body expands to compensate.'

No one could think of a better explanation, and Holy's theory was partly confirmed when the gasping fish died as it was hauled out.

'It can't live at surface pressure,' Holy declared.

The bright colours of the fish gave him a new idea. Cutting it up, he fixed a portion on the hook, which he cast as far away from the ship as he could, before hauling in swiftly. There was a streak of lightning through the water and the coil of line was running smoothly away. At two hundred feet it eased and Holy struck and started hauling in. He had caught a fine barracuda, much acclaimed by the interested on-lookers. This would provide an excellent starter for dinner that evening.

For three days the two ships remained at anchor, with the officers whiling away their time with fishing or bartering or sunbathing, and fretting at the enforced idleness. On the third day they received a wireless report that a suspicious vessel had been sighted by an aircraft three hundred miles north of Cape Town and all merchant ship movements were cancelled. The Captain decided to sail immediately and that evening the two ships headed in a south-easterly direction towards the reported position.

Again the squadrons fell smoothly into their routine of searches and anti-submarine patrols. They were in high hopes of catching their prey. If the suspicious vessel were indeed the German raider, they were in the right position at the right time to catch it. Each search was capable of covering an area of a hundred and sixty miles by a hundred miles. Unless the raider had steamed clean away from the last reported position, he would surely fall within their search pattern. However, the operation did not develop as planned.

Three days out from St Helena, as the two ships neared the target area, a gale-force wind from the south-west developed, setting up a huge and dangerous swell. Flying was difficult, but not impossible. It was decided to maintain two aircraft on A/S patrol, one inner and one outer, but to cancel the afternoon search. The CO and Holy Temple, in A-Abel and B-Baker, had taken off and Killer Compton in L-Love had landed on. Bing Crosby, in M-Mike, was about to land on.

The stern of the carrier was lifting and falling by thirty to forty feet and landing on was extremely hazardous. Bolo Hawkins, senior pilot of the squadron, was watching from the goofers' platform. He saw Bing Crosby make a good approach, keeping well up over the round-down. However, when he was about to cut his engine, the ship, in a huge valley between the swells, had fallen away from him, so that he was too high. Bing reacted by closing his throttle to allow his plane to sink. At the same time the ship, on a roller-coaster, rose rapidly to meet him. The result was a clash of aeroplane against flight-deck, and a broken undercarriage and bent propeller. Luckily the Swordfish did not catch fire.

The deck-party, under the control of the DCO, brought

trolleys and a tail-arm and wheeled the plane onto the forward lift. As the lift descended, an armourer decided to start removing the flame-floats under the port wing. He had removed a float and was about to replace the safety pin in it when the ship lurched to another big wave, which sent him sprawling. The flame-float was flung from his hands and burst into flames, setting the port wing alight. This fire was fanned by the down draught through the lift-well and there was a very real danger of a general fire amongst the assembled aircraft. Already another aircraft had sparked into flame. If a petrol tank blew the hangar would be devastated.

Killer Compton, whose aircraft had landed just before M-Mike, was in the hangar with his aircraft, and he now ran to a fire extinguisher, which he directed onto the flames. The lift had already ascended, thus making the hangar a sealed box and cutting off the down draught.

Bolo Hawkins, who as Senior Pilot wished to inspect the damaged aircraft, had come down with the lift. He saw at once that the fire was in danger of getting out of hand so he pressed the fire alarm. The fire curtains came down and salt-water sprays drenched all sixteen aircraft in the hangar, including those on fire, quickly extinguishing the flames. The hangar floor was running with salt water, inches deep, and all personnel in the hangar were soaked. The ship and all the aircraft had been saved and the immediate danger was over, but sixteen out of the eighteen Swordfish had been put out of action and all the spares in the hangar, wings, tailplanes and engines, had been rendered unserviceable.

The ship's Commander, responsible for damage control, had now arrived on the scene. He ordered the sprays to be turned off and the two lifts to be lowered to create a draught that would blow the fumes away. Then he took stock of the situation.

The scene was like an underwater grotto, with water dripping from the deck-head and running off every object in the hangar. The men, who had cowered under the wings of aircraft during the deluge, now emerged, soaked and shocked. At a stroke the carrier no longer existed as a fighting unit. Its main armament, its Swordfish squadrons, had been rendered inoperable except for the two flying on anti-submarine patrol.

Flying-crews had come up to the hangar and now stood with the maintenance crews silent and subdued, unable to take in the scope of the disaster.

'Lieutenant Hawkins, you had better come with me to report to the Captain,' the Commander said.

As Bolo left the hangar, he heard the voice of Tom Stillson, the Chief Air Artificer, calling in a strong voice, 'Come on, you men. We've got some work to do. Let's be having you.'

On the bridge, Bolo reported what had happened to the Captain.

'There will have to be an enquiry,' the Captain told him, 'but in my opinion what you did was right. The safety of the ship is paramount and had the fire obtained a hold the ship would have been in jeopardy.

'Your CO is flying at the moment. I've sent for the Commanding Officer of 998 Squadron, but while we are waiting for him will you give me an estimate of the damage?'

'All the aircraft in the hangar and all spare parts are unserviceable, sir.'

'How long will it take to make them serviceable?'

'I'd like to consult the two Commanding Officers and the ship's Air Engineer Officer, sir, but I would estimate at least a week. All aircraft will have to be washed thoroughly with fresh water, checked for corrosion, and moving-parts cleaned and greased. The engines must be stripped and cleaned thoroughly.'

The CO of 998 Squadron agreed with Bolo's estimate, but the Air Engineer Officer was convinced that it would take longer than a week, perhaps as long as a fortnight, before he

208

would be satisfied. Some of the aircraft, he thought, might have to be replaced.

The Captain made his decision.

'I see little point in continuing with this operation,' he said. 'We have neither the aircraft to carry out searches nor the aircraft to attack the enemy should we find him. We shall return to Freetown. Our first duty is to make the ship and our air squadrons operational again.'

He turned to the Commander and to Commander Flying.

'Will you see to that, gentlemen?'

'Aye, aye, sir,' they both replied.

Throughout the next week, the two ships made their way steadily northwards to Freetown. A-Abel and B-Baker were used alternately for A/S patrols, flying fifteen miles ahead of the ships.

Bolo spent much of his time in the hangar, often with other pilots, encouraging the men working on the aircraft. It was painstaking and backbreaking work. First the hangar itself was thoroughly scrubbed out with fresh water; then the hands started on the aircraft. Chiefy was a ball of fire, energising the men, supervising their work. He set meticulous standards: every part of every aircraft had to be scrubbed clean. Each engine was taken out of the aircraft to the workshops where it was dismantled and reassembled, and finally reinstalled in the aircraft. Every connecting rod in the aircraft, every wire, was individually wiped and given a light coating of protective grease. Rusting parts were replaced or cleaned up until they looked new.

The air-mechanics were determined not to let the air-crews down and they were encouraged by pilots, observers and air-gunners who frequently visited the hangar to discuss the problems with the mechanics. The electrics provided some of the more intransigent problems and the Chief TAG had to decide that some of the wireless and R/T sets were not salvable. Where possible they robbed Peter to pay Paul, using spare parts from otherwise useless sets to build up those that were capable of being recovered. When an aircraft was finished and serviced, the men were available to clean and lubricate the spares stored in the hangar.

Seven days after the fire, as *Peregrine* entered Freetown harbour, Chiefy declared that he could see the end in sight.

'Another three days,' he said, 'with some new parts and stores from Freetown, should see us home.'

Chapter 18

Janet and Bill

Work continued non-stop during daylight hours in harbour and the damaged M-Mike was off-loaded into a lighter. Apart from when they were on watch-keeping duties, the flying-crews were free to go ashore after lunch, and Bill took the first opportunity to telephone Janet. He waited tremulously for his call to be answered, not sure whether she had already left for England, and he felt a sense of relief when he heard her voice. She told him of a dance at the Harbour Hotel that was being arranged by local residents for the following evening. Could he come? Bill was delighted and very quickly agreed that Ann, Janet, Killer and he would make a foursome and they would call for the girls in a taxi in time to take them to dinner at the hotel.

The next day, as he helped Janet into her chair, Bill thought how much dinner and dances had become a main thread in the pattern of their lives. Janet had told him that Ann and she with the party of wounded would be boarding the transport in three days' time and this would be their last dance before she left for England. How long would it be before they would attend another dance together?

Whilst Bill was ruminating, Killer, ever practical, was selecting their wine and ordering food. Bill shrugged off his momentary melancholy. He remembered their last dance at Cape Town and decided that this, too, would be a memorable one, a satisfying one, not a sad one.

211

The food was good and the mood was merry, full of light-hearted conversation and banter. Killer was in full flow, his conversation pointed with ironical observation and humour. Ann responded readily, Janet and Bill with rather more reserve at first until Killer's more outrageous comments had them all laughing. The war was far away. By unspoken consent they decided to leave the dancing until after they had finished eating and the music became a background to their conversation.

At length the coffee cups were cleared away and both the young men rose to invite their partners to dance. Janet slipped easily into Bill's arms. Unlike Killer, who chatted to his partner throughout the dance, Bill was silent, letting the dance speak for him.

Janet loved the firm feel of Bill's right arm round her, supporting her left arm, which she rested on his shoulder. Dear Bill. How often he had been her support when she had needed him! Her thoughts went back to Durban, where Joel had been a real menace to her. Bill had been like a rock, protecting her from Joel's violence. And yet he had been gentle with her, easing her fears and not intruding himself. This strength and gentleness was symbolised in his dancing. His steps were strong and purposeful and yet he held her lightly if firmly. He was so easy to follow; it was as if they were one, united in the spirit of the dance.

Then she thought of the lifeboat. On that last night she had not expected to survive. Her last thought had been that Bill had not made love to her on Chapman Peak, and she had awakened to see Bill peering at her from his Swordfish. When she needed him most, Bill had come to rescue her. She remembered what she had said to him on the way to church in Durban, 'You are my verray parfit gentil knight', and as she looked at his face, serious and concentrated, a deep feeling of love flooded through her. For a moment she nuzzled her face against his and Bill looked at her enquiringly.

Ann had told Janet of Bill's devoted nursing through the critical night of her illness. Throughout that night she had been dimly aware of Bill's presence. At times she had felt the waters of death closing over her and she had nearly let herself go. It would have been so easy to give up and let death submerge her. Somehow, Bill's quiet voice had reached through to her, calling her back to life, never giving up. The touch of his body had put life back into her, warming her and cherishing her.

She felt the touch of his body now, hard and muscular, her body softly responding to his. She remembered her first dance with Bill when she had become aware that he was sexually aroused and embarrassed by it. She had liked him then both because of the arousal and because of his shyness. He was no longer shy with her, and he danced now, in close contact, completely relaxed. Her liking had turned into love, and she too could wait, as Bill wanted, until they were married before satisfying her love.

The dance was over. Bill was leading her back to their table, gay and relaxed, talking to Killer and Ann who had joined them. The next dance was a quickstep and Bill and Killer exchanged partners. Janet now found it much easier to dance with Killer than when she had first met him. He is an aggressive, pugnacious character, Janet thought, but, with Ann's influence, he has channelled that into controlled discipline. Formerly, Killer would have seen the other dancers as the opposition and he would have ploughed his way through them. Now, although he made comments about the ability of dancers who got in his way, he steered round them. He had also learned to do chassés and natural and reverse turns, and no longer relied on a walking step that had been the basis of all his dancing. He was now fun to dance with, and Janet enjoyed her dance with him.

Killer had a soft spot for Janet. Not only was she his friend's girl, but he, with Bill, had rescued her, and that in itself was a reason for liking her. He treated her much as the young sister he never had, and enjoyed every minute of his dance with her.

Ann, too, enjoyed her dance. She was a good dancer herself and was well aware of Bill's ability. They danced well together and once Ann thought that if it weren't that Bill was Janet's man and she was in love with Killer, she could … Her thoughts stopped there. She had shared Bill's torture during his night's vigil with Janet. She would never intrude. Even so, he was an attractive man.

Laughingly, the four joined forces at the end of the dance and made their way to their table. Killer replenished their glasses and they took time off during the next dance, an old-fashioned veleta. The following dance was a slow foxtrot, Bill's favourite. This is the most satisfying and the most difficult of all ballroom dances, and the floor was not crowded. Bill had the opportunity with Janet to express himself in long, slow steps as they glided over the dance-floor.

How I love this girl! Bill thought. I have grown from boy to man since I first met her and she now means more to me than life itself. For a moment he tightened his grip round her waist and felt her ready response. Half our lives together have been spent in dancing. I think I fell in love with her when we first met and all our subsequent meetings have only confirmed that. She dances so beautifully, as though she is an extension of me. She makes me feel strong, unbeatable. Together we shall face the future, our future. Such strength she has! She saved all the others in the lifeboat and almost sacrificed herself. She nursed me when I was wounded. She brought the little boy back to life in Mombasa after he nearly drowned. Then recollections faded before the present as Bill gave himself up to the sensuous, dragging steps of the slow foxtrot.

The next dance was a quickstep, which Bill danced with Janet. This was a laughing dance, a devil-may-care dance, and

214

Bill danced it exuberantly. A series of reverse turns was followed by three chassés following each other, a kind of romping, skipping step; this led to a half-dozen natural turns followed by turns with short running steps, each partner following the other like ice-skaters. They both danced with abandon, their feet almost flying over the dance floor, perfectly in time with each other and with the spirit of the dance. Neither had time for thoughts during this dance and they returned to their table at the end of it, flushed and breathless.

So the dance progressed, sometimes with a lively exchange of partners, more often Bill and Janet together, sometimes lost in their reveries, sometimes living in the sensuous present, always influenced by the dance. It was time for the last waltz; not their last meeting, for Bill had arranged to take Janet for a walk and a picnic the next day. This was their last waltz, the last time they would dance together before they met up again in distant England. By some quirk of fate, the tune was 'Soon we'll be sailing, far across the sea'. It was very poignant for Bill and Janet as they danced beneath the darkened lights and sang the words softly to each other. The floor was crowded. There was no room for normal dance-steps, but they were content to rock to and fro, close together, intensely aware of each other, savouring each other's presence.

As the dance came to an end in the almost dark ballroom, Bill whispered, 'Thank you, my love.'

Janet turned her lips to his and kissed him. Her emotions were too strong for her to speak.

The following day broke fair, and by ten o'clock Bill's taxi had deposited him at the Rest Home. Janet was waiting for him. She had obtained a picnic lunch from the Rest Home kitchen to add to Bill's bottle of wine and the groundsheet in his knapsack. Janet had been told of a route that would take them through the forest, round the mountain without losing height, to a waterfall in one of the tributaries of the Sierra Leone River.

Initially, the path was broad and well defined and they walked easily, hand in hand, accompanied by the chatter of monkeys overhead. The monkeys, some quite small, swung in the trees high above them, watching them and no doubt commenting in monkey language.

'Do you remember the monkey family at Mombasa, Bill?'

'Yes, I do. That was a magic moment when I opened my eyes and saw them above us.'

'Are we going to have a family, Bill?'

'Of course we are, darling. How many do you want? Enough for a football team?'

Janet laughed.

'Not quite as many as that! In any case, I hope some of them will be girls,' she said. 'As an only child, I've missed having brothers and sisters. It must be wonderful to be part of a large family.'

'It has its moments,' said Bill. 'Growing up with my brothers was fun. When I was thirteen we used to go off to the forest for the day. Our headquarters was a hollow oak, but we roamed all over the forest. I knew where to find bluebells and primroses, where we'd meet up with wild deer and even where a nest of grass snakes hid out. We used to swim in the pond and catch newts and tiddlers. We always arrived home grubby, tired and hungry, but we were happy enough.'

'It all sounds delightful to me,' said Janet. 'I spent all of term-time at a girls' public school. But I think I'd rather have been grubby and tired after a day's play in the forest.'

'What are we going to do now that we're parting?' said Bill, suddenly changing the subject. 'How are we going to keep in touch?'

'I've written down my parents' address and telephone number,' said Janet 'Even if I'm not at home when you arrive back in England you can contact me through them. Be sure to let me know as soon as you arrive. I'll put the banns up.'

'How will your parents feel about our getting married, Janet?'

'I'm sure they'll be delighted. My mother will love you. I think she always wanted a son. My father will probably ask you what you intend to do with your life and how you propose to support his daughter. He's a little bit old-fashioned, but he's a dear.'

'How am I going to support you?' Bill said. 'What I'd like to do is to go up to university to complete my education. I had a place offered at Cambridge, you know.'

'That's wonderful, Bill. And I'll continue nursing to bring in some money until you've obtained your degree. What will you study?'

'I'm not sure,' said Bill. 'I'm very interested in archaeology, but I don't suppose there's much future in that. I doubt whether it will support a family. The other career that attracts me is writing, I'm not sure what. If I do that, I'd like to study English at Cambridge.'

'English was my favourite subject at school,' said Janet. 'I'll study with you. Well, that's settled. You tell my father you are going to Cambridge to study English in order to become a writer.'

The path had now given way to rocks and boulders and the trees had disappeared. They could hear the waterfall and as they approached it Bill offered a helping hand to Janet at the more difficult places. Janet was athletic and quite capable of managing on her own, but she loved to accept Bill's help.

Suddenly they were there. They passed through a narrow defile and there was the waterfall, splashing into a pool forty feet below. Beyond the pool it became a river again, rushing on between boulders and rocks and throwing up a smoky spray. On their side it shallowed to a small beach of grey sand. They were enchanted; the perfect place for a picnic.

217

'We have the place to ourselves!' Bill exclaimed, 'Apart from the monkeys, that is.'

A small troupe of monkeys had escorted them to the pool, but, as they watched, the monkeys drank from the pool and then retreated back along the way they had come. They laughed as the monkeys disappeared, chattering.

'I'm very hot after our walk,' said Bill. 'What about a swim before lunch?'

'I haven't brought a costume,' said Janet.

'Nor have I,' said Bill. 'Does it matter?'

Janet gazed at him, searchingly.

'No,' she said slowly. 'It doesn't matter at all.'

Bill quickly stripped to his boxer shorts and waited for Janet. She was now down to panties and bra and she looked at him questioningly.

Bill held out his arms and she moved towards him.

Slowly Bill undid the straps holding the bra and released it. Then he knelt before her and hooking his thumbs in her panties lowered them gently to the ground. Janet stepped out of them, regarding Bill intently. She saw his eyes travel down her body from top to toe and back again. She was naked and unashamed.

'My God, Janet,' Bill murmured. 'You are beautiful.'

With a small cry Janet ran into his arms. Bill stood holding her for a few moments, then, stepping out of his own shorts, he led her to the small beach. Hand in hand they walked slowly into the cool water.

Janet felt the cool of the water on her feet, climbing up her legs to her waist and breasts. Never before had she been so aware of the sensation of cold. It was excruciatingly satisfying, and she was sharing it with Bill.

Bill looked at her and said, 'Here goes,' and they plunged forward together, striking out for the opposite shore and back again, swimming together. The brisk swim made their blood tingle and their flesh warm. Laughing and splashing, they raced across the pool again. They were young, they were happy, and they were in love.

For several minutes more they swam with a leisurely breast-stroke and then, holding hands, floated on the surface of the water and let the sun beat down upon them and fill them with gladness and joy. They climbed out of the water together and threw themselves down on the groundsheet to dry in the hot sun.

The picnic was a great success. Janet had brought a pâté, ham, chicken and salad, and cheese to finish. Bill produced his precious bottle of Mouton Cadet. This time he had even provided glasses for the drink.

'*Dejeuner sur l'herbe,*' he said, referring to Monet's famous painting. 'Though I have to say that unlike the painting, none of us here are dressed at all.'

Janet laughed. It was so easy now to accept their nudity, to enjoy it and share it with Bill. She thought their marriage would work very well and she looked forward to their wedding night.

After lunch they lay on the groundsheet, Bill with his back to the rock and Janet leaning against him, loving the hardness of his body. His hands rested lightly on her thighs. Totally relaxed, and at peace after their war experiences, committed to each other, they fell into a loving and dream-less sleep.

Chapter 19

The *Suffren*

The next day Bill climbed up to C deck to watch the activity going on all round him in the harbour. Through his binoculars he saw Janet and Ann and their patients taken out by motorboat to the *Canberra Queen*, a passenger ship carrying troops to England, which was anchored in the middle of the harbour. Later, in the afternoon, he stood with Killer on the quarterdeck of *Peregrine* to watch the convoy depart. All over the harbour anchors were being weighed and large vessels were on the move. Some forty merchant ships, with a large escort of destroyers and a cruiser, were leaving.

'Not much chance of their being attacked by *Hohenlinden*,' said Killer.

'No. I think they'll be safe this time,' Bill replied, 'and I expect they'll pick up a carrier at Gibraltar to escort them to England. They'll need fighter protection against Focke-Wulfes and Swordfish protection against U-boats.'

'A pity we're not going with them,' said Killer.

'Well, we've a job to do down here. Hopefully, when we find and sink the *Hohenlinden* we'll be able to go home.'

The *Canberra Queen* was now getting under way and Bill gazed through his binoculars as she steamed slowly past. A group of passengers was clustered at the stern, behind the swimming pool. Amongst them he saw Janet and Ann, looking towards them. He raised his arm in farewell and saw Janet raise hers in return. She had spotted him. Sadly he watched the great convoy gather pace, one ship after another, until the harbour seemed empty and desolate. Then he and Killer went down to the hangar to discuss problems in their aircraft with Bailey and Riggs, their fitter and rigger.

By Wednesday, the twenty-fifth of July, all aircraft aboard *Peregrine* were fully restored and ready for service. A replacement for M-Mike was waiting ashore at the aerodrome to be flown on by Bing Crosby when *Peregrine* put to sea. This he did soon after dawn the next day. Five miles out of Freetown, the new M-Mike landed on and the first two anti-submarine aircraft took off to begin their patrols. *Peregrine*, accompanied by *Daventry*, was on her way to St Helena, to resume her search for *Hohenlinden*.

During the next three days nothing was sighted. Anti-submarine patrols took off and landed every two and a half hours and parallel track searches were mounted at dawn and in the late afternoon. The squadrons settled down to the routine, each crew having a daily flight. They caught up with a backlog of their squadron duties, played deck-hockey or sunbathed during the day and often enjoyed a game of bridge or poker or mahjong in the evening. The weather was good, the wind light, the flying easy. After the anxiety of the fire, a feeling of relaxation descended on the squadron as the two ships moved southwards.

On the fourth day, St Helena was sighted and the two ships anchored to await events. Again, no shore leave was permitted and the ship's crew and the air squadrons became increasingly restless. Four days later came news of a sinking. There was no SOS, but the survivors of a British merchant ship had been picked up off the coast of Argentina and taken to Montevideo. *Peregrine* weighed anchor.

The course was west-south-west for more than three

thousand miles towards the mouth of the River Plate. Captain Bentley did not expect to find the raider in that position; his method of hunting was to sail towards the raider's last known position and hope that he would be near enough to pinpoint the target by aircraft search. For the first five days there would be little chance of meeting the *Hohenlinden,* so only anti-submarine patrols were flown. Captain Bentley was saving his aircraft for the testing time when they would be closer to the target. Intelligence, however, had reported the presence of new long-range U-boats in the South Atlantic, preying on traffic from South America to Cape Town or Britain. Because of this threat, an A/S patrol was regularly flown off. Nothing was sighted.

On the sixth day, searches began at dawn and late afternoon, searching parallel tracks ahead of the ships. The period of comparative rest was over. The search of the endless sea was resumed in deadly earnest. On the seventh day out from St Helena, the search bore some fruit.

Bill was relaxing in his cabin in the middle of the morning when he heard the Tannoy broadcast, '999 Squadron range nine aircraft armed with bombs.'

Almost immediately, as Bill came out into the cabin flat, it was followed by another broadcast.

'D'ye hear there?'

The familiar tones of the Captain halted Bill in his tracks and, with several other officers who had emerged from their cabins, he listened to the broadcast.

'One of our aircraft has sighted a suspicious vessel. When it closed to investigate, this vessel fired on the aircraft. 999 Squadron is being armed with bombs to form a striking-force. Briefing for all flying-crews in the briefing-room in fifteen minutes. That is all.'

From all over the ship, from cabins, the wardroom, the mess-decks, the hangar, the squadron office, the goofers' platform and C deck, 999 Squadron flying personnel made

222

their way to the briefing-room. Bill joined Killer, Bolo Hawkins and Dicky Burd on the way up.

'Do you think this is *Hohenlinden?*' Killer wanted to know.

'It doesn't sound like it to me,' Bolo replied. 'I think we'd arm with torpedoes if we knew it was *Hohenlinden.* It's more likely to be a tanker or supply ship for the long-range submarines, or even for *Hohenlinden.* We know she's received supplies and fuel from ships coming from South America.'

In the briefing-room a full briefing team was waiting to address the assembled flying crews. Wings spoke first.

'One of 998 Squadron's search party has reported being fired on by a suspicious vessel,' he said. 'P4G spotted a tanker, flying a Uruguayan flag. He flew close to identify it and was immediately fired on by the tanker's Bofors and other short-range weapons. P4G was hit several times, but is still airborne and has remained to shadow the tanker. The CO of 998 Squadron, in P4A, who was on anti-submarine patrol, has been instructed to fly out to relieve P4G. Uruguay is a friendly, if neutral, country and would be most unlikely to fire on a British aircraft. We have to assume, therefore, that the tanker is an enemy one. P4A will take over the shadowing of the tanker and report its movements.'

He was followed by the Air Staff Officer.

'The tanker at 0900 was on a bearing 250 degrees from *Peregrine,* distance ninety miles. It was heading on a course of 200 degrees at a speed of twelve knots. You are timed to take off at 0945. Your call sign is "Ilford"; 998 Squadron is "Hector"; and *Peregrine* is "Mother". Hector Abel will confirm the identity of the tanker as you approach.'

He then gave them their W/T frequencies and call signs and made way for Schooley. Schooley's message was brief. Wind was westerly, force three; visibility beneath the clouds was twenty miles; at three thousand feet there was five-tenths cloud.

Finally, Lieutenant Commander Simpson addressed his squadron.

'It's several months since we had a target at sea,' he said, 'so let me remind you of our procedure for a dive-bombing attack. I'll keep the squadron together until we're ahead of the target, using whatever cloud cover is available. I'll approach at six thousand feet. Five miles from the target I'll give the order on R/T to form line astern. About a mile away I'll order the attack. Then it's up to each individual pilot to do the best he can. After the attack I'll drop a smoke-float five miles east of the target where the squadron will re-form for the flight back to the carrier. Any questions?'

There were none.

'Right, chaps, let's get to it and good luck.'

Collecting his canvas holdall containing his chartboard and navigation instruments, Bill joined Killer and L/A Gibbons and made his way down to the flight-deck, where the Swordfish, their wings already unfolded and each bombed up with six 250-pound bombs, were waiting. Air-mechanics were sitting in the pilots' cockpits revving up the engines, and air-riggers were waiting to help the crews aboard. Dodging past the whirling propellers, Bill and Killer made their way to L-Love, in the third sub-flight.

Killer went through his pre-flight routine, testing his controls and, with the mechanic and rigger leaning on the tail-plane, running up his engine against the brakes and the chocks.

'All ready, Bill?'

'OK, Killer.'

'You ready, Gibbons?'

'Yes, sir.'

Killer watched as the carrier turned into wind and the wisp of smoke at the forward end of the flight-deck trailed aft. He saw the green flag raised by Wings on the bridge. The DCO signalled the chocks away and waved the CO off. The

Swordfish, bumping a little, moved ponderously forward, like an ungainly elephant, gathering speed slowly at first and then accelerating. It disappeared from view below the forward end of the flight-deck, as if it were about to plunge into the sea. A few seconds later, it reappeared, climbing laboriously.

B-Baker was already under way, following his leader. Soon it was Killer's turn. His chocks were removed; he revved his engine hard, holding it back on the brakes until the Pegasus engine was giving him full power. Then he released the brakes and let the aircraft build up speed, holding it down on the deck. He had barely reached flying speed when he left the forward end of the flight-deck. Fifteen hundred pounds of bombs need a lot of lift in a small aircraft. To help build up flying speed he put his nose down towards the sea before pulling up to climb away gently from sea level.

Ahead of him the Swordfish were spread out in a long line to where the CO was already circling his smoke-float.

'Permission to reel out the aerial?' came the voice of his TAG.

'OK, Gibbons.'

The trailing aerial was needed to receive and transmit on W/T. Then came the voice of his CO.

'Hello, Ilford aircraft, this is Leader. Form up on me round smoke-float. Please acknowledge.'

As they climbed steadily, Bill listened to the replies.

'Hello, Ilford Leader, this is Baker. Wilco. Over.'

'This is Charlie. Wilco. Over.'

And so on to M-Mike.

'Hello, Ilford Leader, this is Mike. Wilco. Out.'

All the aircraft were in touch and now R/T silence was maintained. Bill carefully noted the time, course and speed as they headed towards the enemy, and plotted them on his chartboard. He might well find himself navigating back to the carrier. He had switched on his ASV and checked that it was working, using the carrier and cruiser as targets.

Half an hour later he picked up the tanker on his ASV at a distance of twenty-five miles. His height was five thousand feet and they were still climbing. Banks of fluffy, white cloud rolled beneath them, broken by gaps of grey-blue sea. One W/T signal from 4PA was received, reporting that the tanker had altered course to the west, presumably making for Buenos Aires. Bill noted the alteration of course made by his leader to compensate for this. When the target was ten miles away on his ASV he instructed his TAG to wind in his trailing aerial. At the same time he heard an R/T message from his CO.

'Hello, Hector Abel, this is Ilford Leader. Am ten miles from target. Over.'

'Hello, Ilford Leader, this is Hector Abel. Target confirmed enemy. Now flying German flag. Over.'

'Hello, Hector Abel, this is Ilford Leader. Roger. Out.'

'Hello, Ilford aircraft, form line astern. Go. Go.'

The attack was on. Bill glanced up to see Bolo Hawkins wheeling his sub-flight away from the leader and then waving Love and Mike to form line astern. He led them back astern of the second sub-flight.

Below them was thick cloud, with no sight of the tanker. He looked at his ASV and reported to his pilot.

'Target five miles to port.'

The CO was taking them round the tanker to attack from ahead. The blip remained constant at five miles to port. A little later it moved towards the centre. The C/O was turning in.

'Target ahead, three miles,' Bill reported.

A gap in the cloud, and there was the tanker, two miles ahead of them. 'Ilford aircraft. Attack. Go, go.'

Tracers and shell-bursts from the tanker were already bracketing the CO as he dived towards his target. Bill saw the ship swing ponderously in towards the CO, making him overshoot. Holy Temple, following him in, was hit by tracers, and pulled away, his bombs falling harmlessly short of the target. Hatters Dunn in C-Charlie pressed home his attack, but his bombs dropped alongside – a near miss.

Bolo was almost in a diving position and Bill knew that it would soon be their turn. Biddy Bidwell, leader of the second sub-flight, was going in now, miraculously avoiding the flak and pressing home his attack. One of his bombs burst on the foc's'le. The ship heaved out of the water, but did not stop. Hank Phipps in G-George followed his leader down and scored a second hit astern of the bridge. He must have damaged the propeller shaft, for the tanker faltered, putting Midshipman Cartwright off his stride. His bombs fell ahead of the ship.

Now it was their turn. Every gun in the ship was now firing at them, the tracers they could see and the bullets they could not see. Bolo was going down straight into the thick of it. The tanker was almost beneath them when Killer banked his aircraft into a screaming dive. Bill, hard up against the forward bulkhead, felt his stomach move up to his chest with the negative G. It was strangely quiet. Killer had closed his throttle, allowing gravity and his bomb load to give him speed and using the drag of the biplane to hold him back.

Four thousand feet. The tanker was getting larger, appearing to revolve as Killer lined up his aircraft. On the bridge a group of people were staring up at them. Streams of tracers were passing them on either side. An enormous explosion forward of the bridge marked where Bolo's bombs had straddled the ship, scoring two hits.

Three thousand feet. Two thousand feet.

The ship looked enormous, smoke pouring from where the bombs had hit, men running hither and thither, most of the men on the bridge lying killed or wounded on the deck.

One thousand feet.

'Bombs gone.'

Bill felt the judder as the bombs left and saw them leave

227

the wings, bucketing and swaying as they fell. Then his stomach moved down towards his feet as Killer pulled up and away. He had prepared himself for the attack by attaching himself to his G-strap to avoid being thrown out of the aircraft and by setting his camera. He took two snapshots, one recording Bolo's hits and one as their own bombs burst right across the bridge.

Bing Crosby, in M-Mike, following Killer, dropped his bombs into an already dying ship. The tanker was settling in the water. Men were struggling to release the lifeboats, only one of which got away. As they circled, Bill could see about ten men in the lifeboat. The tanker was ablaze from end to end and burning oil was spilling out across the sea. Those in the lifeboat would escape but there was no chance of any other survivors. It was time to go. War was a horrible business and Bill had the sick feeling he always had after a successful attack. His thoughts were for the victims and the fine ship destroyed.

'There's the smoke-float,' exclaimed Killer, and L-Love joined the stream of aircraft forming up on their leader.

No aircraft had been lost, though both B-Baker and H-Howe had been hit. No one was wounded. Bill listened wearily to the reports as they came in until it was time to give his own. As the squadron approached within sight of the carrier, a message came through on the W/T. The enemy tanker had sunk. Keeping his squadron together, the CO led them in a fly-past before breaking off to land on.

It had been a successful strike and U-boats in the area would feel the effects of it for days to come. However, *Hohenlinden* was still at large and the searches must still go on. The aircraft of 998 Squadron that were not flying were brought up on deck to form the afternoon search, whilst the aircraft of 999 Squadron were taken below to the hangar to be serviced, refuelled and, where necessary, repaired. The repairs took much of the night, but by morning both 998 and

999 Squadrons were fully operational. In the morning, Bolo, accompanied by the CO, made a round of the hangars, thanking the weary mechanics.

999 Squadron was to form the first search party, and at first light all nine of their aircraft were ranged on deck, together with two aircraft of 998 Squadron who were on the first A/S patrol. It was to be a full-scale search, nine aircraft flying thirty miles apart to cover as large an area as possible.

At the briefing the crews were told to look out for anything, the *Hohenlinden*, or perhaps a supply ship, or even a submarine. All ships were to be closely investigated and photographed and, if they acted suspiciously, reported. Wireless silence could be broken if necessary.

'We are right in the heart of the enemy area,' Wings told them, 'and we can't afford to miss anything. We know that the Germans use subterfuge and are good at disguise, so be prepared. Don't be put off by the obvious. In fact, if it's too obvious, like the Aussie hats when we last saw *Hohenlinden,* be more suspicious.'

The crews were very determined as they walked down to their aircraft. They had now been searching for six months. *Hohenlinden* had slipped through their fingers once; it would not do so again. Moreover, they had a debt to settle for when the two VADs and the naval wounded had been sunk in the ship carrying them home.

The third sub-flight was on the extreme left of the search, and Killer and Bill had Bolo Hawkins in K-King on one side of them and Bing Crosby in M-Mike on the other. It was L-Love that first sighted *Suffren,* Bill spotting the ship on his ASV.

'Killer, I've a blip at twenty-two miles, almost ahead. Let's go and investigate.' Five minutes later Killer exclaimed, 'I've got it! I can see smoke.'

Bill studied the ship curiously as they approached. She was a fine, modern fruit ship, especially built to carry fruit speedily from South America to Europe. She probably had a top speed of eighteen knots. She certainly wasn't *Hohenlinden.*

'Fly alongside, Killer,' said Bill. 'I'll challenge her, then take some photographs.' Killer brought his aircraft to within a quarter of a mile and flew down the starboard side of the ship.

What ship? Bill flashed on his Aldis lamp.

There was no reply.

'I'll go round the stern,' Killer said, 'and we can read her name.'

He passed the stern only fifty yards away and they could both read the name, *Santa Lucia,* and identify the Spanish flag.

'Strange they don't reply to my signal,' said Bill. 'Let's try again.'

Again Killer flew down the side of the ship and Bill repeated his request.

Again no answer.

'They must have someone who knows a little English,' said Bill. 'I don't like this. Fly past again, Killer, and I'll take some photographs.'

This time Killer flew past two hundred yards away and Bill took several pictures.

'Now fly overhead, Killer. Look out for anything suspicious.'

Killer brought his aircraft over the ship at five hundred feet.

'Bloody hell!' he exclaimed. 'They've got a gun there. They're going to fire at us. Man your gun, Gibbons, and give them a burst.'

Killer, never one to duck a fight, now brought his aircraft down in a shallow dive and fired his single Lewis gun at the two men firing at them. He saw them both collapse as his bullets hit them. Meanwhile, Leading Airman Gibbons sprayed all the men on deck with his Lewis gun, sending them running for cover. While this was happening the Spanish colours had been hauled down and a German flag hoisted.

'Get a message off to the carrier, Bill,' Killer said. 'I'll circle round and if any of them come up on deck I'll give them a squirt.'

Quickly Bill wrote out a message in code for Leading Airman Gibbons to transmit:

German ship bearing 230 degrees from you, distance 102 miles. Steering 250 degrees. Speed 18 knots.

Again two seamen ran towards the gun and again Killer dived on them, cutting them off with his machine gun.

'Message passed and received, sir,' said Gibbons.

'Good show,' Bill replied. 'Stick to your gun now and shoot anything that moves.'

'Message from the ship, sir,' said Gibbons a few minutes later. 'K-King and M-Mike to join us and help out.'

'Good!' exclaimed Killer. 'The beggar fired at us before he put up his German flag. If he can do that we can stop them leaving. Let's go down and shoot up the lifeboats.'

Again he circled and dived on the ship, aiming his gun at the starboard lifeboat whilst Gibbons fired at the boat on the port side.

'Hello, Ilford Love, this is Ilford King. Do you read me?'

Bill was glad to hear Dicky Burd's voice. The situation was getting complicated. 'Hello, King, this is Love. Receiving you loud and clear,' he said into his microphone.

'We'll be with you in five minutes,' Dicky said.

'Hello, Ilford Love, this is Ilford Mike. Over.'

'Hello, Mike, this is Love. Receiving you loud and clear. Over.'

'Hello, Love, this is Mike. Am approaching you now. Over.'

'Hello, Mike, this is Love. Roger. Out.'

'Hello, Love, this is King. What's been happening?'

This was Bolo's voice and Killer answered him. Briefly he

told of their approaching the ship and being fired upon whilst it was under false colours and his decision to fire back.

A long pause ensued. At length Bolo's voice came through.

'I'll take control now,' he said. 'I want you both to space yourselves out round the ship and circle it as close as you can. If you see anyone try for the boats, go in and fire ahead of them and frighten them off. If you see anyone going for the guns shoot to kill.'

'This is like Red Indians,' said Killer, as he settled into position, circling the ship.

'Message from K-King to *Peregrine* in code, sir,' said L/A Gibbons.

'Decode it please, Gibbons, and let me know what it says.'

A few minutes later the TAG read out his translation.

Three aircraft circling target. Crew kept below by our gunfire. Request instructions.

The reply soon came back.

Continue your action. Relief on way.

An officer appeared at a doorway with books in his arms. Bolo immediately dived at him, firing just ahead of him. The man dropped the books and fled back to safety.

'Code books, I expect,' said Bill, who had been watching carefully.

The cat-and-mouse game continued sporadically for the next hour until a new voice came over the R/T.

'Hello, Ilford King, this is Hector Abel. Over.'

Dicky Burd replied.

'Hello, Hector Abel, this is Ilford King. Receiving you strength four. Over.'

'Hello, Ilford King, this is Hector Abel. Have target in sight. Be with you in five minutes. Over.'

'Hello, Hector Abel, this is Ilford King. Roger. Out.'

A minute later the CO of 998 Squadron called again on his R/T.

'Hello, Ilford, this is Hector. My sub-flight will take over in two minutes. Mother has turned towards target and increased speed to twenty-four knots. Escort dispatched at twenty-eight knots. Over.'

A bit cryptic, Bill thought, but he got the gist of the message. It gave them the carrier's new course and speed and they would be able to plot the return course to the carrier accurately.

'Hello, Hector, this is Ilford. Message received and understood.'

The 998 sub-flight quickly slotted into the group circling the enemy and Bolo ordered his sub-flight to withdraw and form up on him in loose formation. Forty minutes later Bill saw *Daventry* making a brave show as she steamed at her maximum speed of twenty-eight knots towards the enemy.

The carrier was already in sight, turning into wind as they approached and flying off two A/S aircraft, before landing them on together with the returning A/S patrol. The officers were told to report to the Captain on the bridge. He listened carefully as Killer made his report.

'You are sure the enemy ship fired at you before he showed his true colours,' he said.

Both Killer and Bill assured him that this was correct.

'In that case, I don't blame you for firing at them. You have put us in a position to capture this ship. *Daventry* has been dispatched at full speed to intercept her and take over. We have increased to our maximum speed of twenty-four knots. We are sending off a relief sub-flight every two hours, organised by Wings and the ASO. The orders are to continue what you have started – keep them below decks, even if it means firing on the boats.'

This was a relief to Killer. He had been rather worried at firing on unarmed men and on the boats, but, apart from those manning the guns, he had fired ahead of them not at

233

them, aiming to frighten them back below decks, not kill them.

'Would you have fired at them if they attempted to escape in the boats?' Bill asked him as they made their way down to the wardroom.

'I don't know, Bill. What I did was in the heat of action. Firing at the boats with no one in them was deliberate, intended to stop them leaving. I don't think I could have fired in cold blood at men escaping in the boats.'

The patrols continued throughout the day, never relaxing the threat to the crew of the enemy vessel. Sub-flights from 998 Squadron were followed by sub-flights from 999 Squadron, each sub-flight leaving every two hours. It was 999 Squadron's second sub-flight led by Biddy Bidwell that was circling the target when *Daventry* arrived. Later, in the wardroom, before dinner, Hank Phipps and Dorrie Dorrington told Killer and Bill what happened.

'We were still circling like Red Indians when *Daventry* arrived,' said Hank. 'She stationed herself a quarter of a mile away and trained her guns on the enemy ship. She must have ordered her to stop because both ships slowed down and became stationary.

'Then she lowered a boat and sent a naval party to board the other ship. It was like a novel. The Germans came out with their hands up and *Daventry*'s people took over. All the Germans were taken into custody and *Daventry* put a prize crew aboard.

'That was as far as we saw,' continued Hank. 'Our petrol was getting low and it was time for us to leave.'

Much later, when *Daventry* rejoined *Peregrine*, the full story came out, related by the ASO over the Tannoy. The captured ship was a brand-new German fruit ship, converted into a supply ship. It had torpedoes, fuel and supplies for German submarines in the area, together with a relief submarine crew. It was also thought to have supplies for *Hohenlinden*. It was the German submariners who had tried to resist and reach the guns. The ship's name was *Suffren* and it had been sent to Freetown for onward passage to England.

Chapter 20

Search the Southern Ocean

It was now known that *Hohenlinden* was in the Southern Ocean. But after the long search to St Helena and across the Atlantic, ending in the high-speed chase of *Suffren,* both *Peregrine* and *Daventry* were low on fuel. It had been planned for them to rendezvous with a tanker in position thirty-five degrees south, fifty degrees west. This they did on August the seventh, two days after the capture of *Suffren.* The weather remained good, the wind light and the sea calm, ideal conditions for refuelling at sea.

A new method of refuelling was to be attempted, requiring the tanker to tow the carrier broadside on at a rate of one knot. While this was a good system for the tanker, it placed *Peregrine* in a dangerous situation. U-boats were known to be in the area and, almost stationary, she would be vulnerable to U-boat attack. *Daventry* would circle protectively round her, using her Asdic for detection, but this would leave large gaps, which a U-boat could penetrate. It was essential to have an aircraft in the air, armed with depth-charges, patrolling round the carrier. It would be impossible for a Swordfish to take off from, or land on, a stationary carrier, but it was quite feasible for a seaplane to land in the calm water to leeward of the carrier. With this in mind, floats, carried in the hangar for just such a purpose, were fitted to the CO's machine, 5PA.

By 1000 all was ready. The tanker had warps out to the fo'c'sle and stern of the carrier and was towing it broadside on into wind at a very slow speed, enough to keep the warps taut and the fuel hose out of the water. In the lee of the carrier, on the opposite side to the tanker, the Swordfish was lowered into the sea, complete with crew, by Jumbo, *Peregrine's* crane.

The CO was in the cockpit, with Sandy Sandiford as his observer and CPO Cutter his TAG. A crowd of aircrew from both squadrons gathered on the flight-deck to watch the take-off. Keeping about a hundred yards from the carrier, the CO taxied towards the stern, turned the way the ship was pointing and took off, to the cheers of the watching men. This was the first time most of the airmen had seen a Swordfish on floats and they were impressed with its performance. A-Abel took station five miles from the carrier, circling it at that distance.

During the day, a long, coded message was received from *Suffren*. *Daventry's* First Lieutenant, who had been transferred to the prize as its captain, had made further searches in the ship and had found references to *Hohenlinden*. She was to meet a tanker for refuelling in position fifty-five degrees south, fifty degrees west, halfway between the Falkland Islands and South Georgia.

This was the lead the Captain wanted. Twelve hundred miles to the south, in the icy waters of the Southern Ocean, was the German raider they had been searching for for so long. They now had a chance of coming up with her, but first both ships must be refuelled. The chase could still be a long one and they needed all the fuel they could hold. It took the whole of the day to complete the operation. When *Peregrine's* refuelling was complete, the tanker linked up with *Daventry*. The Swordfish on floats was hoisted aboard and anti-submarine patrols were flown off from the deck of the carrier, which steamed in a tight circle round the cruiser. By dusk refuelling was completed and the two ships set off to the south.

As they progressed southwards the weather became progressively worse. They were steaming into the southern winter. Shorts and khaki slacks disappeared, to be replaced by blue serge battledress. The wind grew in strength, sometimes reaching gale force. Heavy rain clouds appeared, and once the squadron was caught in low cloud that might have resulted in calamity.

On the third day after refuelling, 999 Squadron was carrying out a full-nine aircraft search. They were beginning to approach the latitude of the Falkland Islands and there was always the possibility now that *Hohenlinden* might be in the area. The weather forecast had been poor. At briefing, Schooley had warned them of low clouds and low overcast with visibility down to two miles. In these circumstances, normally, aircraft would not have taken off.

'The circumstances are not normal,' said Wings, addressing the squadron. '*Hohenlinden* is somewhere in this area and we cannot afford to miss her. You will use your ASVs for the search and to help find the carrier on your return.'

Bill shivered as he walked out onto the flight deck to his waiting aircraft. He was wearing his Sidcot flying-suit with kapok lining, fur-lined flying-boots and skin-fitting silk gloves under his leather gauntlets. He could navigate in these silk gloves and would keep them on throughout the flight. Killer, nearer the engine and warmer, was wearing his Irvine flying jacket.

'A bit different from the Tropics,' murmured Killer.

Just for a moment a recollection of the waterfall at Freetown came into Bill's mind and of that sunny interlude by the pool. He thrust these thoughts aside and concentrated on his immediate problems, settling into his cockpit, arranging his navigation gear in their familiar places and beginning his plot. The nine aircraft had to fly out to their allotted search lines, twenty miles apart, and then fly due south along them until it was time to return. They must be back at the carrier two and a half hours after take-off. The search had been shortened by half an hour because of the appalling conditions.

As soon as they took off Bill became aware of how bad the conditions were. At five hundred feet they were flying in and out of the low cloud. Two miles from the carrier, both ships had completely disappeared; so had all the other aircraft on their diverging courses. Bill felt they were on their own and very vulnerable. Nevertheless, they had a job to do and they would do it to the best of their ability.

The cloud-laden wind was gusty and the aircraft bucketed about, sometimes rising or falling a hundred feet with breathtaking suddenness. Shortly after leaving the carrier Bill took his first wind and found it was twenty-five knots from the south-west. He applied it carefully to correct his course. If the ASV failed, pinpoint dead-reckoning navigation would be essential; so would Killer's accuracy in following his compass course.

During the flight, Bill took two more winds and found that while the direction was constant the wind strength varied from twenty knots to thirty, reflecting its gusty nature. Apart from navigation, Bill spent all his time watching his ASV with straining eyes. Visibility was never more than two miles and sometimes down to a few hundred yards. At five hundred feet his range would be little more than ten miles and he kept it tuned to the fifteen-mile band.

By the time they were nearing the carrier on the return track Bill was stiff with the cold. He could see the sea below him, bleak and wind-wracked, but there was very little visibility ahead. He was relying entirely on his dead-reckoning navigation and his ASV.

Twenty miles from the carrier he tuned his ASV to the forty-mile range, but sea returns were the only signals he was receiving. There was no blip. He had not expected one, but, after a quick look downwards, he thought how dreary the sea was and how lonely his aircraft.

'Any sign of *Peregrine* on the ASV?' came Killer's voice over his intercom.

'Not yet, Killer.'

'How far on dead-reckoning?'

'Just under twenty miles. We won't pick her up until we're within ten miles, so I've switched to the fifteen-mile range. Even then, I'm not sure with all this cloud. It's giving us interference.'

Killer was now flying on his instruments, in thick cloud.

At nine miles Bill caught the flicker of a blip that came and went and came again.

'Turn ten degrees to port, Killer,' he said.

'Ten degrees to port. Course now three-four-oh degrees.'

'The wind has increased and blown us to the east of our course,' said Bill. '*Peregrine* should now be dead ahead, distance six miles. I've a firm contact.'

'More than I have,' said Killer. 'Visibility is zero. I can't even see the sea.'

Pilot and air-gunner peered ahead anxiously, whilst Bill concentrated on his radar. Gradually the distance came down until Bill called, 'We're overhead now.'

'I can't see a damn thing,' exclaimed Killer. 'I'm going down to sea level.'

Slowly and anxiously he brought his Swordfish down, steering the courses given by Bill to keep him close to the carrier. Using his ASV, Bill was aiming to circle the carrier at a distance of one mile. Suddenly, the aircraft pulled up sharply.

'Sorry, chaps!' Killer's voice was deliberately drawled. 'We nearly went in then. The white horses saved us.'

'Hello, Ilford aircraft, this is Mother. We can hear you flying close to us but cannot see you. The top of the cloud is

240

at about four thousand feet. Climb above it and orbit the carrier, using your ASVs. Out.'

'Good idea!' Killer exclaimed. 'At least we won't hit each other. Whoops!'

The Swordfish made a violent turn to port and Bill saw the huge shape of another Swordfish, only feet away from them.

'Let's go out to about three miles from the carrier,' Killer said. 'We should find more room there.'

Bill carefully directed him. Fifteen minutes later, as they climbed to four thousand feet, the grey of the cloud became paler, then luminous, and finally gave way to clear, blue sky. To port Bill could see two other aircraft, with another coming through the cloud. Soon all nine aircraft were visible, circling an invisible carrier.

'Hello, Ilford aircraft, this is Leader.' Sandy Sandiford's voice came loud and clear over the R/T. 'We are going to look for a clear patch. The rest of you continue orbiting Mother. Over.'

As the 'wilcos' came in, one after the other, Bill saw a Swordfish break off on a course ahead of the carrier, gradually descending into the cloud. Ten minutes later Sandy's voice came again over the R/T.

'Hello, Mother, this is Ilford Leader. There is a clear patch bearing two hundred degrees from you, distance eleven miles. Over.'

From *Peregrine* came the response.

'Hello, Ilford Leader, this is Mother. Roger. Have altered course towards it.'

A minute later.

'Hello, Ilford aircraft, this is Leader. Carry out the following instructions carefully. Approach Mother on a heading of two hundred degrees. Steer two hundred degrees for ten miles, descending to five hundred feet. There you will find a patch of clear visibility. I will drop a flame-float in the middle of it. Orbit the flame-float until Mother arrives. Please acknowledge.'

As the acknowledgements came through, Bill directed Killer to a position over the carrier on a course of 200 degrees. Once again they entered the murk. Again the icy fingers of the cloud clawed in through the open cockpit as Killer, using his instruments, controlled his descent. Even the radar could not help now. It was only Killer's flying ability and instinct that could save them. Bill stood against the forward bulkhead, his face close to Killer's, watching the instruments: speed steady at ninety knots; compass course steady on two hundred degrees; turn and bank indicator steady; descent steady. The altimeter recorded their descent: three thousand feet; two thousand; one thousand; five hundred. They were through. There was the flame-float, symbol of life and safety. Thankfully, Killer joined the circuit, orbiting the float at four hundred feet, just below the cloud base.

Half an hour later the grey shape of *Peregrine* parted the mist, followed by the leaner *Daventry*. Never before had the Swordfish pilots been so eager to land. Never had they landed so quickly. In twenty minutes the last aircraft touched down. Five minutes later the carrier was again enshrouded in mist.

For the next twenty-four hours all flying was cancelled as the ships made their way southwards through the sea mist. When they passed latitude fifty-five degrees the wind, now from the west, grew stronger and the sea more violent. They were now south of Cape Horn's latitude, with no landmass to form a wind barrier. When flying was resumed, the accidents started. With the pitching of the carrier in the huge seas, the stern was rising and falling forty feet. Both squadrons had experienced similar conditions when they had last ventured south and had learned to avoid the round-down by landing towards the middle of the carrier, where they could pick up the third or fourth arrester wire. However, they were still caught out by the unexpected. A sudden surge of water sent the flight-deck upwards to meet the descending Swordfish with a crack, breaking oleo legs and tail wheels. An unexpected roll of the ship turned a waiting Swordfish onto its side, damaging a wingtip. On one occasion, a Swordfish took control of its handling party and slithered across the icy deck to finish up against the island.

Down below, in the hangar, life was equally precarious. All aircraft were fastened to ringbolts with triple tethers, but when aircraft were being moved to or from the lift accidents happened. It was impossible always to maintain control of the aircraft on the slippery, gyrating deck. The maintenance crews worked long hours to repair their damaged machines and keep them serviced, and when not working on aircraft they were often called to help move them.

Nevertheless, morale remained high. The sinking of the tanker and capture of the supply ship had lifted the hearts of the riggers and fitters and, although they grumbled, they turned to willingly when required, often working late into the night.

Chapter 21

The End of the Search

Two days after the stand-down more news of the *Hohenlinden* came in. A patrol vessel from South Georgia reported seeing a large ship being refuelled by a tanker south-west of South Georgia. This could only be the German raider. The hunt was on again. They were closing in on their quarry.

At 1400 the next day, in the half-light of the southern winter, Killer and Bill moved carefully out to their waiting aircraft. Conditions were appalling. The deck was slippery with icy patches and moving wildly under the heave and thrust of the sea. Huge waves, with half a mile between their crests, came thundering from astern, blown by the near gale-force wind. Nine aircraft of 999 Squadron, with wings folded, were packed herringbone fashion behind six aircraft of 998 Squadron. 999 Squadron was armed with torpedoes, 998 Squadron with bombs.

As he sat in his cockpit waiting for take-off, Bill reflected on the events leading up to this. A dawn search by 998 Squadron had revealed the *Hohenlinden,* a hundred and thirty miles ahead of the carrier. The raider had not attempted to escape by subterfuge. No friendly merchant ships would be in that latitude, and when challenged the *Hohenlinden* had opened fire on the Swordfish. From that moment she had been shadowed by aircraft of 998 Squadron. The remaining aircraft had been recalled to join with 999 Squadron in a combined strike: six aircraft of 998 Squadron armed with bombs, nine aircraft of 999 armed with torpedoes.

At the briefing, Wings had outlined the plan of attack. Using cloud cover, 998 Squadron would endeavour to get into position for a dive-bombing attack on the raider, which was to take place immediately before 999 Squadron began its run-in with torpedoes. The object was to create as much damage and havoc as they could and provide a diversion, during which 999 Squadron would have an opportunity to get in close enough to drop torpedoes.

Every spare man from both squadrons was utilised to assist the deck handling party to hold down the parked aircraft. In normal circumstances in weather like this flying would have been cancelled. No one gave a thought to cancellation. The only concern was how to get the aircraft off safely.

As the ship turned almost a hundred and eighty degrees into the wind, every man was needed to hold the aircraft down and stop them from sliding one into the other. Broadside on to the sea, *Peregrine* rolled alarmingly, testing the will and determination of the men to the utmost. Then she was round and the wind was coming from ahead in great gusts, bringing with it blown spume that drenched men and aircraft with icy spray.

At last the green came from Wings on the bridge and the first aircraft was off. Each pilot had to fight for control as wind and sea attempted to take charge, but, because of the strong wind, most were airborne before they reached the end of the flight-deck. Each aircraft, as it reached the starting-position, had its wings unfolded and locked into position, to be held by half a dozen men and prevented from falling to one side or the other. Others hung on to the tail plane as the engine was revved up. The chocks were removed and the plane was off.

At last it was Killer's turn. Bill could feel the force of the wind buffeting the aircraft, particularly when its wings were unfolded. A revving-up of the engine, a green light, and they were away, gaining control and manoeuvrability as they gained speed. As the seal, awkward and lumbering on land, gains grace and control when it enters the sea, so with these clumsy aircraft as they became airborne. With a wind-speed over the deck of sixty knots, L-Love was quickly airborne and Bill was glad to see the deck dropping away from them.

Ahead of them Bill could see the line of aircraft, rising and falling, as they slowly caught up with the leader. The CO took them up to three thousand feet, just beneath the cloud base, and ordered a loose formation of three vics of three. In the buffeting wind close formation would have been impossible.

The CO had presented his plan of attack at the briefing. It was one the squadron had developed in the Mediterranean when attacking Italian battleships. He would lead them to a position about five miles ahead of the enemy ship and give the order to break away into attack positions. His own sub-flight would attack from ahead, the second sub-flight from starboard and the third sub-flight from port. In each sub-flight, aircraft would form line abreast at a distance of two hundred yards from each other. This would prevent the aircraft from bunching up and thus make them more difficult targets for the German gunners. The whole attack would be co-ordinated with 998's dive-bombing attack and would require accurate, stopwatch timing.

It was very cold in the open cockpit, with the temperature well below freezing, but Bill was unaware of it. At first he was busy with his navigation, plotting all the moves of the squadron so that if he had to he could navigate back to the carrier. Killer's attention was completely taken up by his need to maintain formation on Bolo Hawkins, his sub-flight leader.

Although their airspeed, with the heavy torpedoes slung beneath the aircraft bellies, was only seventy-five knots, because of the wind, their speed over the sea averaged a hundred and fifteen knots. After fifty minutes' flying Bill picked up the German ship on his ASV, eighteen miles ahead. A few minutes later he saw 998 Squadron, which had been flying in formation just ahead of 999 Squadron, start to orbit to port. This would give 999 Squadron an opportunity of getting ahead of the target before the attack began.

The ship was now in sight, barely distinguishable in the murk. Bill felt sure that they would not have been seen against the grey clouds. He watched as they passed the ship five miles to port of them, gradually circling round it until they were five miles ahead, with the *Hohenlinden* now on their port beam.

'Hello Ilford and Hector aircraft, this is Leader. Attack five minutes from – now.'

'Hello, Ilford aircraft. Sub-flights break formation. Go, go.'

Bill saw Bolo wave his arm and break away, taking Love and Mike with him. Bolo circled to port until he was five miles to starboard of the target.

'Hello, Love and Mike, this is Ilford King. Attack formation. Go, go.'

The order came loud and clear in his headphones and Killer responded immediately, taking up a position two hundred yards abreast of Bolo, with Bing Crosby at a similar distance on Bolo's other side.

'Hello, Ilford aircraft, this is Leader. Attack, attack. Go, go.'

From ahead and on either beam the sub-flights began their attack, so that whichever way the target turned a sub-flight would be in a good attacking position. At the same time, 998 Squadron, cloud-hopping astern, would begin their attack, hopefully undetected.

As the three aircraft plunged forwards in line abreast the flak started. Shell-bursts from the six-inch guns splayed out ahead of them and Killer began to weave to and fro to avoid them. Their speed had built up to a hundred and thirty knots. Soon they would meet the tracers and close-range weapons. Bill gritted his teeth, and crouched over the forward bulkhead, his face close to Killer's to give him support. He could see the German ship, its guns blazing in all directions, but principally, Bill thought, at them.

At four thousand yards range Killer put his nose down into a dive to get into dropping position. To port Bill could see the other Swordfish and these gave him some comfort. Lines of tracers were coming towards them. Could they survive that barrage? On his left he saw Bolo's aircraft hit by a shell-burst, falter – and continue flying. Tracers passed through their own port wing, damaging the lower mainplane. They would never survive this. Then Bill saw the dive-bombers, breaking cloud just astern of the raider. They were almost overhead and undetected. The leader plummeted down in a near vertical dive and Bill saw the first explosions. Immediately the German defences switched to the attacking dive-bombers, giving the torpedo-bombers the breathing space they needed, when they were most vulnerable. One of the dive-bombers did not pull out and splashed into the sea beside the ship.

Three thousand yards. Two thousand. They were now at sea level and the three aircraft were still racing towards their target. The ship was turning towards them. A bomb hit the stern. Another hit the bridge. The ship was one thousand yards away and still Killer held his fire. Bolo, in K-King, had dropped his fish and was staggering away. Eight hundred yards. Guns swivelled back towards them. A judder, and then came the quiet voice of Killer.

'Torpedo gone.'

Now Killer was turning away, weaving and jinking up and down, dodging the flak. Bill saw the torpedo running true. A minute later came the first explosion, then another, and a third. Three torpedo hits. The German ship was doomed.

Looking back, as they raced away, Bill saw the German raider ablaze amidships and settling low in the water. Seamen were already taking to their boats.

'Hello, Ilford aircraft, this is Leader. I am dropping a flame-float two miles north of the target. Form up on me.'

Bill saw the flame-float start up and directed Killer towards it. L-Love was flying clumsily, its damaged port wing causing considerable drag.

'I can't make more than eighty knots,' said Killer. 'Keep an eye on the port wing, Bill.'

Bill could see where fabric had been ripped away by tracers, leaving a gaping hole in the lower mainplane. He reported this to Killer.

Bolo was just ahead of Killer, also flying clumsily. His starboard upper mainplane was damaged and he, too, was flying slowly.

'Hello, Ilford Leader, this is Ilford King. I have a damaged wing and am unable to maintain more than eighty knots. Over.'

'Killer, that was Bolo, reporting the same trouble as we have,' said Bill.

'Hello, Ilford King, this is Leader. Roger. Out.'

'Bill, report our problem to the CO,' said Killer.

'OK, Killer.'

'Hello, Ilford Leader, this is Ilford Love. We also have wing damage and cannot maintain normal speed. Over.'

'Hello, Ilford Love, this is Leader. Roger. Out.'

By now all the aircraft were orbiting the flame-float and Killer had formed up loosely on Bolo's port quarter. No other aircraft of 999 Squadron appeared to be damaged, although Bill knew that at least one aircraft of 998 Squadron had been shot down.

The CO's voice came through the R/T.

'Hello, Ilford aircraft. All Ilford aircraft, except King and Love, are to form up on Ilford Fox who will lead you back to

Mother at best speed. I will stay with King and Love to escort them home. Over.'

Bill listened to the acknowledgements as they came through and watched the six aircraft as they departed for the carrier. The CO had formed up on the starboard quarter of Bolo, leaving him to lead the formation at his best speed, no more than eighty knots. Bill did some quick navigation on his chartboard, then spoke to his pilot and air-gunner.

'Listen, fellows,' he said. 'We've a problem. If the wind's as high as fifty knots, we are making only thirty knots over the sea. We're not going to be able to reach the carrier.'

'It's worse than that, Bill,' said Killer. 'I'm using more fuel than normal just to maintain eighty knots. This will cut down our endurance.'

'I expect that's why the CO is staying with us,' said Bill.

'I've a message to the carrier from the shadowing aircraft, sir,' said Leading Airman Gibbons. 'The *Hohenlinden* has sunk. He is returning to base.'

'Good show!' exclaimed Bill.

Five minutes later L/A Gibbons reported another W/T message, from Ilford Leader to the carrier, reporting the damaged condition of the two aircraft.

The situation looked desperate to Bill. Killer was doing his best, nursing his engine as much as possible, but the damage was not helping him and Bill could see that it was getting worse. The light was already beginning to fade in the winter afternoon and the sea beneath them looked dangerous, with wind-swept, breaking waves and blown spume.

'A message from *Peregrine,* sir.' L/A Gibbons' voice was raised in excitement. '*Daventry* was sent ahead at full speed at 1430 to meet us.'

'That could make all the difference,' cried Bill. 'It'll be thirty miles nearer to us, an hour's flying. If we have to we can ditch alongside her.'

His thoughts were confirmed a minute later when Bolo's voice came through on the R/T.

'Hello, Ilford Leader, this is King. We'll not be able to make base. Intend to ditch alongside *Daventry*. Over.'

'Hello, King, this is Leader. Roger.

Hello, Love, this is Leader. What is your situation? Over.'

'Hello, Leader, this is Love. We are in the same boat. We can't make base. Will ditch alongside *Daventry*.'

'Hello, Love, this is Leader. Roger. Out.'

'Hello, Leader, this is King. Submit, you leave Love and King and make for base at your best speed. Otherwise you may be forced to ditch with us. Over.'

Bill noted that Bolo's voice was very steady as he made his recommendation, even though it meant leaving the two crippled aircraft to their own fate.

A pause ensued and then the CO's voice came through.

'Hello, King and Love, this is Leader. I'm going to leave you now and try to make the carrier. Good luck. Over.'

'Hello, Leader, this is Bolo. Thank you, sir, and good luck to you. Out.'

Bill watched as the CO waggled his wings in farewell and surged ahead of them. Now the two crippled aircraft were on their own, with at best a ditching in that dreadful sea ahead of them. At least, Bill thought, we have each other for company. We are not alone.

'Hello, Killer, this is Bolo. Listen carefully. As soon as I can contact *Daventry* I shall report our condition and tell them that we have to ditch. I expect they will make a slick for us. That means they'll turn in a broad circle round and through the wind. This will make a calm patch on their leeward side. Land in that as close to the ship as you can. I'll be right behind you. If you can manage it do a belly-flop. This will prevent you from nose-diving into the sea. Have you got that? Over.'

'Hello, Bolo. Killer here. Yes, I understand. Over.'

'Right. All three of you make sure your harnesses are attached so that you don't get thrown out. But be prepared to

251

release yourselves and your dinghy immediately you are down. Over.'

'Roger, Bolo. Wilco. Out.'

They had been flying for nearly four hours and Killer's fuel gauge was very low. Their height was now one thousand feet.

'Killer, I've got *Daventry* on the ASV, eleven miles ahead.' Bill's voice was excited.

'Report it to Bolo, Bill,' said Killer.

When Bill did this, the reply came back from Dicky Burd.

'Thank you, Bill. Our ASV was damaged in the attack. I shall now try to contact *Daventry*.'

Bill heard Dicky call the cruiser on R/T and receive a reply. When they were a mile away *Daventry* would begin to circle to form a slick. A boat would be lowered to pick them up.

They could see the cruiser now, only three miles ahead of them.

Two minutes later came the message from *Daventry*: 'Am turning now. Good luck.'

Bill fastened his jockstrap and saw that Gibbons had done the same. Then he braced himself on his stool, his arms against the forward bulkhead. He heard the engine note change as Killer went into fine pitch.

Killer watched the cruiser manoeuvre out of the wind and then make a broad curve, within which the sea was relatively calm. *Daventry* was now stopped and Killer could see the boat being lowered into the water. He was close now. The waves were still high, but not breaking. Easing his throttle and maintaining a nose-up position, he glided down towards the sea.

'Stand by,' he called sharply.

The tailwheel struck first and the aircraft made a perfect belly-flop with a great splash, a hundred yards from the cruiser. After the shock of the landing, Bill's first awareness was of the extreme cold of the water seeping into the cockpit, which was filling up. The aircraft was flat in the water, but rocking violently in the swell. The dinghy was released and already inflating and all three crew began to clamber into it. Thank God! Bill thought. There appeared to be no bones broken.

Bill released the dinghy as soon as the crew were all in it and turned to see the ship's boat approaching. Helped by the boat's crew, they transferred to the boat, which then turned towards K-King. Bolo had successfully landed just astern of L-Love. The three crewmembers were sprawled on the wing of their aircraft. Their dinghy had failed to inflate and they had chosen to stay with their aircraft rather than risk the freezing sea. They were soon in the rescue boat and it was not long before all six were safely aboard *Daventry*, wrapped in blankets in the sickbay with a brandy each to warm them up. Whilst their clothes were being dried, the medical officer gave them a brief examination and pronounced them all fit and well.

'We've been lucky,' said Bolo. 'I was on the last knockings of my petrol.'

'So was I,' said Killer. 'Until Bill reported picking up the *Daventry* on his ASV, I didn't think we'd make it.'

'It was a great moment, Bill, when you told us you had picked up *Daventry*. Until then, we were flying blind. Our ASV was knocked out of action by the shell-blast.'

'Do you think it was our torpedoes that hit?' asked Killer.

'It's likely that the two on our side came from our sub-flight,' said Bolo. 'The *Hohenlinden*'s turn put us in a good attacking position, but it doesn't matter whose torpedo hit. It was a team effort and as a team we won. We sank the enemy.'

As soon as their clothes had dried out, PO Mercer and L/A Gibbons were taken down to seamen's messes, and the officers to the wardroom. From here they were summoned to meet the Captain in his sea-cabin. He questioned them

253

closely on the action and particularly about the German sailors abandoning ship and the British aircraft shot down. Did they think there were any survivors from this aircraft?

Bolo and Killer had seen the aircraft splash down, but had both been too occupied with their own problems to pay close attention to it.

'I saw it,' said Bill. 'It made quite a good belly-flop and was lying flat on the water. I saw some movement in the rear cockpit, but then we were hit and my attention was taken up by our own difficulties.'

'Well,' the Captain said, 'we are making our best speed towards the position where the enemy ship went down, to look for survivors. We expect to get there just after dark. Then we'll rejoin *Peregrine* so that both ships can make for St Helena where you'll be transferred back to your carrier.'

May we go up to the bridge, sir, and help to look out for survivors?' Bolo asked.

The Captain paused for a moment and then said, 'Four more pairs of keen eyes will help. Yes. All right. See the Commander and he'll supply you with night-glasses.'

An hour later, all four, wrapped in their flying-clothing for warmth, stood on the bridge peering into the night. Killer had particularly good night vision and he was the first to spot the winking light on the starboard bow. The Captain reduced speed and turned *Daventry* towards the light. Soon they could pick out the dim shape of a ship's boat and then another. Fifty-four German sailors and four officers were rescued, but not the Captain. He and several other officers had died on the bridge in the dive-bombing attack. There was no sign of the Fleet Air Arm officers.

Dicky Burd approached the Captain.

'The German ship continued for at least a mile after the plane was shot down and then began to turn in a slow circle to port,' he said. 'If they escaped in their dinghy our chaps could be two miles away.'

'Go and discuss this with the navigating officer and come up with a position.'

In the chartroom Dicky Burd plotted what he remembered of the movements of the German raider after the aircraft was shot down, and produced a bearing and distance from their present position. The Captain ordered *Daventry* to turn along this bearing and searchlights were switched on to illuminate the sea. Again Killer was the first to spot the dinghy. As the ship was brought alongside there seemed to be no life in it. The bodies were sprawled out along the bottom.

Seamen from *Daventry* climbed into it and carefully lifted the bodies aboard the cruiser. They appeared to be frozen to death, but miraculously, under the doctor's careful treatment, they were thawed out until a flicker of life was restored. The pilot and observer were both injured and the TAG was the first to recover. He told how he and the observer had pulled the pilot out of his cockpit before he also collapsed from his wounds. None of them had been immersed in the sea, and this and the protective hood of the dinghy had probably saved them.

A wireless message was sent to *Peregrine,* informing her of the rescue of three aircrews, and this was received with jubilation aboard the carrier. The CO, too, had made it safely back to his ship. He was on the bridge as *Daventry* approached and he watched as the two ships flashed their messages. The ship's companies cheered each other as *Daventry* passed close to *Peregrine* to take up her station astern.

During the following week, the 999 Squadron personnel recovered completely from their ordeal, as did the TAG from 998 Squadron. The pilot and observer from that squadron had suffered more severe injuries and were still bedridden when the two ships anchored off St Helena. All the Fleet Air Arm crews, however, were transferred to their carrier, whilst the German prisoners were taken ashore in St Helena to await transport to South Africa.

The two squadrons celebrated their victory with a special dinner. There was even more to celebrate the next day. At twelve-thirty the Captain spoke over the Tannoy system.

'I have received congratulations from the Admiralty on our recent victories. *Peregrine* has been ordered to pick up a convoy at Freetown and escort it to Gibraltar. From there we shall escort a second convoy home to England. All being well, we shall be home by Christmas.'

The sound of cheering could be heard throughout the ship. Most of the ship's company had been away from England for nearly four years when they had first set out for the Far East. War had started in Europe since they had been away and they had seen action in the Mediterranean, the Red Sea, the Indian Ocean and the South Atlantic. Now the long search was over. They were going home.

For two officers, the Captain's words had a special meaning. In his cabin, Bolo gazed at the picture of Joyce, the girl he would marry on his return to England.

In the wardroom, Bill and Killer raised their glasses.

'Killer, will you be my best man?' said Bill.

Glossary

ack-ack	anti-aircraft fire
air artificer	highly qualified technician
Aldis lamp	a powerful portable lamp for signalling
angels	altitude of aircraft in thousands of feet
armourer	technician who looks after weapons and ammunition
arrester wires	spring-loaded wires that stretch across the flight-deck to be caught by a hook on the aircraft
A/S	anti-submarine
ASO	Air Staff Officer – the ship's senior observer
ASV	an early form of radar, showing a single vertical line with blips across it denoting ships
bandits	enemy aircraft
Barracuda	a high-winged monoplane that replaced the Swordfish as a TBR aircraft
battleship	the heaviest unit of the fleet with fourteen- to sixteen-inch guns

257

bigsworth board	a portable chartboard with a parallel ruler on a flexible arm
Blighty	Great Britain
black gang	engineers and mechanics who work in the engine-room
bumph	official documents
bumboat	small craft in Asian ports that come out to visiting ships to sell their goods
bumboatmen	natives who sell local produce from bumboats
buzz	rumour
chinwag	discussion
chow	food, a meal
C-in-C	Commander-in-Chief
comb torpedo tracks	turn towards a salvo of approaching torpedoes and pass between them
Commander Flying	the ship's senior Fleet Air Arm officer, normally a pilot – usually known as 'Wings'
confab	a discussion
cruiser	fast, large, lightly armoured ship, usually with six- to eight-inch guns
cutter	large open boat
destroyer	fast ship of one to two thousand tons, with four- to five-inch guns; they carried torpedo tubes and depth charges
dhow	large commercial sailing vessel with a single lateen sail
dish up	wash up
DCO	Deck Control Officer, who controls movement of aircraft on deck
DLO or DLCO	Deck-Landing Control Officer,

	sometimes called 'Bats', who controls landings and take-offs
ETA	estimated time of arrival
FAA	Fleet Air Arm
felucca	small sailing vessel with a single lateen sail
Fiat CR 42	Italian biplane fighter aircraft
fiddle	a low guard rail round a dining table to prevent china from sliding off
fitter	engine mechanic
Firefly	fast monoplane that became the Navy's bomber-reconnaissance plane towards the end of the war
fish	torpedo
flak	anti-aircraft gunfire
flame-float	a float, dropped by aircraft, that emitted a flame for several minutes; used as a marker
flaming onions	tracer shells of various colours
flap	emergency
flat	an area of deck space surrounded by cabins or offices
Fulmar	a naval two-seater fighter aircraft
G	force of gravity
gen	information
gharry	horse-drawn carriage
gimlet	gin and lime
Gosport tubes	speaking tubes
Gladiator	naval biplane fighter aircraft
G-string	a safety line for observers and air-gunners that prevented them from being thrown out of the open cockpit

goofers' platform	a space on the island of an aircraft carrier reserved for flying-crews where they could watch landings and take-offs
hook	a hook beneath the aircraft lowered when landing on a flight-deck to catch an arrester wire
horse's neck	brandy and dry ginger
hostilities only	for the duration of the war
IFF	Identify Friend or Foe – an electronic aircraft identification device
island	the superstructure on the starboard side of an aircraft-carrier that housed the bridge, chartroom, operations room, etc.
jellabah	Cloak, worn by Arabs, resembling a nightshirt
line-book	permanent record of any outstanding or outlandish events
mae west	inflatable life jacket
make and mend	a period free of duties
MV	motor vessel
NAVEX	navigation exercise
parallel search	organised search by a number of aircraft following parallel tracks ten to twenty miles apart
Pilot	ship's Navigating Officer
PMO	Principal Medical Officer
rigger	an airframe mechanic
roger	message received and understood
round-down	after end of flight-deck sloping downwards
R/T	radio telephony
Schooley	the ship's schoolmaster whose

	duties included teaching, meteorology, navigation, etc.
SM 72	Savoia Marchetti – Italian high-level bomber or torpedo bomber
smoke-float	a float dropped by an aircraft that emitted smoke for several minutes; used as a marker
SOS	emergency distress signal
square search	a search in which each leg is at right angles to, and longer than, the previous one
SS	steamship
TAG	telegraphist-air-gunner
tally-ho	target in sight
taffrail	guard rail
TBR	*torpedo-bomber-reconnaissance
TSR	*torpedo-spotter-reconnaissance
tell off	'Each aircraft in turn is to report receiving me and the strength of signal.'
VAD	Voluntary Aid Detachment – a women's service with a nursing branch
Verey pistol	a pistol that fires a signal cartridge in various colours
wardroom	officers' mess in the Navy
Wavy Navy	Royal Naval Volunteer Reserve
wilco	'will comply with your instruction'
Wings	Commander Flying
WRNS or Wrens	Women's Royal Naval Service
W/T	wireless telegraphy – requiring Morse
yashmak	veil worn by Moslem women

* all Swordfish were capable of either function

zog   method of signalling with the
forearm, using the Morse
Code